The Card

Other Five Star Titles
by D-L Nelson:

Chickpea Lover

The Card

D-L Nelson

Five Star • Waterville, Maine

First Edition
First Printing: October 2005

Published in 2005 in conjunction with Tekno Books.

Set in 11 pt. Plantin by Elena Picard.

Printed in the United States on permanent paper.

Library of Congress Cataloging-in-Publication Data

Nelson, D. L., 1942–
    The card / by D.L. Nelson.—1st ed.
        p. cm.
    ISBN 1-59414-417-6 (hc : alk. paper)
    1. Female friendship—Fiction. 2. Christmas cards—Fiction. I. Title.
PS3614.E4455C37 2005
    813'.6—dc22   2005016254

Dedication

To Mardy Willson, more than a foul-weather friend

1982:
Boston, Massachusetts

"The Card came, Mom." The intercom distorted Kate's voice.

"Fantastic!" Jane balanced her groceries against the door as she struggled with her four locks. The last had been getting harder each night. Like her South End neighbors, she worried about robberies. She glanced over her shoulder at the footsteps coming from the direction of Pour Vous Antiques. It was her next door neighbor, who nearly dropped her Samurai Sushi bag as she waved.

"Merry Christmas," Jane said as she jiggled the key, impatient to see Diana's card.

Snow spat. Gaslights couldn't dispel the gloom of a night that arrived much too early. In December she felt like a mole, scurrying from home den to work den. As the lock gave, she hugged her bags to keep them from spilling into the dark hallway.

Beef and onion smells greeted her from the first floor apartment. When she was first married, David had complained about apartment living, citing cooking smells as a major problem. She loved them, feeling it told of life behind closed doors, but this evening she was too rushed to enjoy them.

She hit the switch, bathing the oak wainscoting in soft light. When she'd bought the building after her divorce, she found the wood buried under layers of paint. She'd spent eight months, sitting cross-legged on the stairs plying a heat gun, watching multi-colored paint curls, relics of a hundred years, fall in her lap.

Kate had unlocked their own apartment door. A small, fuzzy, black and white body hurled himself into Jane's arms. Milk, hamburger, bread, oranges, carrots and two cans of Campbell's tomato soup spilled on the floor. She managed to keep the second bag in one arm, while holding the squiggling dog in the other. He looked at her with unabashed love as his long tongue licked her face. She kept her head averted so Main Man's kisses stayed on her cheek.

Baking odors of chocolate and sugar filled the one room divided by furniture into cooking, eating and living areas. A balcony hiding three bedrooms jutted over the kitchen. Like most South End homes, it had exposed brick, rosetted ceilings, natural wood floors and Indian print rugs scavenged from flea markets and garage sales.

"The Card's by the angel chimes. I didn't open it, even if it's addressed to both of us." Kate put a sheet of cookies on the kitchen counter. "Diana must think I'm a real person."

"You've been real for a long time," Jane said. The chimes were in the center of the oak slab mantle. To the left was a wicker basket for mail. She shuffled through the envelopes ignoring the VISA, phone and plumbing bills without finding The Card.

"The manila envelope under the chimes," Kate said.

Jane found it and tore it open. The familiar white dove, having survived fifteen mail trips and one in-person presentation, looked a wee bit tattered. His wish for peace on earth was no less sincere for the many times he'd delivered it. Every possible space on the card had a message written in different colored inks. One was typed on a Post-it Note.

Jane carried The Card to the sofa. She slipped off her boots and tucked her feet under her. David used to lecture her how that position was bad for circulation. She thought both then and now that if she died before her circulation gave out, she'd have sacrificed years of comfort for nothing.

Kate had lit a fire in the wood-burning stove. The black cast iron threw enough heat to warm Jane. She slipped her arms out of the sleeves of her down coat.

Her daughter came up behind her and looked over her shoulder. "Can you find the new message? You guys have so much stuff written on it."

"That stuff covers a lot of living, child-of-mine. Here it is. Under where I wrote, 'This year was a bitch, but at least I'm out of jail.' "

Kate ran her finger under the new message. "Diana says, 'See y'all soon.' Maybe she's coming to Boston. I hope so."

"That's because she sides with you against me," Jane said.

Kate waggled her ear lobes at her mother. On one visit, Diana had told Jane that Kate was old enough to get her ears pierced and then had taken the girl to have them done.

Jane left The Card on the trunk serving as a coffee table while she hung up her coat. "So, Brat, what's cooking?"

"Christmas cookies. If this were January, I'd call 'em chocolate chip. Wanta taste the dough?" Both loved batter more than the finished product. The night they'd moved in, Kate had made celebration brownies. Sitting on a ladder, one above the other, they'd devoured the batter while watching J.R. cheat on Sue Ellen. When the program was finished, so was the batter—not even a spoonful was left to bake.

"Green dough?" Jane asked peeking into the oversized bowl they'd found at the Salvation Army store.

"I said Christmas cookies. We're out of food coloring. I put it on the list." Kate pointed with her wooden spoon to a paper on the refrigerator fastened with magnets shaped like a strawberry, a Japanese Chin like their dog, the state of Florida and their favorite that said, "Fuck housework."

Jane swallowed anti-mold comments along with the dough. "Not bad. How was your German test?"

"I think I passed. And your presentation?"

"I got a good order. New client, too." Jane took more dough. "I just love these in-depth mother-teenager conversations." She slid her feet into her slippers, which were in the dog's bed, not by the door where she'd left them.

"Take what you can," Kate said.

Jane took another cookie and picked up The Card. She remembered Diana described them as identical twins from separate wombs.

Main Man hopped from a chair to the divider. His long tail brushed the African violet planted in the white enamel teapot. Lots of tea and Diana had seen Jane through her first few months without David. When the pot had rusted, Jane had thrown it out.

Diana had found it in the garbage, "An abandoned war orphan," she'd called it. "I won't allow such a crass disposal of a loyal servant." She'd bought the violet, planted it in the pot and given it back to Jane.

"Get down," Jane said to the dog, whose ability to understand was in direct relation to his desire. He did nothing. She scooped him up and carried him and The Card to the couch. Settling in with the dog on her lap, she looked at everything they'd written. Their lives were contained in each pithy sentence.

10

Fall, 1963:
Boston, Massachusetts

Chaos! An hour earlier Jane Andrews had left a well-ordered dorm room to walk her parents to their station wagon for their drive back to Connecticut.

Good-byes took longer than expected. Until Jane saw tears in her mother's eyes, she hadn't thought about the change her leaving the farm would make in her parents' life. She'd been too excited about starting Boston University. Her expectations hadn't covered devastation-in-the-dorm.

There wasn't a spare inch of space visible on the floor, two desks, mismatched dressers or the night table between the single beds. Her new calico puff and sham were hidden. Suitcases and boxes, helter-skelter, were open, their contents strewn every which way.

"A cyclone must have gone through," she said aloud.

"No cyclone, just me," a voice said from the doorway. Jane turned towards the voice, which belonged to a redhead hovering at least ten inches above Jane's five-foot frame.

Amazon flashed through her head, but years of her mother's nagging about being polite stopped the words before they escaped her teeth.

"Hi, I'm Diana Bourque. You must be Jane," the Amazon drawled softly. Diana was abundant, not fat. Her hair

11

flowed in unmanageable curls, a Botticelli's Venus without a shell. Her breasts flowed freely under a smocked Indian linen blouse. Slate-blue eyes peeked from a tanned and freckled face. She stuck out her hand.

"Did you make this mess?" Jane's small hand shook Diana's paw as her free arm swept over the room.

"I'll get it away," Diana said.

"When?" Jane asked.

"You some kind of neat freak?"

"I prefer not to risk my life crossing the room."

"God, you would like one of our housekeepers," Diana said.

Jane had never met anyone who had a housekeeper. "Are you rich?" Her olive complexion hid her blush. "Forgive me. That's rude and nosy."

"It's OK. How else do you find out stuff?" Diana plunked herself down on her bed amid her clothes. "Are we going to start living together with a fight?"

"Sorry. Want some help?"

Diana nodded.

Jane wound her black hair around her hand and reached for a barrette to fasten it off her neck. While she neatly folded sweaters before placing them carefully in drawers, Diana stuffed things anywhere she found a spot.

"Everything has price tags," Jane said.

"I'm from Florida. I never needed winter clothes." Diana bit her tongue rather than say, "I wish I didn't now." Sitting cross-legged on the bed during a work break, she produced two Cokes from her straw shoulder bag. They began the let's-get-to-know-each-other ritual being duplicated in rooms all over campus.

"My dad publishes the *Sarasota Journal*. Most of my childhood was spent in the city room."

12

"Wow! That's different." Jane took a swallow of Coke.

"I learned my alphabet on Gino's lap. He's our linotype man. I'd press the keys and read the hot lead as it dropped out, only it was backwards. It's a miracle I can read frontwards. While most kids read about Dick, Jane and Spot, I was reading 'Mayor jailed for fraud.' "

"How come you spent so much time at the paper?" Jane asked. In Connecticut everything was so ordinary.

"My mother flipped when I was born. Most parents complain their kids drive 'em crazy. I really did—just by being born." Diana's statement sounded casual, but the tone hid how all her life she'd hated being the only motherless child at school.

Jane didn't know what to say, but Diana went on. "It was better than if she'd been home. Jim, that's my dad, took me neat places. Like following a circus clown for a day or seeing Alan Shepard take off for space."

What Diana didn't say was how much she'd missed having someone who could tie her sashes in pretty bows or French braid her hair. Silence hung heavily as Diana drifted into her memories. For no good reason a housekeeper making terrible tasting cookies for Valentine's Day flashed into her mind. It was the only time she'd been able to take something home-baked to school.

Diana regretted starting the let's-get-to-know-each-other game. She wondered if moving so far from home had caused her to dredge up these unwanted memories, but she couldn't pull herself away.

Until she was ten she'd worried she might be just another problem to Jim. Eavesdropping on his conversation with Bill Reed, his editor-in-chief, put her mind to rest. She should have been in bed, but she had slipped out to listen to them talk.

"You worship that kid so much, I bet you burn incense at the foot of her bed," Bill had said. Diana had pushed her body into the floor and held her breath waiting for Jim's answer.

"Only mentally," Jim had said.

Diana's thoughts drifted to her mother. As a little girl, she'd dreamed if she could only talk to that lady wearing a wedding dress and standing next to her father in a silver filigree framed photo on his bureau, everything would be fine. The Bourques could be a real family again. No matter how much she'd begged to be taken to see her mother, her father had always refused.

When Diana was twelve, Jim gave in. Together they went to the sanatorium where Jim had committed his wife the day after he found his infant daughter stuffed in the refrigerator above the roast beef.

The meeting snapped Diana, not her mother, into reality. She had been ushered down a hall stinking of urine by a nurse whose thighs made funny sounds as they scraped together. The nurse had grabbed keys, too many to count, and had unlocked a door. The room had two barred windows, a sink, a toilet and a metal hospital bed. From a chair, a creature stared at Diana without seeing her.

The child walked over to her, reached out and touched the face. The skin was dry to her fingers, reminding her of the snake the naturalist had brought into her classroom. A groan, more animal than human, knocked Diana's planned speech from her head. A wall clock clicked the minutes as she searched for the magic words she'd dreamed of saying. The claws tied to the chair twitched. After another groan from the woman, Diana fled.

In the car her father held her, letting her cry herself out. Her mother's eyes, slate-blue like her own, haunted Diana.

For months she moaned with nightmares of harridans, to wake to find her father next to her bed. He'd rock her back to sleep like a baby, but he would never tell her why her mother went mad.

Sometimes Diana worried she carried a seed of madness. Seeing Patty McCormack in *The Bad Seed* reinforced her fear. If hormonal changes from giving birth had driven her mother nuts, would puberty, pregnancy, the pill or menopause, push *her* over the brink, too?

The fear wasn't constant, more like a toothache triggered by ice cream. Then Diana would picture herself tied to a chair next to a barred window. This information was too scary to share with a stranger.

Diana shivered waiting for Jane to comment. If she lived with the disadvantages of a crazy mother, she might as well enjoy the advantages, even if only for the drama.

Jane didn't know what to say. None of her friends' mothers were crazy, at least not certifiably. Most were like her own—bakers of pies and dispensers of advice, wanted or not. She started hanging up blouses.

Diana broke the silence. "Tell me about your life."

"Disgustingly normal in comparison." Jane sat on her bed, now clutter-free. She picked up some records. "Where do you want these?"

"On the shelf there," Diana motioned with her hand and watched Jane put the records between her legs. "What are you doing?"

"Putting them in alphabetical order." Jane flipped them back and forth, inserting one, pulling another out.

"By singer or title?" Diana asked. She was joking.

Jane noted the variety of music: rock, folk, jazz, show and classical. "Singer first, then title."

Diana threw up her hands.

"Want to hear my life story?" Jane asked.

Diana nodded.

"I grew up on a farm. We raised strawberries and pota-toes. My father made me gather both, so like you, I spent a lot of time at my dad's work."

"Sounds hard," Diana said.

Jane finished putting the records on the third and fourth shelves of the bookcase. "Hot and sticky anyway, especially the strawberries. To make the time go I pretended things— like I was working in a rice paddy near the Great Wall of China. I would be a nobleman's daughter thrown out when I refused to have my feet bound. My peasant husband adored me, but we had to work so hard."

Jane felt stupid recounting how in all her daydreams there was always a handsome man. They would share hard-ships, their souls and hearts locked in eternal love. "What's your major?"

"Communication-journalism. Business minor. I wanted to work for my dad right after high school, but he insists I get a degree. And yours?"

"Liberal Arts. All I really want to do is get married, have lots of kids, and be a wonderful wife and mother."

Boston is a city of red bricks. Residents speak with an ac-cent made identifiable by President Kennedy. Locals ex-change Rs for Hs. But with or without an accent, Bostonians created a series of abbreviations confusing to the uninitiated. By October, Diana and Jane knew they went to BU not Boston University on Comm Ave not Com-monwealth Avenue. They rode the Greenline cars of the Massachusetts Bay Transit Authority, called The T. From there they could travel to BI or Beth Israel if they needed more medical care than BU's infirmary could provide.

If they adjusted well to the city, classes and being away from home, they adjusted more slowly to one another.

"Have you an allergy to hangers?" Jane stepped over Diana's clothes. The room was hot, because the window was closed. Diana found the October air too cold. Jane found it easier to wear less than watch her roommate shiver.

When Jane got into bed, Diana was already propped up with pillows, working on a paper, "Advertising and the Media." Scratching out the sentence she'd just written, she bit on the stub of her pencil while trying to think of a better one. She used her pencils until the eraser met the point.

"You're an Olympic gold medallist nag." She reached over to her desk for a magazine. The corner was just visible under a mass of texts and notebooks. When she pulled, everything toppled. She left them on the floor.

Jane's desk next to Diana's looked unused. Books were arranged on her shelf above the desk. Papers were stacked in a single pile. Pencils, pens, rulers and paper clips were in a tray in her middle top drawer.

"Maybe we should ask for new roommates, except you'd have to request someone of the pig persuasion," Jane said. She put out her lamp.

"Very funny! Except for your religious obsession with neat, we get along great." Diana snuggled under the debris. "Guess I'll go to sleep, too." She switched off her light.

"Darn," Jane said after five minutes of twisting.

"What?" Diana asked.

"I think I got my period." Putting on the light, she stomped to her bureau for a pad, kicking Diana's jeans out of the way.

"Why don't you wear tampons?" Diana asked. "They're comfortabler."

"I'm a virgin."

"Virgins can wear tampons."

Jane thought of the Barbara Marshall scandal her junior year of high school. Someone had discovered Barbara wore tampons leading to immediate speculation about her sexual habits. Barbara, the class brain, had a black belt in karate. At a donkey basketball game, Greg Brown had the nerve to touch her breast. She decked him in front of the entire school.

Jane wasn't ready to test tampons. Taking her pad and belt, she headed for the toilet, three doors down the hall. "I'll shut the light off so you can sleep."

Diana mumbled a drowsy thanks.

Returning, Jane heard Diana breathing regularly, but she wasn't letting out the funny whistle that she normally made. She tried to get into bed quietly, but her covers were no longer thrown back. In the dark as she patted her hand around the bed she realized that everything was smooth.

Diana giggled.

"What did you do?" Jane flicked on the light. Her bed was perfectly made.

"Boy, what a slob leaving your bed unmade like that," Diana said.

"You made my bed when I went to the bathroom?"

"I had to. My roommate kept calling this room a pigsty. She's a farm girl so she knows a lot about pigsties."

"OK! OK! I give up," Jane said. She went to her closest, pulled her BU sweatshirt from the hanger and dropped it on the floor. Then she emptied her wastepaper basket. She rolled the papers into balls and threw them against the wall. Most landed on the scatter rug her mother had braided. Others rested on Diana's clothes. "I tell you what. I'll try not to be so neat, if you try to be neater. Deal?"

"Deal! Let's get a Coke to celebrate."

The last thing Jane said before she fell asleep was, "I can't believe you made my bed."

"Believe," Diana said.

The ground work for their friendship had been laid.

Winter 1966:
Massachusetts

"Hey, hey, LBJ, how many kids did ya kill today?" Muted chants floated from five stories below through the closed dormitory window. Diana watched protesters snake up Comm Ave. Two mounted policemen sat in their saddles to one side of the group. She imagined the tight set of their jaws and their nails turning white as their hands clenched the reins.

"Look at those bastards. They're just waiting for a kid to step out of line," Diana said to Jane, who sat on a huge pillow serving as an easy chair. Her legs were crossed, Indian style. A book, *Pre-Elizabethan Drama*, was propped on her lap. She joined Diana at the window, stepping carefully not to disarrange file cards surrounding the pillow. Diana pointed, "Look. There's the FBI. Two of 'em."

"Where?" Jane asked.

"Left of the lamp pole. See, with the pressed jeans and crew cuts. God, they stick out."

"Maybe they want us to know they know." Jane returned to her pillow and book. "I feel guilty not being there."

"You do your share. We both do."

"But Fred really got on my case today," Jane said. "I told him I put in three hours fixing that damned mimeograph. It's pro-establishment. Only breaks down when we put out anti-war stuff. Never when they run exams."

Diana shrugged. She'd gone out with the sociology professor who let the students use his department's machinery when no one was around. Since they stopped dating, she'd avoided the office. "Fred thinks everyone should put in at least two hundred hours a week."

"He's just this side of SDS." Jane wrote a note on a file card and tucked it into the third pile from the right. "I'm not sure our protests do any good." She found her place in *Gammar Gurton's Needle*, her assignment for Early English Drama. Her empathy for the medieval woman, who'd lost the only needle she would ever own, was limited. Her sympathy for students, forced to read about it, was greater.

A knock on the door was followed by Sandy Jones sticking his head in. "Phone, Diana."

"Who is it?"

"A man. Not HIM."

In the hall, Diana, relieved it wasn't the sociology prof, reached for the receiver. Last month, when he told her he was going back to his wife he'd added, "It won't change our relationship." They'd been riding in his car, and he'd patted her knee.

"Wrong!" She'd jumped out of his car at the next traffic light.

The prof had called last night, whining that it was really his kids that made him go back. Her last words before she hung up on him were, "Lie to me if you must. Don't insult my intelligence."

"Hello," Diana said.

"Hi, kid."

"Jim!" She slouched against the wall settling in for a pleasant chat with her father.

"Thought I'd call. Those clips that you sent—great. Great that you're selling stuff."

Diana glowed. She'd loved writing the article about how demonstrations were planned and then convincing the *Boston Phoenix* to buy it. She'd sold another on drug sales to *The Boston Globe*. For the articles she'd earned an A in Investigative Journalism. She blushed at her father's professional recognition.

"You've got printers' ink in your veins, chip off the old block, etc. Righto, kid?"

"Good reporters don't talk in clichés," she said. "Besides when I come to work for you in June . . ."

"Whoa! I never said that you'd work for me after graduation."

She stood up straight. "What do you mean? That's why I'm exiled here—to learn the theory side of the business."

"And your next step is to work for another paper," he said.

"I gotta go. There's a line waiting for the phone." She hung up without waiting for his, "I love you."

She stood alone in the hall, shaking, then ran to her room, where she threw herself across the bed, sobbing. As she landed, books and her teddy bear went flying.

Jane had never seen her roommate cry: not when she broke up with any of her boyfriends, not when she'd been humiliated by a professor who'd falsely accused her of cheating—never. Jane rushed to the bed. "Did someone die?" She wrapped her arms around Diana.

Five minutes went by before Diana regained enough control to speak. "Too bad, you're so (choke) little. You (hiccup) can only give a half a (choke) hug. Where's the toilet paper?"

Jane reached into her desk drawer and pulled off several

sheets. Diana honked into it.

"Wanta talk about it?" Jane asked.

"No." Diana then spent the next half hour talking about it.

Jane threw in comments like, "He just wants you to get some training," or "You know he loves you." Jane liked Jim. She'd gone to Sarasota for spring break each year, just like Diana spent Thanksgivings with Jane's parents in Connecticut. "Did he ever tell you after graduation you could start on the paper?"

"I assumed. He always said the paper would be mine one day, if I wanted it." She made a face. "If I wanted it. That's funny. I've never wanted anything else." She rubbed her eyes with the back of her hand leaving it black with mascara. "I must look horrendous."

Gazing at the blotched and bloated face, Jane said, "You've been more glamorous. Go take a shower, you'll feel better."

Diana did, dressing afterwards in Dr. Denton's. As she got into bed, Jane handed her a consolation Coke and sour cream potato chips from their junk food stash. Other students might keep LSD, uppers, downers or grass in their rooms, but Diana and Jane hid potato sticks, pretzels, Oreos, jars of marinated mushrooms and sweet pickles.

At 2:14 a.m. Jane woke, sure she felt Diana thinking in the dark. "You awake?" Her voice was less than a whisper in case she was wrong.

"MMMhmm."

Jane flicked on her Raggedy Ann lamp, Diana's Christmas gift to her. "What's up?"

"I've been thinking. If I can't work for Jim, I think I should have an adventure and write about it. Like Hemingway."

Jane propped herself on one elbow to listen.

Diana mirrored her friend's position. "Maybe the Peace Corps?"

"They'd send you to the jungle. There are lots of snakes in the jungle. You hate snakes."

"Paris then. Only human snakes are there. Want to come?"

Jane thought about it. She'd never been anywhere outside of New England except for visits to Diana's in Florida and a couple of weekends in New York. She'd sent out applications for teaching jobs, but nothing had come in. No Prince Charming had appeared for her to start her real life. "Why not? We can be Stein and Toklas." They had just finished reading *The Moveable Feast* for the one class they'd ever taken together.

Diana jumped out of bed to hug Jane. "We'll get T-shirts that say 'Paris or Bust'."

"OK." Jane turned Raggedy Ann off.

After about five minutes, Diana said, "Let's cut classes tomorrow? Go skiing."

They approached Prospect Hill, a single ski slope in Waltham, west of Boston where they skied whenever they could steal time from classes and demonstrations. Because it was early and midweek, they were alone for the first three runs.

Originally, Jane had great difficulty convincing Diana even to try skiing. A true southerner, she had defined skiing as an activity where a boat drags a person on wooden planks, preferably over temperate water.

To both their amazements, Diana found zooming down a mountain produced a thrill like no other. She loved the air stinging her face and the way her muscles felt after a

24

morning on the slopes. A natural athlete, she surpassed Jane's skill in three lessons. Jane, who had skied since nursery school, cheered her friend on.

Diana's nickname was Bitty Bladder. It had come from her one vice—an addiction to Coca-Cola. She drank it in place of coffee with breakfast, claiming she preferred her caffeine cold and bubbly. The many bottles consumed were matched by many frequent dashes to the toilet.

At the top of Prospect Hill, after the girls' fifth run, Diana's need arrived suddenly as it usually did, and mounted. "God, I have to pee." She wished she were a child with the luxury of holding tightly onto the offending organ. "I'll never make it down," she moaned.

Thanks to Diana, Jane knew every public toilet in the Greater Boston area. She'd threatened to write, *A Potty Guide to Boston and Cambridge*, rating toilets with one, two or three stars. The girls had stopped at a gas station on the way out, and Diana had used the toilet in the shack at the bottom of the hill before their first run.

"Go behind that bush." Jane pointed to a small pine.

Despite doubts, Diana's discomfort was too great. Jane's tree was too small, too sparsely needled, but to its left Diana found a group of baby pines.

She dropped her pants. Had she taken time to unstrap her skies everything would have been fine, but her crouching movement propelled her downhill. The stream of urine was lost in the snow. A professional skier couldn't have stood up from that position fully clothed, much less a novice with pants around her ankles.

Jane, hearing the scream, turned. As soon as she saw the problem, she skied to help her roommate. Diana was almost at the bottom before Jane could maneuver in front of her. The force of Diana's body knocked Jane over. Together they rolled in the snow. A tree stopped both of them.

"You OK?" Jane struggled to her feet. Diana undid her bindings, stood up shakily and pulled up her pants.

"I think so."

"Let me see your bottom," Jane said.

"No!"

Ignoring her, Jane pulled at the elastic waistband of Diana's ski pants. "You're bleeding. Let's go to the hospital and get you cleaned up."

"I'd be too embarrassed."

"Suppose you get gangrene and need your bottom amputated. Think how embarrassed you'd be then. Supposing . . ."

Waltham Hospital was quiet. The doctor, who had been on duty for twenty-three of his required twenty-four hours in his shift, had handled three heart attacks, a suicide attempt, a battered child, a knife fight and an epileptic seizure since midnight. He wanted to sleep out his remaining hour.

The first thing the girls saw as they entered the emergency room was the doctor disappearing into the physicians' lounge. The second thing they noticed was the desk nurse who weighed in at three hundred pounds. They had no way of knowing the woman had two fantasies in life: chocolate and making love to the doctor, who by then had removed his shoes and stretched out on the cot.

While Diana told the nurse her story, the nurse was thinking that no healthy, pretty college kid stupid enough to pee on a ski slope, and especially one with a cute-as-a-bug friend, would be allowed to disturb the rest of her medical hero.

Had Diana or Jane been old and ugly or in real distress the nurse would have delightedly wakened her doctor. He'd have looked at her and would have said, "Thank you, nurse," blinking with his sleep-saturated eyes that out-Newmanned Paul's.

So when the nurse placed Diana in a room with four beds, handed her a hospital gown and told Jane she could stay with her friend, neither girl expected a long wait. The nurse went back to reading *Valley of the Dolls*, forgetting both of them.

Diana positioned herself gingerly on her side in the first bed, her head resting on her outstretched arm. "I feel really dumb."

"You should," Jane said.

"You told me to pee behind a bush."

"I didn't tell you to go down the slope."

The door burst open. Two ambulance drivers, weight lifters by appearance, rolled in a stretcher bearing a moaning man. They gently shifted him to the bed next to Diana's. He moaned louder.

"We're being as careful as we can, buddy," the older of the two attendants said as he folded the blanket that had covered the man. He put it back on the stretcher. The younger attendant found a blanket in a warming cabinet and threw it over the new patient.

"Good luck, fella," the younger one said, pushing the stretcher out the door.

"Want me to close this?" Jane pointed to the drape, the same mud green as Diana's hospital gown. She amazed herself that she could speak to this specimen of human perfection in a normal voice. Had they been in a movie, a flash of light would reflect off his white teeth and a xylophone would sound, "Ping!"

"It's OK," the man whimpered. "But could you get me a drink of water, please?"

Jane ran water into a blue plastic pitcher and carried it and the matching glass to him. He struggled to lift himself but fell back in pain.

Jane found a straw and put it in his glass. Just coming near him sent electric quivers through her body. As she lifted his head by sliding her arm under it, she noticed pine needles and pieces of bark in his golden hair. "What happened?"

"You wouldn't believe me."

"Try me," she said.

"I was skiing at Prospect Hill. Know it?"

Jane nodded.

"Anyway, this woman came down ass over tea kettle with her rump bare naked. I skied into a tree." He groaned, "I think I broke my arm."

The girls believed him. They exchanged a look that said *don't you dare tell him*. At the same time they were formulating opinions of this beauty.

Diana was thinking: conceited, know-it-all, imperious, whiny, inconsiderate. Her feelings were based on instinct.

Jane's list included handsome, articulate, sexy, intelligent, charming. *How can I see him again?* thoughts dominated her being. Hormones took control of her brain.

David Johnson, Brandeis University senior, entered her life.

Spring 1967: Boston

Jane threw herself into her romance with David Johnson with the enthusiasm of a suicidal lemming.

"He's selfish," Diana said, taking off her coat as her roommate typed her beloved's term paper.

"It's not his fault he can't type." Jane pictured David hacking away at his Smith Corona, one finger at a time. She'd felt so lucky that he'd chosen her to type his paper, "The Prolonged Effects of Chlorinated Water on Plants," that she was sacrificing her paper, "Shakespeare's Attitude Towards Women." Both were due the next day. She could think of at least three rivals who would gladly type in her place.

Jane, with a pencil in her mouth, searched through two piles of yellow legal paper. One pile was covered with scrawls, the other with her tight handwriting. Next to the typewriter sat a four-inch pristine pile of white paper and on the bed three sheets of completed work.

Jane's statue of Ho Tai looked down from the larger of the two bureaus. A stick of violet incense burned next to the Chinese god of luck. Nightly, Jane lit a stick before rubbing the god's tummy and chanting, "Make him marry me, make him marry me."

Diana would lie in bed biting her tongue.

"You just missed David." Jane reached for the Snopak. She dabbed the paper and waited for it to dry. "You'll never guess what he told me tonight."

Diana didn't want to hear any more David Johnson litanies—not how David's straight A average earned him early acceptance into Harvard Medical School, nor about his difficult childhood, nor about his brilliant future in medicine.

Jane held a sheet of paper to the light to decipher a formula. Although she'd asked David to print, he'd forgotten. That had meant that they had to discuss the paper, and they'd stopped to make love. For once Jane found herself eyeing the clock, hoping he'd leave instead of wishing their time together could go on forever. Finally, at 7:30 p.m. David had left for a basketball game.

Despite Jane's time pressures she wanted to try for the umpty-umpth time to convince Diana how right he was for her. "He's my destiny. I want to support and nurture him. David needs plenty of nurturing." She nodded her head several times emphasizing the point.

"Did he ever say, 'I need to be nurtured?' " Diana asked. She took two Coke cans from her bag and opened one for Jane, setting it next to the typewriter. She opened the second for herself.

"No, but I know. He had such a sad childhood." Jane thought of the nights spent in his arms listening to, "Tales of David's Youth."

She knew if she created a loving environment, like the one she grew up in, she could erase his unhappy past. He would open like a bud into a rose, a caterpillar into a butterfly. Even her mother had said that she had to train father. He'd become a wonderful husband.

Diana, intrigued by her roommate's change into hopeless love addict, said, "Tell me more!" with a willingness of a good friend to consider she might be two percent wrong about David. She hoped she was. She doubted it. "But Jane, I'm sorry, I find it hard to see a tragedy in being the son of a successful Philadelphia doctor. I mean, how can I feel sorry for a family that has one Mercedes Benz per household occupant?"

"He's got lots of pressure on him," Jane said. "His father is a backbone specialist."

Diana, who'd flopped on the bed, looked confused. "I thought you said he was a GYN."

"It's got nothing to do with medicine. Dr. Johnson believes in building the hardest, strongest, best backbones in his sons. Hard work. No emotion. But his theories backfired."

Diana didn't have to encourage Jane to continue. Stopping her from sharing the latest David information— that would have taken encouragement.

Jane pushed her chair back. "David's oldest brother is living in Sweden."

"What's wrong with that?" Diana asked.

"The way he did it. He didn't tell his commanding office that he'd booked a flight from Saigon. There's still a warrant for his arrest," Jane said.

Diana nodded. "God! The good doctor must have been mega-bullshit." At least this type of information was less vomit-producing than listening to how cute David looked when he slept.

"Not just mega-bullshit. He disowned him. You see, Dr. Johnson also had to give up his hopes of a medical practice of Johnson, Johnson, Johnson and Johnson."

"What about brother number two?" Diana asked.

"The middle brother? In his sophomore year at Harvard

he dropped out all the way to Sunset Strip where he does drugs all day."

"So it's down to Johnson & Johnson, like baby care products," Diana said.

Jane glowered for a moment. "All his hopes rest in David . . ."

Diana only half listened to Jane's babble about her projected care and feeding of David. When her roommate finished Diana said, "You're nuts." Throwing her Coke can away, she added, "Listen, since you'll be typing all night, I'm going to sleep in Sandy's room. He's with Gail tonight. However, I'll be back if she throws him out."

"You're wonderful," Jane rolled a piece of paper into the machine.

"I know." Diana picked up her books, teddy bear and pajamas. "I hope you get both papers done. If you need help, call." The door clicked shut behind her.

Turning the page she'd just finished typing, Jane decided maybe she and Diana would never agree on David, a conclusion Diana was reaching in the room across the hall. While Jane wondered if Diana were jealous, Diana thought Jane a fool for falling for all the *Ladies Home Journal* and *Good Housekeeping* garbage that she devoured monthly. Neither would risk their friendship by voicing their opinions.

Jane glanced at the clock. She looked at the back of the yellow sheet that she'd finished copying. There was a note written on it. "Darn," she said. The note belonged halfway through the completed page. She picked up the perfectly typed piece of paper and threw it away before starting over.

Not sure of a word, she looked it up in the scientific dictionary which David had left with her. "He was so sweet to leave this book knowing it would help," she said to Ho Tai.

The god beamed his ceramic smile.

Finishing David's paper at 1:30 a.m., Jane started hers, integrating the foot notes from separate cards and writing the conclusion. Typing the final word at 5:08 a.m., she tumbled into bed at 5:08:30. As she fell asleep she imagined David taking the paper, dropping to his knee and saying, "Not a typo, marry me."

Instead the next day when he picked it up, he kissed her on the forehead and said, "Thanks. Maybe see you Friday night after my chem lab."

By 10:30 p.m. Friday, when Jane still hadn't heard from David, she went to bed. She was happy that Diana had gone to New York. She didn't have to wonder why he hadn't called and defend him at the same time. A knock allowed her to stop pretending to sleep.

"Telephone, Jane," a voice said outside her door. Jane hopped out of bed and ran barefoot to the hall. She slept in an oversized Brandeis sweatshirt, a gift from him on the second month anniversary of their meeting. Putting the receiver to her ear she prayed, "Let it be him."

"Meet me in Harvard Square," David said.

"Where?"

"ZumZum."

Jane threw on her jeans and wrapped a scarf around her forehead Indian-maiden style. She used another as a belt for her jeans. They were loose. She'd lost six pounds lately. Worry about David had destroyed her appetite.

The new leaves of the trees rustled slightly, but the breeze felt gentle, not cold. She thought about going back for a jacket, but didn't want to take the time. The T came immediately. Changing at Park Street for the Redline, Jane wasn't as lucky. She waited twenty minutes and then three subways came back to back. She hopped in the third to avoid being a human sardine.

She found David pacing between the Harvard Co-op and ZumZum. In the alcove next to the Co-op entrance a guitar player counted the money people had dropped in his case. David didn't kiss her. "What took so long. If I heard him play 'If I Had a Hammer' or 'Amazing Grace' once more, I was going to break into the music store and get him new sheet music."

"The T didn't come."

"Tell me something new. We're too late for ZumZum." Taking her by the elbow, he marched her across the street to The Wurst Haus. It smelled of beer and cabbage. Except for one couple and a man sitting at the bar, it was empty. They slid into a dark wooden booth. The waitress appeared within seconds, her pencil poised on her pad.

"I'll have two bratwursts, German potato salad, and a giant coffee. No, make that a Dunkle Dinkelacker. Want anything, Janie?"

She really wanted a Schwartzwald steak. It cost $6.95. Since she never knew when David would pick up the check or suggest they split it, she ordered pork chops cooked with cabbage and fries for $3.95.

The waitress brought the food within minutes. David cut a generous piece of one of the wursts, spread it with mustard and began chewing. After he swallowed he said, "Enjoy this now, because after we're married, we won't be able to afford to eat out."

Jane's hand stopped part way to her mouth, and the carefully cut bite of pork chop fell into her cabbage. "Even though I'll be working?"

"My father insists I pay as much as I can myself, so we'll need every penny you can earn." He took a long drink of beer. "I don't expect you'll earn all that much."

Her childhood fantasies of the great Wall of China flashed into her head. She wondered if she should tell him how much she loved him before he told her.

David cut another piece of wurst, then put his knife down and took her hand. "We got an A on my paper."

They ate for a few minutes. Or David ate. Jane pushed her food around her plate.

"It'll be hard, Janie, but I do love you."

"I love you too," she said. In her mind she was already preparing the home that would melt through David's brusque surface to the loving man she knew was waiting to escape.

A mosquito woke Jane on graduation morning. It buzzed in her ear then zigzagged across the room. Her eyes followed it until it disappeared.

The room looked strange. The bookcases were empty, their contents in cartons. Ho Tai had been wrapped in paper and placed in his own cotton lined show box for the trip to Connecticut.

The walls had large white spaces where posters of Joan Baez and Flower Power had hung. The closet's open door showed their academic gowns. Their mortar boards painted with "stop the war" sat on the otherwise bare desks.

The mosquito woke Diana, who groaned, "I wished we didn't have to go through today."

Jane stretched. "So who is going to tell our parents? They'll demand we repay all our tuition and want us to pay for last night's dinner, too."

Mary and Paul Andrews, the girls, Jim Bourque and Bill Reed, the editor-in-chief of the *Sarasota Journal* who had come to see "his professional daughter graduate," had eaten together at the Café Budapest. The restaurant was the type that when a customer put a cigarette in his mouth, the waiter lit it before the client could reach for a match.

"I'm still full," Diana said. "You're right. Our respective families, paid almost thirty thousand dollars for a photo with us in our caps and gowns, holding out diplomas and saying . . ."

". . . My daughter the college graduate. I wish we could do something that meant more to us. Our own ritual, just for the two of us." Jane's eyes filled. It wasn't spring allergies.

Diana jumped out of bed and opened her trunk, and started throwing things about. "Here it is." She grabbed her Paris or Bust T-shirt. "Where's yours?"

Jane sat up in bed and pointed to her trunk in the corner. "T-shirts are the third layer down. Don't go through my stuff like a gopher."

Diana carefully unpacked Jane's trunk and found the shirt. "Do you have any wrapping paper left from David's present?"

Jane pointed to a sealed box which Diana slit open and grabbed the roll of duck covered wrapping paper. Instead of retaping the box she interlocked the four parts on the top.

"Scissors? Tape?" Diana asked.

"Same box. You didn't retape," Jane said.

Cutting the paper carefully, Diana gift wrapped the two T-shirts together. Then she made a paper three dimensional star that she fastened onto the package. "This, my friend, is how we'll commemorate the farewell to our youth."

Both girls would start jobs July first.

Diana had gone to one campus interview more out of curiosity than anything else. An MGM Studio recruiter was looking for someone to write press releases. The man could have come from central casting. He wore jeans, a plaid coat and puffed on a cigar. Corporate recruiters wore blue pin-striped, three-piece suits. He'd taken one look at Diana's long hair and longer legs and said, "Baby, you really want to be an actress, don'tcha, not a press hack?"

"Why would I want to do that?" she'd asked, genuinely confused.

"Everyone wants to get in the movies." He'd brushed a fallen ash off his jeans.

"Well not me. Either look at my portfolio or not." She handed him her case. He opened it. Five minutes later she had a contract.

Jane had been hired by John R. Pringle, Inc., a textbook publisher. She was to churn out copy making the immediate purchase of those books the only acceptable alternative.

Their working lives would not start for a month. First they needed to graduate and get Jane married off.

Together they walked to the Charles River, looking for a place for their own rite of passage. On the way Diana handed Jane the gift wrapped T-shirts, and reached into her pocket for an elastic to pull back her hair into a ponytail. Frizzies escaped, making a wispy halo around her face.

"We'll melt in our robes." Jane darted across Storrow drive. She shifted her canvas bag that was somewhere between a pocket-book and a small suitcase to her other shoulder. The sack carried a microcosm of her life.

"What's your idea?" Jane asked as soon as Diana caught up.

"We're going to burn our T-shirts," Diana said.

"Our childhood will go up in smoke," Jane said.

"That's the idea. But our friendship won't. Not ever," Diana said. "I'll miss you."

"Me, too." Jane hugged her friend. She stood on tiptoes. Diana had to scooch down.

Summer 1967: Connecticut

The Johnsons and Andrews met for the first time two days before the wedding, scheduled for the last Saturday in June. David had come to stay at the Andrews' the night before his parents were due.

Jane went to bed knowing David was down the hall, properly tucked on the day bed in her mother's sewing room. When she got up to go to the bathroom she heard her mother saying softly, "Don't you think David's a bit cold?"

Her father's silence told Jane that he agreed, but then he said, "We won't have to worry about her. Doctors make good money."

"Money's not everything," Mary Andrews said.

Jane tiptoed back to bed with her father's "I know" ringing in her ears. She would warm David up as her mother had broken in her father.

The next day, as her mother prepared canapés for the great meeting and as the Johnsons drove from Philadelphia, Jane almost mentioned the conversation. She changed her mind, preferring to list David's strengths, his grades, his entrance exam scores. She didn't say what a wonderful lover he was.

Mary nodded at each virtue and then said, "I wonder what the Johnsons are talking about?" It was better she didn't know that Dr. Nathan Johnson mumbled half the way to the Connecticut farm that his son was marrying into a family of hicks. Lucille Johnson, immune to his mumbling, navigated them with homing pigeon accuracy directly from their long driveway into the Andrews' in four hours eleven minutes.

David, seeing the Mercedes pull in, went to greet them. He shook his father's hand and kissed his mother's up-turned cheek while Jane stood on the porch shifting her weight from foot to foot. When they joined her, she showed them inside.

Welcomes, questions about the drive, usherings first to the toilet then to the library soothed the first few minutes. Dr. Johnson settled himself in Paul Andrews' leather chair. A Bach concerto played in the background. "At least they weren't wearing coveralls," the doctor whispered to his wife as the Andrews went to the kitchen to get the hors d'oeuvres, wine and sangria that Mary had made for David because he said he liked it. Nathan's voice carried through the closed kitchen door.

Mary Andrews ignored the remark as she handed a tray to Jane with the last of their asparagus converted into finger sandwiches. A second plate had shrimp and avocados with a cocktail sauce. This she carried as Paul held the door for them.

Setting the Chardonnay on the table, Paul pulled out the cork and sniffed it. He poured a mouthful into his glass and tasted it before serving Mrs. Johnson. Jane and David chose the sangria. Then Paul lifted his glass. "To our kids' happiness."

Everyone watched Dr. Johnson examine the room. The

library was small, but every spare piece of wall was covered with books, not *Reader's Digest* condensations, but classics, some literary works, some popular novels, a lot of history and art books and agricultural texts. The only place there weren't shelves was over the fireplace where a primitive of a farm scene hung.

"Does the fireplace work?" Dr. Johnson asked.

"Of course, Nathan," Paul Andrews said. "Why wouldn't it?"

Jane said, "This was my favorite room growing up, especially when it snowed. I'd curl up on the couch with a book and hot chocolate."

"And she'd be there all day," Mary said. "Those nights we'd play games but in the kitchen. These old homes have such nice big kitchens."

"When did you buy the place?" Dr. Johnson asked.

"We didn't. It's been in my family since the early 1800s," Paul said.

"This is a real New England Yankee family," David said.

"Come over on the Mayflower?" Nathan's tone bordered on mockery.

"Two boats later." Paul measured his words.

"My family are the newcomers. We didn't arrive until 1672," Mary said. "But let's talk about our children. We'll help as much as possible."

"If my son marries, then he'll have to bear the consequences. A little hardship will develop his backbone." Nathan bit into a shrimp.

Jane choked, spewing sangria and an asparagus tip onto Lucille Johnson's white linen suit. As the stain spread, she felt as if she were watching a slow-motion film. She thought of blood from a gunshot wound.

Dr. Johnson jumped up to wipe his wife's skirt. "Water," he yelled.

Jane prayed her mother wouldn't say, "A stain is a memory," as she did when guests spilled something on a tablecloth or furniture.

"Salt will help," Mary said.

"No cockamamie 'Hints by Heloise' stuff," Dr. Johnson said.

Mary led Lucille into the bathroom to rinse the spot while Paul sat and listened to the ills of coddling the young. Jane noticed how her father's face became immobile and how his hands clutched the chair arms. When she guessed he was about to erupt, the women returned. The spot on Lucille's skirt was a damp memory.

"Excuse us, but I need my husband's help in the kitchen," Mary said, adding as soon as the door closed, "Pompous asshole."

"I wanted to punch his lights out," Paul said. Then he turned to see Jane's horrified face. "Honey, herd your future in-laws into the dining room."

Jane did as she was told, swallowing her tears. The last time she had heard her mother use crude language was when she was twelve. The man who had fixed their cesspool tank had miscalculated and sewage had spilled on the lawn making it smell worse than a pig farm.

At dinner the atmosphere grew colder than the chilled cucumber soup when Nathan said, "Last time we had this was at Allison Potter's. Remember David? Lucille, why are you grabbing my thigh?"

"Allison has a face like a horse, not pretty like Janie's," David said.

Jane wondered who Allison was and why this day kept going so wrong. Everyone else who she'd ever brought home had basked in her parents' warmth.

"My son has no idea how hard medical school will be," Nathan said, taking a last mouthful of soup. The spoon squeaked as it scraped the bowl.

Mary offered fresh beet salad to Lucille. "I'm sure Jane will have her hands full too."

Jane recognized her mother's tone. She'd used it with Paul's mother, who'd lived with them and had driven Mary Andrews almost crazy until the month her mother-in-law had died. The reason it wasn't until the *day* she died was that the woman had a stroke and was speechless the last fourteen days of her life.

Mary Andrews switched to her *I-won't-put-up-with-any-more-nonsense* tone. "I for one will do everything possible to help this young couple. Before you say no, Nathan, why should they buy furniture when our barn is crammed with pieces from Aunt This or Uncle That?" She went to get dessert—fresh strawberry shortcake.

A crash came from the kitchen. Paul Andrews started to get up, but Jane motioned for him to sit down. "I'll go, Daddy."

She found her mother sweeping up shards of a plate. "I needed a little fresh glass to decorate Nathan's dessert." She smiled sweetly and handed the shortcakes to Jane who looked at Nathan's portion very carefully before putting it in front of him. The sparkle was probably moisture on the berries.

By 7:30 p.m. the Johnsons had left for their hotel, having refused to stay at the farm. David had waved good-bye then suggested he and Jane go for a walk.

"It could have been worse," David said as they passed the cornfield. The plants were six inches high. They had a

42

long way to go before Mary Andrews would start the water boiling before telling her husband to pick six ears.

Jane looked at David in disbelief. "Other than that, how did you like the play, Mrs. Lincoln?"

"Don't exaggerate. I know my father comes on a little strong."

"And the Rock of Gibraltar is a pebble," Jane said.

David draped his arm around Jane's shoulders. "Let's not fight."

They walked past the rock which, as a child, Jane had painted yellow then pretended it was a palomino. The paint had worn away a long time ago. She started to tell David then stopped. Too often in the past, when she'd tried to talk about her feelings or childhood, he'd hushed her with a "don't be silly" or "stop talking nonsense." When it happened, she comforted herself with the thought that his devotion to medicine made him serious.

They walked hand-in-hand, not talking, enjoying the last of the day's sun on their faces. Jane broke the silence. "Let me show you something." She led him to a circle of trees. The center was moss carpeted. "When I was little we picnicked here." Kneeling, she ran her hand over the moss that reminded her of a velvet Christmas dress.

David hunkered down to feel it. He pulled Jane to him and kissed her. Their skins smelled musty from sweat and sun. He touched her breast, leading into the pattern of lovemaking established in his dorm room. The glade was far roomier than his single bed.

David came quickly, his eyes tightly shut. Jane followed. "Was it good for you?" he asked.

"Yes, but when I was little I never imagined making love here."

While David struggled into his cutoff jeans, Jane

43

watched him dress. She began to twirl, her arms stretched toward the sunset.

"You're so cute," he said. "I love you."

Fifty friends and relatives were invited to the noon, backyard wedding and reception. The temperature soared to ninety degrees before the clock struck nine.

"At least the tent will give some shade," Paul Andrews said as he carried another rented table. He rolled up the sides of the tent to give some air. Chairs for the guests were lined up outside the tent, twenty-five on each side of the flagstone walk leading to the rose trellis where David and Jane would exchange their vows.

As Mary Andrews finished decorating the cake she'd baked, the caterer carried ice cream molded like grape clusters resting on spun green sugar to the cellar freezer. Instead of a plastic bride and groom, pink frosting roses cascaded down the four tiers of the cake intertwined with real lilies of the valley anchored in hidden vials.

Two and a half hours later, Jane peeked out of her bedroom window at guests fanning themselves with whatever they could. Diana sat on the bed watching Jane pull on her lace gloves.

"Help me button these, please." Jane held out her hands. The fingers were open to allow the ring to be slipped on.

Diana broke a nail struggling with the tiny buttons. As she grabbed nail clippers, she asked, "Aren't you afraid David will turn out like his dad?"

"Bite your tongue," Jane said.

The girls were alone. Mary Andrews, who had been in and out, up and down stairs, checking details already checked, had left to fix her make up—to both girls' relief. "I never saw my mother dither before."

They looked at each other and the same thought passed between them. Diana would never have a mother dithering over her. Jane hugged Diana who said, "It's OK."

Placing the wide brimmed straw hat on Jane's head, Diana pulled strands of Jane's pixie haircut until she felt her friend looked like a bride should. "You never got married before. That gives her dithering rights."

Diana wore a simple blue dress. Her hair had been forced into a French braid with flowers entwined. Even so, tendrils escaped. She grabbed Jane by the shoulders and spun her around to look in the mirror of her Victorian dresser. It resembled a throne with its marble covered arms. Jane's bouquet was on one, Diana's on the other.

"Are you absolutely, drop-dead sure you want to go through with this?" Diana asked. "We announce the wedding is off, make it a big party. Return the gifts. Save yourself writing thank you notes."

"I'm absolutely sure," Jane lied.

There was a double rap on the door. "Time to give my baby away," Paul said through the door.

"Onward and outward." Diana pushed Jane out the door.

Two boy cousins, eight and ten, rolled out a white carpet. The four-year-old girl next door scattered petals.

Diana started down the carpet ahead. Not seeing a bump caused by an uneven flagstone, she tripped. Jane fell on top of her. Mr. Andrews helped them to their feet. "Pretend it didn't happen," he whispered.

The organist, playing the rented organ in the living room, had her back to the window and kept playing.

Summer and Fall 1967: Boston

The young Johnsons began married life in backbone-weakening luxury. Dr. Johnson's university roommate lived on Beacon Hill. Like many of the residents, he could trace his family history to the early Boston Brahmins. In his case, he traced it back to John Quincy Adams.

Because the current Adams family had rented a tall ship for the summer, they needed house sitters to guard the family antiques, water plants and walk the family's Japanese Chin.

"I wonder what a presidential descendent looks like?" Jane had asked, ringing the door bell. The brick townhouse, built in 1803, still had more than half of the original violet-tinted glass windows.

"Like anyone else, dummy," David said, ruffling her hair. He'd known Dr. Adams since his childhood. "Except for the powdered wig, of course."

A squirrel darted through an iron railed fence. Scampering up a tree in the grassy area that served as a communal neighborhood lawn, he chattered to the newcomers.

"Are you two coming in or spending the next two months watching that squirrel?" They turned to see Dr. Adams in cutoff jeans, a Celtic T-shirt and wet, but unpowdered hair. "Sorry I took so long to answer. I was in the shower."

They went into a hall cool from air conditioning. A small black and white dog eyed them. "Meet Saki. He loves everybody," Dr. Adams said.

The doctor may have remembered to tell David and Jane which plants needed what kind of care, what days the cleaning woman arrived and about the idiosyncrasies of the house, but he forgot to tell Saki that he was supposed to love everyone. The dog did fall passionately in love with Jane. As for David, the moment Doctor Adams shut the door behind him, Saki lifted his leg on David's suitcase. The two males' relationship did not improve for the eight weeks the couple house-sat.

The Friday before Labor Day, Jane and David went to Harvard's Medical School for their housing assignment. Standing in front of the Med School's grassy quadrangle surrounded by marble buildings, they watched two students throw an orange Frisbee.

"Fun," Jane said.

"Maybe you'll have time to play Frisbee. I won't," David said.

Jane touched his arm. "It won't be like your nightmares," she said referring to his dreams that had kept them both awake. Since she knew he didn't like to talk about them, she asked, "Where do we go?"

David took a paper from his shirt pocket. "Fanny Tackaberry Building."

Inside the office, a desk, bookcase and chair occupied most all of the available space. Jane and David squeezed in. David motioned for Jane to sit while the woman flipped through the card file.

"Studio 3B, 475 Park Drive." She almost threw the key at them.

They cut across The Fenway to their new home. The six-story building was white stucco, a former apartment house converted to married student housing. Small glass panes lined each side of an ornately carved door.

After David unlocked 3B, he slung Jane over his shoulder, "Consider you've been carried over the threshold." When he set her down, he kissed her nose.

The apartment smelled of fresh paint. Because of two floor-to-ceiling windows, it was bright.

Jane opened the half-sized refrigerator, two cabinets and turned on the tap. The water ran rusty. "I've two burners but no oven." She could prepare most of the meals she'd copied from "Twenty-five meals under $1.50" in *Family Circle*.

The bathroom door was open. The tub had claw feet and a permanent green stain from years of dripping water. Everything was operating-room clean. "This whole place isn't as big as the Adams' library." She'd meant it as a statement of fact.

"You knew it would be tough," David said.

Paul and Mary Andrews drove from Connecticut with a desk, kitchen table, two chairs, bookcases and a sofa bed from the Andrews' barn. Mary and Jane found flowered chintz and reupholstered the couch. They painted the two chairs and table the same yellow as the flowers in the fabric.

"The apartment looks good. I'm surprised," David said as they set the last piece in place.

"Never underestimate the power of a woman," Mary Adams said.

"We won't tell your father," Paul said. "Let him think

the school furnished the place."

The Johnsons weren't the only ones moving in that day. Up and down Park Drive, in fact all over the city, yellow U-Haul trucks parked as students from the city's fifty-four universities settled in for another year. This annual migration was as regular as geese flying south in October.

The Andrews didn't stay. "Gotta make way for the next truck." Paul kissed his daughter and patted his son-in-law on the back. Mary kissed both of them. David looked startled.

As soon as her parents left, Jane unpacked the wedding gifts: pots, pans, dishes, glasses, towels, sheets, blankets. Standing back, she admired Auntie Helen's spice rack, then arranged her most original gift. Mrs. Brown, who lived on the next farm, had filled a basket with small kitchen utensils, like a vegetable peeler and garlic press. The things that were too cheap for individual gifts but together cost a fortune. Jane couldn't remember feeling so content.

When she finished, they made love on new sheets. *I have everything I want,* she thought.

After David arrived home on his first day of classes, he sank in a chair.

"How did it go?" Jane asked. She draped her arms around him. He pushed her away.

"The profs said no one flunks out." What he didn't say was that nothing else they said made much sense. The handouts hadn't helped. "I've got lots to study, so please be quiet." He opened up a text book. Jane could smell the new paper.

Jane made up the sofa bed. She read the issue of *Life* she'd borrowed from the office and then fell asleep with the magazine on her chest. She woke and looked at the clock. It was after midnight. David slept, his head on his folded arms that rested on his text.

If David had adjustment problems in school, Jane had had none at work. She settled quickly into her new job under the watchful eye of Lucy La Flamme, an old maid fifty pounds overweight. Lucy's bleached hair, piled at least three inches above her forehead, defied gravity. Lucy's personality and drill sergeant voice made everyone at JRP quake. The department secretary told Jane that even President Harrison Codrington III quaked when Lucy spoke.

People listened, but not from fear. Lucy knew the textbook business. When she said, "This book won't sell," editors scrambled to the authors for rewrites or reduced the print run. No one remembered Lucy ever being wrong.

Lucy barraged Jane with information about targeting markets, designing and writing brochures, pushing them through production and selecting lists. In August, she gave Jane sole responsibility to sell a text.

The book, written by an anthropologist, showed how Lobi women in Ghana controlled men by convincing them that touching cooking pots caused their genitals to wither. "Too bad we can't do the same," Lucy cackled. "That's real power. The key to a man's balls and stomach."

Jane and Lucy brainstormed all possible buyers. Jane suggested mainstreaming the book and produced research to back it up. Then she came up with a publicity campaign and budget. Management balked.

Jane found Codrington and Lucy in Lucy's office. For once her boss had no cigarette dangling from her lips, in deference to Codrington's asthma. He offered Jane his chair.

"Are you confident enough that you'd stake your job on this, Jane?" he asked.

Jane looked at Lucy. Lucy looked at Jane. Codrington looked at both of them. Knowing how much she needed the job, wondering how she would tell David she'd been fired, she said, "Yes."

"You agree, Lucy?" Codrington asked.

"I back my assistant."

"We'll do it." He bowed and left the room.

Jane slouched in her chair.

"Honey, you're brave. He won't fire me, but if we don't make your advertising budget, you're out the door. I won't be able to save you."

Never had Jane wished so hard for someone to talk to. She couldn't tell David what she'd risked. Diana still hadn't sent her California address.

The ads broke. Jane pushed the author's agent to wheedle for a *New York Times* book review. It worked. The review appeared the first Sunday in October.

Halloween, when Jane walked into her office, Lucy sat with two chocolate cupcakes decorated with chocolate cats on orange frosting and two cups of coffee. "This is a celebration," she said, tossing Jane the sales figures. In four weeks the book had sold 14,530 copies. Normally JRP, Inc. was content with a 2,000 book run over four years.

Lucy grinned. "When you look good, I look good." She picked up the phone and punched three numbers. "She's here," she barked into the phone.

Within minutes Harrison Codrington appeared. "Young lady, there'll be a five dollar raise in your paycheck. Lucy, next time buy me a cupcake, too." He left, then came back. "And anytime you want to break our sales records, I won't

51

ask you to risk your job again."

Thus Jane felt competent by day, but at night she led a different life as wife of a suffering medical student.

She wrote Diana in care of Jim Bourque, for she had heard nothing from her ex-roommate.

Hi Buddy,

My days are full of the unexpected, but my nights are peppered with knowns. We're like all couples in this building—not enough space, time or money. My raise helps, but we have five ways we need to spend the same money. I miss having a best friend to talk to. Hope your life is more glamorous and exciting than mine. Please write, I miss you.

Love, Jane

As she finished writing, David said, "Please stop rattling the paper Janie. I can't concentrate."

Licking the envelope, she said, "Sometimes I think you think I'm plotting against your studies."

"You said it; not me." He picked up his books and left. Jane guessed he went to the library. Able to make noise, she used the time to vacuum the apartment.

She put cookies on a plate to leave for David when he returned from his studying. Arranging brown and white sugar cubes in a pattern she left it next to a cup with a tea bag. All he would have to do was heat the water. Before she could put it in a pan, the door bell rang.

"Hi, I'm Bridget Saunders." She pointed to the apartment at the other end of the hall. "Come visit. I can't leave the bedroom qualifier too long." Her accent was English.

Jane looked confused.

"Cecil, our baby. Means we get allotted a bedroom."
Bridget opened the door to reveal the man with Dumbo
ears, whom Jane had seen in the hall sitting at the table
studying amid a pile of unfolded diapers. His smile warmed
her.

"Hello, I'm Nigel, your husband's anatomy partner. If
you ladies are going to chatter, I'll hide in the library." His
accent matched his wife's. He hugged her and left.

After that, many evenings while Nigel and David
studied, Bridget and Jane visited. "If you need anything, I'll
be across the hall," Jane would say to David who might or
might not indicate that he had heard. Then over pots and
pots of tea, she and Bridget would talk. Although Bridget
wasn't Diana, she brought lightness back into Jane's life.

Jane arrived home drenched to the skin. Stripping as
soon as she shut the door, she went into the bathroom and
turned the shower to scald. David came in and sat on the
toilet. "What's for dinner?"

"American chop suey." She poured shampoo on her hair
making sure both shoulders boiled under the heat until her
bones thawed.

"Again?"

"It's cheap."

Throughout dinner David had a textbook propped up.
Finally he looked up. "I'm sorry. It's a good meal." He
walked around the table and kissed Jane on her hair. She
turned to hug him, tenderness flooding through her. That
night they went to bed at the same time and made love.

"I know this isn't much fun for you Janie," David said.
"Someday I will make it up to you."

"You've got a lot of pressure on you," she said.

They fell asleep holding hands.

★ ★ ★ ★ ★

JRP, Inc. closed for Veterans Day. Both Jane and David slept in, back to back, her foot trapped between his calves. Nigel's knock woke them. David, dressed in T-shirt and jockey shorts, let him in.

"You're wasting the day. The library is open. Let's go and talk about Mildred and the test." Nigel was talking about their shared cadaver.

David threw on jeans and a sweatshirt. "Stay in bed, Janie. I'll get coffee at Sparr's."

Bridget stuck her head in the Johnson's door an hour later. "Let's go for a walk. It's a super day."

Jane, cozy in her flannel nightie, had been reading *Exodus*. "Agreed." She dressed and spread a slice of bread with peanut butter and peeled an orange. She ruffled her hair, cut extra short to make the cut last longer. As she crossed the hall, she heard Cecil scream.

"He detests getting dressed." Bridget pushed her son's flailing arm through the miniature fisherman knit sweater. Her teeth clenched. She put the dressed baby in the stroller that she called a push cart. Together they carried the baby down the stairs and out the door.

The sky shone brilliant blue. The temperature climbed into the sixties. Whiffs of burning leaves tickled their noses.

The women walked by the superintendent raking more leaves into a fire. He tipped his Red Sox cap.

"Let's go to the Victory Gardens," Bridget said. She put her weight on the handle of the stroller to turn it.

The gardens were tended by nearby residents with yens for country living. The small parcels of land produced fruit, herbs, flowers and vegetables. Some had picket fences. Others were protected by wire.

"Half the city is here," Bridget said. People were

cleaning up for the season. In one, a little boy, not more than five, pulled weeds with his father. He ran to the fence and peeked through.

"Look," he said to the girls. "We still have pumpkins. Mummy's making pie."

Jane knelt so she was face level to him through the chicken wire. "Maybe you can cut a jack-o-lantern face in the pie."

The child wiped his sleeve across his runny nose. "I'll ask her."

His father came over to the fence. "Would you like a couple of pumpkins?"

The women protested.

"You might as well. Kids will smash 'em if you don't."

The little boy opened the gate and pointed out the pros and cons of each pumpkin. Bridget held up an oval one. "If I hollow it out, I can put flowers in it."

"This one has pie written all over it," Jane said.

"Where?" the little boy asked.

Bridget propped the pumpkins on each side of Cecil. He listed over to taste one with his tongue.

They walked in silence, stopping to sit on a bench facing the Muddy River. Jane stared at huge reeds growing along the bank. Suddenly she ran to the water's edge and broke off half a dozen reeds, each about the width of her thumb. Then she placed them parallel to each other.

"What are you doing?" Bridget asked.

"With tiny nails and wires they'll make great blinds. Better than the blankets I use now."

Over the weekend the women made blinds for both apartments. David and Nigel made fun of them until two students saw them and paid the two women to make a set.

Bridget took a sample to a used furniture store where the

owner displayed them. He took orders for a commission. As long as the blind factory stayed across the hall, David didn't complain.

Nigel said, "Our flat is so confusing one more thing doesn't make any difference."

The Boston Globe carried an article about how the parks department had arrived to do their annual weeding along the banks and found it already done.

Neither couple had to worry about paying for text books the next semester. They had made close to five hundred dollars between them.

A snowstorm struck mid-November. The weather stayed cold through Thanksgiving and into the Christmas shopping rush.

Jane's walk to work took forty-five minutes. When leaves layered the sidewalks, the walk had been pleasant. Now it was raw and dark morning and night. Ice-coated bricks made each step a challenge. Even wrapped in scarf, gloves, striding briskly, Jane arrived at either destination chilled.

I'm saving $2.50 a week by not taking the T, she told herself. But three times when the chill factor was below ten degrees, she gave in. Those days she went without buying a Coke to go with her brown bag lunch.

December 13, leaving JRP, Inc.'s offices, she turned. The windows were frosted with lace patterns. New snow covered the brown slush of yesterday's storm. She decided to take the T.

At Park Street Station, a Salvation Army band played "Silent Night." Jane reached into her pocket for her only quarter. She looked at the turnstile leading into the subway. She looked at the coin and threw it into the kettle. Humming the carol as she walked home, she told herself what a really dumb thing that was to do.

She kept warm with fantasies of a cup of hot, sweet, milky tea. Entering the studio, she saw David at his desk transcribing notes. He didn't look up. Her fingers refused to obey her brain's order to undo her coat buttons.

She filled the kettle with water.

"Shhh," David said.

"Thank you, I had a wonderful day. Nice of you to ask."

David looked up. "What's wrong?"

"I'm freezing."

"It's cold out."

"No shit," Jane said ignoring his frown. Walking home hadn't bothered her. However, when *she* got home first, she always greeted David with a hug to make him feel welcome. Being shushed wasn't an acceptable alternative.

"Don't start, Janie; I've lots to do," David said.

Jane made her tea with borderline slams of doors, cups and saucers. Usually she would have made David a cup, training him by example into how to be giving. This time she felt he was training her how to be hard. She opened the refrigerator. There was no milk.

"I asked you to pick up milk," she said.

"I didn't have time."

"You walk by the supermarket on your way home."

"It was too cold to stop."

Jane slammed the refrigerator door. A pot on top rattled. "You have a ten-minute walk. Mine is forty-five. I have to walk past our front door and go another seven minutes beyond," she said.

"Leave me alone," he said.

She leafed up the mail as she sipped milkless tea. A dark blue envelope addressed to her bore a Los Angeles postmark. Her name was written in calligraphy with white ink.

Turning it over she saw a wax seal stamped with a gothic D. Jane opened it without disturbing the wax.

A white dove flying across a smoky sky wished her peace. Inside the card, written in the same calligraphy were the words, "Shit on the whole thing! Love, Diana."

Jane stared at the card. Then she burst out laughing. She couldn't stop. Every time she tried, she'd go off in another burst. David got up, looked at it and shrugged.

Several minutes passed before Jane regained control. "Empty your pockets," she said to David as she wiped her eyes. Without asking he did, piling the change on the table.

"What are you doing?" He watched his wife rummage through her bags and pockets.

"I'm calling Diana." $4.15 in change was on the table.

"That would buy me two lunches," David said.

"Or two weeks of subway rides for me." After tucking The Card into a drawer, Jane went to the hall to use the phone.

February 1968: Florida

A pelican settled on the post next to the Lemon Bay Inn. The Inn's terrace ran almost to the water's edge.

Apart from Jim and Diana Bourque, all the other couples were retirees. Because they sat closest to the water the pelican stared at them, periodically flapping his wings.

"Intimidation won't work, friend," Jim said to the bird. "I'm sharing nothing." He broke off a piece of pecan roll. He noticed his daughter shivering. "Cold, honey?"

She pulled her sweater around her shoulders. "After Boston winters, this is heaven."

The waitress snaked her way between tables pressed as close as possible. "Another Bloody Mary?" She plucked a pencil from deep within her teased hair, which contained a bow matching her pink uniform and cheek rouge. Her name tag read, "Hi, my name's Betty."

Jim pushed his glasses from the bridge of his nose and quickly surveyed his menu. "Pompano fresh?"

"Your dinner swam in the Gulf this morning."

"I'll take the pompano," he said.

"Shrimp," Diana said. The waitress left. Early-bird specials didn't carry choices. One size of vegetable and salad fits all.

The pelican watched Diana take the last pecan roll. She wiped her sticky fingers on her napkin.

Jim watched every move his daughter made. "Let's talk about you."

She avoided his eyes. She'd been avoiding any serious conversation with him since he'd found her on his couch eight weeks before.

The super had let her into Jim's new condo the night before she'd flown in from the West Coast. While waiting for her father, she'd fallen asleep on the familiar furniture in the unfamiliar room.

Jim hadn't been surprised to find her there. He'd thrown his sweater over a chair and asked if she wanted a Bud or a Coke.

He had waited for her to talk that night and every night since. The waiting time was over.

Jim played with his knife. "My condo's spotless. It's painted. I've new curtains, albeit with uneven hems." He put his fingers to his lips to stop her from speaking. "I've enough frozen meals to feed the entire Seventh Army should they drop by for dinner. This isn't any daughter I know. My kid flunked home ec three consecutive years and once claimed vacuuming caused pimples. So tell me—what are your plans?" He tried to put on his hard face but couldn't. He could, however, wait for Diana to talk, a trick learned from interviewing people who didn't want to be interviewed.

Diana toyed with the empty breadbasket. The silence grew louder. Finally she blurted out, "I want to work for you."

"No!"

"Why not? BU gave me good training. I've got some great clips."

"You're not ready," he said.

"You won't give me a chance. I worked for you when I was in high school."

"And Bill Reed spent hours correcting your spelling."

"Never my facts. Or my style. And my spelling's improved."

"Only one way to go." Jim drummed his fingers on the table. She looked at him. He looked at her; master and mistress of the poignant pause.

The staring contest was a draw interrupted by Betty with their dinners. She placed the plates carelessly. Jim ordered a carafe of dry white wine, an afterthought.

When the waitress left Jim said, "Diana. I don't hire anyone without real experience. Fluff and powder Hollywood releases don't do it."

Diana stared at the yellow paint embedded under her fingernails. It matched the new color in Jim's bedroom. She speared a shrimp, then put it down without tasting it. Using the back of her hand, she brushed tears away.

"Level with me. Why didn't you go to Paris?" He rubbed his chest at a contraction not from his physical heart but his emotional one.

Diana bit her lip. When she did speak, it was in the direction of the pelican. "Truth?"

He nodded. The only time he'd caught her lying, she was seven. She had sat on her bed, her lip jutting out and said that the housekeeper had spilled the forbidden chocolate soda in her bed. Jim had spanked his daughter—the first and last time he had ever laid a hand on her. "I will not have a liar in my family," he'd said. After that when he demanded information from her, she repeated either, "Truth?" or "I won't say."

"Fear." She looked at the pelican.

"Still scared?" he asked.

"To go alone without money, job or papers? Ya."

"Afraid of the language," he asked.

"The way you insisted I learn French, Spanish and German? How could I be afraid?" She wrinkled her nose, thinking of Jim embarrassing her with the school principal. The man had said Diana needed two years of one language and no more. She had been the only kid to take Spanish, French and German. Jim had hired tutors for all three. She practiced verbs like other kids practiced piano scales. She continued her pelican studies but certain muscles in her shoulders relaxed.

"Think your French is good enough to be a journalist in Paris?"

Diana switched from bird-watching to father-watching.

"I talked to Maurice DuBois today," he said.

"Who?"

"A kid in the resistance when I covered the war," Jim said. "He's no longer a kid. Has his own paper. He'll hire you, but you gotta start Monday."

Diana stared at her father.

"You'll get your credentials. After that you can work for me. Promise."

"I can't write French like English."

"Maurice publishes in both languages, although it wouldn't hurt to develop your French writing."

Diana upset her chair jumping up from the table to hug her father. Her movement frightened the pelican, who flew away.

Jim drove Diana across the Tamiami Trail to the Miami airport. He talked nonstop about his memories as a Paris correspondent, what she should remember and how he was jealous.

Diana said nothing, enjoying the sound of her father's voice. The two of them checked their watches periodically, although they had allowed more than enough time.

At TWA's gate, as everyone boarded the plane, Jim hugged his daughter, pushed her away but kept a grip on her shoulders. Looking into her eyes he began firing last minute instructions. "If Maurice is late take the Metro. You've enough francs. Don't go with strangers. Watch out for men who want to marry you for a green card and don't forget . . ."

The clerk gathering the boarding passes stood twirling the rope, ready to close off the area. He touched Jim on the shoulder and spoke with a clipped English accent, "Dad, let the little bird fly."

Diana hugged Jim once more before running through the gate. She made the plane as the doors were closing.

Back inside the gate, Jim blew his nose. Hard. He stayed looking out the window long after the plane had disappeared over the Atlantic.

Spring 1968:
Paris

March 15, 1968

You were right Jim . . . or what else is new. None of the horrible things I feared has happened. Of course, no French count has asked me to marry him, although I interviewed one.

Solange and Maurice are wonderful!!!! Solange helped me find my "flat," a room with a bed which looks like a couch, <u>IF</u> I make it up. Guess how many times I've done it???

You're wrong. I actually did—once in a row.

As for Solange, that's one classy lady. I should look that beautiful at forty. I should be that beautiful at twenty-three. She took me to all the "ries"—you know: boulange<u>rie</u>, chacute<u>rie</u>, epice<u>rie</u>—and introduced me to the owners to make sure I wasn't treated like another American brat in Paris.

'Always greet the person and exchange a few words,' she said. I've tested it both ways. It works. Monsieur Thibeau, the butcher, is even giving me cooking tips with every purchase. Too bad I didn't know him when I cooked all those meals for you.

Maurice doesn't play favorites, and I get my chance at

good and bad stories. Now I understand why you wanted
me to work for another paper.
If I get an international by-line can I come home and
work for you???? Just kidding. You can't keep me down
on the farm after I've seen Paree.

Love and kisses,
Diana

Diana reread the letter written on preprinted quad-rangle-marked paper. She'd printed one letter per square. For the first time she could write legibly, unlike what she produced on the lined paper she'd used all her life.

The café table held a demitasse with espresso dregs and an empty Coke bottle. In an ashtray a torn receipt signaled that she'd paid. She was alone except for a man dressed in a black sweater. He drank Pastis as he read *Le Monde*.

As she addressed the envelope, she glanced periodically through the window at a couple arguing. Searching in her bag, she found notebooks, a pick to pull through her tangles, her wallet, a flat metal box of cough drops, several business cards, but no stamp. She left the café for the *tabac* next door to buy stamps.

Diana sat at her IBM self-correcting typewriter. Six desks with typewriters were crammed side-by-side facing a row of another six. Because everyone was out gathering information the quiet was unusual and unsettling.

Two glass-protected offices flanked the entrance. One belonged to Maurice, the other to Bernard, publisher and editor, respectively. When she threw the sixth piece of paper away, Maurice came out of his office to stand next to her.

Diana looked up. "I don't understand it. When I talked

to that deserter, I knew what I wanted to say. Now every-thing's blank. I could just as well bang my elbows against the keys."

Maurice went to the espresso machine. The liquid hissed into two demitasse cups. Beige foam coated the liquid. He dropped three cubes of brown sugar into Diana's and one into his. When he set her cup on her desk, a new blank sheet had been rolled into her typewriter.

He sat on the corner of her desk and drank his coffee. "I have seen you holding your breath. That reduces your ability to think. Your brain needs oxygen. Take some deep breaths."

Diana inhaled and exhaled several times.

Maurice continued, "Put your hands on the keyboard."

She did.

"Put something on the paper," he said.

"I can't even start," she wanted to cry.

"Give me a noun."

"Deserter," she said.

"Type it."

She did.

"What does it mean?" he asked.

She thought a moment, turned to the typewriter and began pounding out the story. Maurice patted her on the back as he left.

Thirty minutes later she knocked on his door and handed him eleven sheets of paper, six in French, five in English. He transferred a stack of paper to another pile, making room for Diana's story. He'd once bet his staff that he could find any document that they named in his chaos within thirty seconds. Each reporter lost a hundred francs. His editor knew better than to bet.

Maurice leaned forward in his chair to read. He reached

for a pencil to make a couple of marks.

"What's wrong?" she asked.

"Relax. An accent was missing. Stop fidgeting. I've never shot a reporter."

He placed the stories side-by-side on his desk. "This is excellent writing. In both languages. I am calling Luke Harris at AP. Maybe we can get the English on the wire service." He reached for the phone then put it down without dialing.

"You changed your mind. You think it's too amateurish," she said.

Maurice shut the door. "Diana! You are so anxious to do a super human job that you are wearing yourself out. You're wearing *me* out."

Diana said nothing.

Maurice took out his cigarettes and lit one. "You're a talented kid."

For the first time she noticed his thick lashes. "I guess I'm afraid you hired me because of Jim. I want to prove myself in my own right."

"Is that what this is all about? Let me show you something." He walked to his file cabinet and pulled out a folder fastened by elastics at the corners. The folder was labeled, "Jim Bourque."

"Your father found me my first job. Now, do not think that is why I hired you." He showed her a letter stapled to copies of clips she'd sent Jim from Boston. Diana read the letter.

"Your father said to hire you based on these articles and my need, not on our friendship. I did. When I received his letter, Marc had quit me to write for television. I needed a new reporter." He paused. "Any other problems?"

"No." She felt really, really dumb.

"Good. The reason I wanted you to call Luke is you need contacts if you want to build the career your talent says you should. Now remove yourself from my office. I need to finish my work."

Diana picked up her story and the paper on which Maurice had written the AP number. Before she shut the door Maurice said, "Breathe more." He didn't look at her when he said it. He was already working on his next project.

The clock next to Diana's bed buzzed. She clasped it between her breasts while deciding how much longer she could stay in bed. Then she remembered. It was Sunday.

She groggily wondered what to do with her day. Too lazy to make a decision, she fell into a hazy state of half thoughts and dreams. Ideas floated through her head, some in French, some in English. One stuck. Nothing in her studio apartment said, "Diana lives here" except for piles of clothes and dirty dishes.

"That's what I'll do today. Work on my apartment. But later," she said to herself.

When Diana had begun talking to herself a few weeks ago, she pictured herself in a rocking chair, next to a barred window. Then she decided she would only be considered crazy if nonexistent people answered.

Fumbling for the latest issue of *Paris Match* on the floor, she puffed up her pillows. "I can read or nap as long as I want," she said.

Her isolation was self-chosen. Danielle, another reporter, had invited her to go to the forest in Fontainebleau. She'd said no but not because the ride on the back of Danielle's motorcycle would make her pray hard.

Solange had invited Diana for lunch—just her, not the rest of the staff. Despite the temptation of an excellent meal, she'd said no.

Pierre, the paper's film critic, had suggested a movie. She'd asked for a rain check. When he looked confused, she'd explained the idiom.

Since her arrival she had been occupied every minute. "I need time to decompress," she said.

"Meow," Lily, the landlady's cat, announced herself from the ledge outside her window.

"Hello, you daredevil, you." Diana twisted to open the window latch without leaving the warmth of her duvet.

As Lily settled in the sunbeam bisecting the bed, Diana twisted to stroke her. The cat licked her paw then rubbed her face. They stayed in companionable silence until Diana got up to go to the toilet. Lily wound herself around her legs. When Diana sat on the toilet, the cat sat next to her. Then when she flushed, the cat put her paws on the seat and watched the water swirl. "Flushing: a new spectator sport," Diana said.

She opened her refrigerator, which was under a board balanced between the sink and table. A hot plate rested on the top of the board. The cat rushed from the toilet to the refrigerator. Carefully, Diana shut the door easing the cat out. "Cats don't like Coke. If you want milk, you'll have to wait until I shop."

On Sundays a *marché* set up under the overhead metro tracks a block from Diana's apartment. Stands sold vegetables, meat, bread, cheese, wine, clothes, linens, books. Several merchants already knew Diana, calling her *La Grande Américaine*.

This Sunday, shopping basket in hand, Diana passed the

old man from whom she bought the vegetables that would rot in her refrigerator during the week. As soon as he saw her, he held out a handful of fresh peas.

"Picked this morning. Come look, *La Grande*," he said.

Diana took one and smelled. "They're so tiny."

The man scratched his beard, scraggly as usual, and leaned across the table hitting his scale as he did. When he spoke his voice was confidential. "That's the idea."

He looked around as if divulging a secret affecting French security. "Heat cream, but not to boil. Drop in these baby peas. Two minutes. No more." He put his fingertips to his mouth and kissed them, the ultimate French compliment. "Tell me next week how right I was." As he wrapped the peas in a newspaper he called, "Marie-Claude."

The woman at the next table looked over.

"Give *La Grande* some cream for her peas," the man said.

Many of Marie-Claude's customers brought their own bottles, but she had a few extra for those that didn't. Diana bought enough cream to share with Lily.

As soon as Diana poured cream into a saucer, Lily jumped to the counter. She had to push the cat to one side to lower the saucer to the floor.

Diana put a long metal coil into a pot of water and plugged the cord into the wall. She filled a metal net ball with tea and put it in a bowl. When the water was hot, she poured it over the ball. Following the instructions on how to cook the peas, she then cut some fresh bread. They finished eating about the same time.

When Lily returned to her sunbeam, Diana returned to the bed and *Paris Match*, two beings enjoying species-defined pastimes. Twenty minutes later, Diana put her magazine down. "Lily, it's too beautiful to stay inside. Definitely too beautiful to clean. I think I'll go play tourist."

Another tourist caught Diana's attention as she emerged from the metro. An American woman with a thick Texas accent demanded of a street vendor, "Is this spoon the real McCoy?"

"That's a real spoon, don't worry," Diana said. The street vendor winked at Diana. The woman glared.

Diana headed for the market a block from Notre Dame where every Sunday merchants sold everything possible for birds as well as the birds themselves.

"They make nice pets," a woman said. She was heavy. Wisps of grey hair escaped her black scarf. A white apron, covering her black dress, ended at her stocking and shoes. "What kind of birds appeal to you?"

"Live ones. My landlady's cat would consider it a snack." Diana noticed the woman had two gold teeth.

"You English?" the vendor demanded as she arranged packets of bird seed.

"American."

"Student?"

Diana said she worked in Paris.

"Good."

Diana felt the warmth of the woman's breath on her cheek as she stood on tiptoe to whisper in Diana's ear. "It's dangerous to be a student these days. My son is. All he talks about is revolution. Even today he and his friends are on the Left Bank. Plotting." She spat. "Meetings won't change anything. Life is meant to be hard."

Diana nodded. *"Bonne journée."* She ran to the nearest taxi.

* * * * *

The taxi deposited her on the Left Bank. As she tipped the driver an extra fifty francs for his speed, she wondered how she would trace a pre-revolution meeting without saying to strangers, "*Bonjour,* planning a revolution today?"

She remembered an article she'd read on overcrowding at the University of Paris. Was it five or ten times capacity? Was the student failure rate twenty or twenty-five percent? She could check statistics later if she needed them for her story—if she found a story.

First Diana searched for posters that might tell of a meeting. Posters told of concerts, a union meeting, a sale and a play, not a revolution. She walked the streets looking for a gathering without success. Stopping outside a book-store, she watched the pedestrians.

She spied a young woman, probably a year or two younger than herself. The girl's long hair streamed as she strode along, her arms crammed with flyers. She held them into her body so as not to drop any. Diana ran ahead, then turned so she was facing her while walking backwards.

"Excuse me, where's the student meeting? I was sup-posed to meet Colette there?" Diana turned to walk beside the girl.

"Follow me. I'm going. Help me carry these." She shoved half the flyers at Diana who grabbed them without dropping one. She could read the headline proclaiming rev-olution. "Aren't you excited about Danny speaking?" the girl asked.

Diana nodded. Although the girl was tiny, she walked so fast, Diana almost had to run to keep up.

They rounded a corner. A narrow side street with an even narrower sidewalk permitted walking single file. Stu-dents, looking like their stateside counterparts, walked towards them as another group spilled out of a house.

Everyone cheered. The speaker had arrived. Two students boosted a short man onto a Renault Dauphin. His red, shoulder length hair was tied back. He held his hands over his head to silence the group. Not a sound came from the crowd as he spoke.

Diana turned to the girl and whispered, "That's . . ." hoping the girl would fill in the blank.

"Daniel Cohn-Bendit. Danny the Red. Isn't he incredible?" She didn't look at Diana but kept her face on the speaker.

Incredible wasn't the word Diana would've used. Danny lacked the style of American protesters like Abby Hoffman, Fred Proctor or Angela Davis. That he didn't match Diana's idea of a revolutionary leader didn't matter. Hitler wasn't glamorous either.

"How long must we suffer?" Danny asked the crowd.

"No more!" yelled the crowd.

"When do we act?" he hollered.

"May 1st."

"Where?"

"Nanterre."

As he whipped the crowd into a frenzy with his catechism, Diana estimated the number of people at about four hundred. Then he was gone, leaving people behind standing with signs reading, "It's forbidden to forbid" and "No more de Gaulle."

She wandered around picking up pieces of conversations, asking questions. She saw no one who looked like an undercover cop. Maybe French *flics* were better at infiltrating than the FBI.

When Diana had heard enough, she grabbed the first

taxi she found. Throwing money at the driver as he pulled up in front of Maurice's apartment, she ran to the door and pressed the entrance code. The door clicked, and she pushed it open, then raced up the stairs. The elevator, with its delicate iron grill and ancient pulleys, would have taken too long.

The knocker on the door to Maurice's and Solange's apartment was a brass ring held in a lion's mouth. Maurice answered. His annoyed expression changed to a smile when he saw Diana.

She paused for a moment. He was dressed in jeans and a peasant shirt. His feet were bare. At some subliminal level she noticed how broad his chest and how flat his stomach were. Solange appeared behind him wearing silk lounging pajamas, looking as elegant as ever.

"Diana! What a surprise. Come in." Solange kissed her on both cheeks.

Not wanting to waste time on preliminaries, Diana gasped, "I'm onto a great story."

Solange smiled. "I do enjoy you Diana. You are so direct, so American. Go into the study of Maurice. We were about to have tea and strawberry tarts. Begin your talking, and I will bring them in."

"It's big. I want to break it," Diana said as Maurice ushered her into the library. Bookcases lined three sides of the room. The fourth wall had two floor-to-ceiling windows. Maurice drew the drapes to keep the sun streaming in from blinding Diana as she sat on the couch. She told him what she'd seen.

"France will break apart," he said. He reached into a desk drawer and pulled out a pipe. He tamped the tobacco until satisfied that it was ready.

Diana, having told him everything she knew, waited.

"The students will break it open. The adults will follow." Maurice sucked in on the pipe.

"In the States it's just the kids," Diana said.

"The adults are content there. Here they are not. Tell me what you know about the leader," Maurice said between puffs.

"He's a German who came during the war. He's an anarchist and a student at Nanterre."

"*Alors.* Nanterre took most of the University of Paris overflow. Have you ever visited there?" When Diana shook her head, he said, "It has about as much charm as a car factory. Maybe less. It is terribly overcrowded."

Solange wheeled in a cart with a tea pot, three bowls, sugar, cream and four strawberry tarts. As she poured the tea into bowls, she asked, "What has our Diana discovered?"

Maurice told her and said, "I think I will assign Pierre or Philippe to it." He picked up the phone.

Diana jumped up and disconnected it. "This is *my* story."

Maurice shook his head. "Negative. Too dangerous. I cannot risk you becoming hurt." Instead of redialing he sat on the couch.

"What would he tell your father?" Solange asked.

"Whoa!" Diana said. She paused, thinking of the best way to win her point. "I appreciate you wanting to take care of me, but I can't become a good reporter behind a desk. If you forbid me, I'll cover it anyway and sell it to the AP."

Maurice took his bowl of tea from his wife. Steam fogged his glasses when he took a sip. Taking his handkerchief, he wiped them clean. "Do that and I will sack you."

Diana sat across from Maurice. Their eyes met across

the tea cart. "Do what you have to do. I will do what I have to do. I am not missing this story."

Solange put her hand on her husband's knee. "*Mon cher,* you are making an emotional decision. If Diana were not the daughter of Jim what would you do?"

Maurice relit his pipe. "I would want someone more experienced."

Diana pointed to herself. "That's me. Think of the demonstrations I've covered already. You've read my clips. You showed them to me the other day."

Maurice gave a face shrug, typical of the French, where he pursed his lips, raised his eyebrows and jutted his chin out all at the same time.

Diana took it as the beginning of conciliation. "And . . . and . . . and I can give you more reasons. One, I look more like a student than Philippe with his gray hair or Pierre with his fat stomach. Two, they'll trust me because of my age. Three, I know how to move during a demonstration because I've been a demonstrator. Four, the kids think that newspapers are merely a mouthpiece for de Gaulle. As an ex-demonstrator I can offer them something and . . ."

Maurice blew air out of his mouth. "I will send Pierre with you. As a photographer and guard."

Diana hugged him as he reached for his tea. Some sloshed on the linen cloth lining the tea cart. Diana blushed and helped Solange clean it up.

As Diana left the apartment Maurice said, "If you are killed, you will have to telephone your father. I refuse to."

"OK."

"And one thing more. Reporters don't hug their publishers. It's unprofessional."

Diana knew from his expression he liked reporters hugging him.

The Card

★ ★ ★ ★ ★

Diana spent May of 1968 in hell.

She made contact with the revolutionaries by marching into Danny the Red's headquarters. Recipes for nitroglycerin, tetryl and picric acid were written in crayon on the wall between maps of the city that were covered with circles and arrows. An odor of marijuana hung in the air.

Six students, four girls and two boys, milled around the sparsely furnished room. They barely noticed her as they stacked pamphlets into cartons. Diana stood before the table where Danny was writing on a pad of paper. Although he saw her, he ignored her.

She interrupted him, introducing herself in French.

"So?" he asked in English. He continued writing.

"I work for *Le Journal de Paris*. I want to follow you and report to my paper and the AP," she continued in French.

He put his pencil down. "Only if I clear what you write," he said in English.

"I write things as I see them," Diana said in French. She pulled the other chair in the room around so she could sit at a right angle to him. He hadn't invited her to sit down.

"I check everything," he said again in English. The others in the room had stopped to listen.

"I'll show it to you, but I won't give you editorial privilege," Diana said in French.

Danny told two of his workers to get the pamphlets out on the street. "How can I trust you not to savage us?" he asked.

Diana switched to German. "How come you know American slang?"

He laughed. "How many languages do you know?"

"Four. Two, well. What will be ours?"

"French. Follow me." In the café downstairs, a man be-

77

hind the counter dried cups. He nodded to Danny, who helped himself to two espressos and took them to a table as far away from the window as possible and put them down. He turned a chair around and straddled it, resting his hands on the back and resting his chin on his hands. "Before I decide, I need to know more about you," he said. "Americans aren't multilingual. Why are you?"

"My dad insisted."

"Why?"

"To make me a better journalist."

Danny noticed Diana's grimace after sipping the coffee. Without a word he offered her sugar cubes from a small bowl. She took three.

They sparred for thirty minutes. The clincher came when Danny asked, "Fred Proctor?"

"We marched together. You know him?"

Danny said, "*Oui,* the movement is more and more connected. Would he vouch for you?"

Diana remembered the fights she and Fred had about her lack of commitment to the cause. "He'd probably say I spent too much time in class and not enough time fighting. You know Fred's on the FBI's most wanted list?"

"Hot damn!" Danny said. "What did he do?"

"Set off a bomb in a shopping center. And 'hot damn' was one of his favorite expressions," she said. "As if you didn't know. Let's stop playing games."

Danny made half nods with his head as Diana continued. "Even if he thought I was a lazy protester, he'd tell you I wrote some damned good articles about the movement."

"What do you want?" Danny asked.

"Live with you, day and night, until you win or lose. Report it as it happens."

"You've got it," he said.

The Card

★ ★ ★ ★ ★

The riots began at Nanterre. Change was written in blood.

Students barricaded themselves, not even giving up to tear gas. Behind the barricades, Diana helped the injured between reporting great acts of heroism and of cowardice. She scribbled notes when she wasn't bandaging someone.

When police cut phone lines, Maurice knew in advance and sent Diana a walkie-talkie. Pierre, on the other side of the barricades, relayed copy she dictated over it—*Le Journal de Paris* scooping everyone. AP, UPI and Reuters all picked up Diana's reports.

She and Danny fought over every word she released. Exhaustion slivered their nerves. At one point Diana screamed, "You're nothing but a fucking short de Gaulle."

Danny swung at her. Diana decked him. When she reached down to help him up, he pulled her down. "Let's stop fighting," they said together, and they did—until the next story.

The riot spread from Nanterre to the Latin Quarter, then spilled onto the Champs Elysées. Suddenly the students found themselves joined by thousands of workers, not only in Paris, but throughout the country.

The media no longer parroted de Gaulle's line. The battle moved to a calmer site—the television studios. Danny and other anarchist factions were invited to appear on a nationwide broadcast.

"I'll show you some tricks," Diana offered.

"Like what?" Danny asked.

She took a box and pretended it was a camera, then coached him on how to turn to get the best angles. "Move with it," she said.

"How do you know this?" he asked.

79

"Part of my journalism course included three television production classes. We also learned how to be on camera. Let's role play this again, and when I ask you a question, sneak in another point."

Danny held both his thumbs up in approval.

The night after Danny's appearance, Diana staggered home for the first time in days. Before letting herself into her apartment, she knocked on her landlady's door to say she was home. The woman, a widow in her fifties, was impeccably dressed as usual.

"When did you eat last, dear?" the widow asked. Diana couldn't remember.

The widow opened her refrigerator. "I haven't much." Seventeen minutes later Diana looked at a plate of creamed spinach with hardboiled eggs and a glass of apple juice on china and crystal. The napkin was linen and a yellow rose sat in a silver bud vase.

Unlocking her door, Diana felt disoriented. Her unmade bed, books, clothes and desk were as she had left them, but they no longer seemed hers.

She turned on the television to see how the TV stations were reporting the riots. Pompidou filled the screen blathering about peace. De Gaulle had gone to Romania. Diana fell onto her bed without undressing. She slept twenty-six straight hours without being aware of the television running in the background.

When Diana walked into the newspaper office for the first time in fifteen days, everyone cheered except Colette, who was talking on the phone. She waved.

Colette said, "She just came in. Hold on. Telephone, Diana."

Diana hugged Pierre, kissed Bernard on both cheeks and blew kisses to the rest of the staff as she headed for the phone. She shook her hair away from her ear before putting the receiver to it. "Hello."

"I got a scoop for you," Danny said. "The French border guards won't let me in."

"Where are you?" She fumbled for a pen and paper.

"Germany. I went to talk to a group. Now I'm headed for Holland. I'll call you later."

Pierre, Colette, Bernard, Danielle, Maurice and the rest of the staff gathered around Diana. They fired questions as only reporters can, until Diana held up her hands.

As everyone drifted back to their own work, Pierre said, "When they fired the tear gas I was really scared for you, partner. You've got real balls."

"We made a great team. I've got to tell Maurice I lost my walkie-talkie."

"After those stories, he'll forgive you anything," Pierre said. He tossed Diana all her clips, including those from the wire services.

At lunch time, Diana refused to leave in case Danny called. Colette bought her a cheese-filled baguette and a Coke.

Each time the phone rang, Diana jumped for it. She talked with Pierre's wife, a drunk who saw a UFO, Luke Harris of the AP and the mayor of Paris, who demanded to speak to the publisher.

It was late afternoon when she heard Danny say, "They won't let me into Holland either. Can you get some messages to my people?"

When she hung up, Maurice signaled her. She stood in front of his desk. "There's something I want you to think about." He pointed to a paper-covered chair. Diana piled

81

the papers on the filing cabinet and sat.

Maurice cleared his throat. "I am not saying you are wrong, but there is a difference between objectively reporting the news and making it."

She bit her tongue rather than say, "You don't like my work." Instead she told him about Danny's messages.

"What I am saying is you must make sure you know where the difference is. Go deliver the messages of Danny. Then I want an article on the other side. About de Gaulle."

"I'll lose my credibility with Danny," Diana said.

"That is part of the lesson. Learn to keep it in both groups."

Diana spent the next nineteen minutes fighting. When she pounded the desk, Maurice lowered his voice. He refused to budge.

"But if you lose my access, you could lose that whole side of future developments," she said.

"You will not let that happen. Now leave."

Diana stood. Her hand rested on the door handle as she opened her mouth. Maurice shook his head and shooshed her out with a series of rapid hand movements. Diana went.

Despite her misgivings, she filed a story based on what an aide to de Gaulle told her. There were rumors the General was thinking of resigning. Maurice smiled in approval and told her to return to Danny's headquarters.

Without Danny the group seemed disjointed. A new recruit hung around watching everything. He had short dark hair, a light brown beard and wore dark glasses. Suddenly everyone started cheering. "Nothing can defeat me," Danny said under his newly dyed hair.

Diana wrote down his version of crossing the border in disguise, and then she followed a group whose mission was to attack a government building. At first she watched from a distance until police grabbed Danny's closest aide. She left her post and hit the cop from the back. The *flic* lost his grip on him. Diana ran as fast as she could.

When she realized no one followed her, she headed to the office to file her story. The Metro wasn't running. Taxis had quit driving a few days earlier.

Rounding a corner she ran into three policemen. They carried shields. From their dirty torn uniforms, Diana guessed they'd been fighting. She staggered a little from the force of hitting the shield.

"Where are you going?" the tallest asked.

"To my office. I'm a reporter."

The youngest *flic* snarled, "Identification. Now!"

She reached into her pocket where she kept her press pass. There was a huge hole. "I really am a reporter," she said.

"And I'm de Gaulle," the middle cop said as he pushed her against the wall. He had one hand on her shoulder and the other rested on her breast.

Later Diana admitted what she said and did was undoubtedly the stupidest thing possible. She explained that when she felt his hand, she lost control. "Listen you fucking *flic* asshole . . ." She kneed the cop in his balls.

He doubled over. His partners grabbed her and threw her to the ground. The two uninjured cops kicked her repeatedly.

Unable to fight back, she rolled into a ball. When they kicked her head, she put her hands over her face. One cop used her hips and stomach as he would a soccer ball. She passed out on the narrow sidewalk.

Summer 1968: Paris

Voices and lights tickled Diana, but she couldn't reach them. She thought she smelled urine and antiseptic. Maurice, Danny and de Gaulle floated around her. Ever so slowly she forced herself to open and focus her eyes. Jim Bourque, not de Gaulle, stood in front of her.

"What are you doing here?" she wanted to ask, but he fell away from her before she could form the words. When she woke again it was dark. Where was she? Who was snoring? She tumbled back into the warmth and the safety of unconsciousness.

The next time she pulled herself out of the world where she was hiding, pain shot over and through her. She tried to move but couldn't. She saw bars on a window. That she'd gone mad like her mother flashed through her mind.

"*Bonjour.* You awake?" a soft voice asked in French. Diana turned her eyes toward the voice.

No, she wanted to say. She couldn't.

The soft voice continued. "Stay with us a little while." Diana saw a woman with grey hair pushed under a veil. The woman smiled and touched Diana's hand. Wrinkles, so many wrinkles, masked the shape of a face, a kind face.

Diana's eyes darted around the room. She twisted as

much as she could, but her body felt weighted.

"You're in a hospital. You will be all right. I'm Sister Charlotte, your nurse."

Despite Sister Charlotte and her own will, Diana slept again. She dreamed she was being boiled by cannibals. One threw some carrots into the water with her. He added cinnamon and scooped water in a huge spoon to taste Diana stew. The water burned his mouth. Diana felt glad.

She opened her eyes to discover she was bathed in sun from the window next to her bed. The room was so hot. Something heavy encased her, and she was sweating. The soft voice of Sister Charlotte said, "Monsieur Bourque, your daughter is awake."

"Hi, kid." Jim Bourque took Diana's hand and squeezed it. When she could focus on his face she saw he was crying. She had never seen her father cry.

"Am I going to die?" She could only manage a whisper. He had to bend to hear.

"Not if I have anything to say about it. We'll talk when you are stronger."

As she drifted in and out of sleep, facts filtered into her consciousness as people talked about her as if she were not within hearing distance. But she never knew what was real, what was a dream.

She thought Jim talked about an unnamed man dumping her at the emergency ward entrance. Maurice's voice said that Diana was lucky she survived being moved. Slowly her mind accepted that her breathing bordered on miracle status.

"You were hurt real bad, kid," Jim said; "but you'll be OK." He didn't say that the doctors had repaired as much of the damage as they could. He didn't tell his daughter that she'd logged thirty-five hours of surgery time, a hospital record. Nor would he tell her that for a week she had been unidentified, Patient X, hovering on the critical list.

"What day is it?" As Diana's lips moved, Jim bent to hear.

"July 24th."

How had she lost two months? It took too much effort to ask.

"Solange found you by accident," Jim said. "But she'll tell you herself."

"This is Solange's hospital?"

"Certainly is."

Diana turned towards the new voice to see a white coat and a name badge reading, Solange DuBois, Administrator.

"It was our good chance that your rescuer came here," Solange said. "I did not recognize you. Your face was too swollen."

"Mirror?"

Sister Charlotte looked doubtful, Jim unsure. Solange whipped a pocket mirror from her bag and held it so Diana could look at herself.

Diana expected to see scars and bruises. They had healed. Her face was thinner but undamaged. Her hair had been replaced by red fuzz. Her hands flew to her head.

"You were bald. They shaved your head. This is an improvement," Jim said. Diana closed her eyes. Jim and Solange watched her sleep.

"She is becoming stronger," Solange said, shivering.

Every time Solange thought of how close she came to not identifying Diana, she shuddered. Her discovery was surrounded by if-she-had-nots. If she had not walked through the intensive care unit looking for the doctor in charge, if she had not been drawn to the poor woman, if she had not asked to see the person's personal effects, Diana might still be Patient X.

Solange's secretary had brought the blood spattered, torn jeans and T-shirt. An envelope held a western belt with a turquoise buckle that Solange had admired when Diana had been at the apartment.

She'd picked up the watch. It was elongated so it covered most of the wrist. Solange couldn't remember what kind of watch Diana wore. Turning it over she read, "DB, BU 1967, Love JB".

A transatlantic telephone call had brought Jim on the next plane to London where he rented a car to ferry across the Channel. French airports had been closed by the riots.

When Diana hemorrhaged five days after Jim arrived, doctors rushed her back into surgery. Jim, Maurice and Solange watched her fight to survive.

Maurice blamed himself, not for the new crisis, but for letting Diana cover the riots. Jim blamed himself for not letting her work with him. Solange, blaming no one, brought Jim food and insisted he sleep on her office couch. It was one of the few battles Solange ever lost. He refused to leave his daughter.

Jim maintained his vigil, but when sleep overtook him, he always dreamed he heard the monitor mmmmmmmming. Then he'd wake to discover it still drawing peaks and valleys.

"She has a strong heart," Doctor Martinez had told him.

"She has a strong spirit. That counts as much," Sister Charlotte had said.

In late July, Diana was on her way back to them, but the trip was slow. Progress was measured in victories as simple as Diana swallowing three mouthfuls of fluid.

Because of pain, she had been kept drugged. It was August before Diana stayed awake for more than ten minutes
at a time. At some point she realized that she was in a cast
from her chest down. Her legs, spread out on either side,
were in casts as well. The haze between the heat and the
drugs confused her until she said, "No more drugs."

"You need them," Doctor Martinez said.

"Make them stop," she said to Jim. "I need a clear
head."

When he did, blinding pain replaced the haze and dull
pain. The withdrawal left her vomiting and shaking. Diana
absorbed it all. "Can I have a fan?" she asked when
Maurice and Jim were both there. Within twenty-five minutes Maurice had one installed.

Diana was moved from intensive care to a private room
on August 15th. As Jim arranged Diana's pillow, Solange
walked in with yellow roses.

"Does this mean I'm really getting better?" Diana asked
as Solange fussed with the flowers.

"Sure does, kid," Jim said. He would not sleep at the
hospital that night for the first time since he'd arrived. Instead he planned to go to Maurice and Solange's and return
in the morning.

Sister Charlotte came with a bowl as Solange left.
"Lunch time," she said. She spooned mush into Diana's
mouth, scraping the spoon across her chin to make sure
nothing dropped.

"I want to feed myself," Diana said. Sister Charlotte arranged the bowl on the bed and handed Diana the spoon.
"Doesn't taste any better when I do it. When can I have
some real food?"

Sister Charlotte and Jim exchanged looks and the nurse shook her head. Diana saw them.

"What secret are you keeping?"

Sister Charlotte motioned Jim outside. Diana heard them talking. Then she heard Doctor Martinez's voice. She couldn't make out what they were saying but recognized Jim's voice growing angrier.

"I won't be responsible," she heard Doctor Martinez say as Jim opened the door to reenter her room.

"I know my daughter, Doctor," Jim said shutting the door. He took the chair and sat next to Diana. He stared at her, scratched his ear and nodded a couple of times, his lips so tightly together, the area around his mouth was white.

"That bad?" Diana asked.

Jim took her hand and said, "Diana, you nearly died. They took one kidney, part of your intestine, your spleen. For the rest of your life you'll have to be careful what you eat. No roughage." He took a deep breath and continued saying what he had been practicing. "You'll probably need supplementary vitamin shots to make up for what your body doesn't get in its normal digestive process."

Diana listened. Finally, after several seconds of silence, she said, "I can live with that." Instead of looking relieved, her father's Adam's apple bobbed up and down.

"There's more, I can tell," she said.

"They took your womb."

Silence, except for the muffled traffic five stories below, filled the room. Jim whispered so softly that she didn't hear. "Maybe I should have waited to tell you."

When she did speak it was an explosion. "Shit!"

The faces of the three men who stole her reproductive organs ran through her mind, blurred, and disappeared.

89

She tried swallowing the tears but they escaped.

Jim stood next to the bed, his arms at his sides, his fingers twitched. She was too old to lift on his lap even if she hadn't been in a body cast. This wasn't a skinned knee. He couldn't kiss her sore and make it better. He put his hand on her shoulder.

Her sobs were shallow. Deep ones hurt too much. When the tears subsided, she said between hiccups, "I was never sure I wanted kids, but I wanted the choice."

"I know, kid." He had more bad news for her but that could wait.

Diana drifted to sleep, her hand in her father's.

He tiptoed out long after the sun set.

August melted into September. The breeze through the window brought fresh air. The night before the casts were to come off, Diana slept without a fan.

Doctor Martinez was all smiles when he arrived to remove them. Diana had finished her flavored mush. She had cajoled Solange into buying her some nutmeg and cinnamon to improve the flavor.

"Can I go dancing tonight?" Diana asked. She'd reached the point in her recovery where she no longer felt sick. Jim spent hours with her playing cards to keep her amused. Diana felt good enough to be bored.

Doctor Martinez looked at Jim who stood behind Diana's head. She didn't see them exchange glances.

"Mademoiselle Bourque, we are not sure you will be able to walk."

"Of course I'll walk again, Doctor Martinez." Her statement was a declaration of war that later included Diana and Solange on one side and Jim and the rest of the world on the other.

★ ★ ★ ★ ★

Doctor Martinez won the first battle. Diana couldn't walk. Between her hip, raw nerves and shattered bones of her legs, combined with the weakness of being in bed over three months, she barely had strength to sit in a wheel chair. When she moved, pain left her drenched in sweat.

Diana ignored all these facts, forcing herself to spend a little more time each day in her chair than the doctor allowed. Despite the pain, she made the first tentative tries to move around. Within three days she felt some strength returning.

Pushing herself, she began touring the hospital. She visited the geriatric ward where she fed lunch to an old lady who had two cataracts removed. The date was September 15th.

"When does therapy start?" she demanded as Jim entered her room. He carried the latest *Paris Match* with Jeanne Moreau on the cover.

Throwing the magazine on the bed he said, "What happened to hello, how are you?"

Diana wrinkled her nose. "Hello Daddy dear. How are you? When does therapy start?"

"After we get back to Florida. You should be ready to fly in another two weeks." Jim didn't know that he'd fired the opening volley in Battle Number Two.

"I'm not going back. I've a job here, unless Maurice has fired me. I'll walk to work by Christmas."

Jim fought with her. After Maurice arrived, *he* fought with her. Solange, who'd heard their voices down the corridor, burst into the room.

"Out." Solange gestured to the two men.

"Make her see sense," Jim said. He closed the door none too gently.

Exhausted from fighting, Diana asked, "Help me into bed, please." Solange lifted her from the wheelchair. Lying under a crucifix, the cross pointed directly at Diana's head. Solange pulled a chair over to the bed.

"You do, how do you say?—dig your heels in," Solange said after Diana gave a word by word accounting.

"Not bad, considering I can't even walk to the bathroom," Diana said.

The two women stared at each other. Solange, as always, was perfectly everything. Diana felt ugly in comparison. Her red fuzz had grown to about two inches and was too curly for any style. Her slate eyes pleaded more than her words, "I can't let this beat me. Help me make them understand."

Solange understood Diana's determination. As a teenager after being shot, she completed her mission for the Resistance. Only afterwards had she allowed herself the luxury of fainting. Collapsing at Maurice's feet had been one of the best things that had ever happened to her.

"Let her stay, Jim," Solange said as they sat in Solange's office. After twenty minutes of verbal circling, Solange put her hand on his arm. "Her spirit needs the battle."

Jim thought of Diana's mother whose spirit had no will to battle life, good or bad. He knew he had to get back to his paper. Bill Reed could hold the fort only so long.

Solange read his mind. "We will take good care of her. Trust me." Jim did.

When Jim told Diana, she cried. "Thank you." She said it over and over.

Fall 1968:
Paris

Florian Boucher twisted and shoved Monsieur Lassieur's scrawny leg against his chest. "Resist, Monsieur Lassieur." The overhead light reflected off the man's bald head.

The patient groaned. The arranged code substituted for words locked out by the damaged synapses of the man's brain.

A woman, sitting in a tub, was watched by the therapist's assistant. "Work deep, Madame Picard," Florian said.

"Sure will, handsome." She winked. As his dark skin brightened, the woman laughed at his embarrassment.

From the corner of his eye he saw Diana wheel herself into the therapy room. *"Bonjour,"* he said, "may I help you?"

"Bonjour. If you're Mr. Boucher, yes. You and I will make me walk by Christmas."

"Excuse me?"

Diana repeated what she had said.

"This isn't a store where you order recovery like a new dress. I need to evaluate your case, talk with your doctors, set up a program."

Diana handed him the large manila envelope resting on the red plaid hospital blanket covering her knees.

He pulled out two sets of X-rays and several pages of reports. "I have not the time now."

"When will you?"

"Maybe tomorrow, maybe the end of the week." He turned away.

Diana twisted her chair in front of him. "That is the wrong answer. I cannot afford to wait."

Florian swallowed his anger. "I run this program; you don't."

"You may run the program, but I run my body. It's out of order." She inhaled deeply. "And I need your help to fix it."

"I am totally booked today, but I will try and look at your history tomorrow. Then we will talk."

After Diana left, his assistant said, "Handle her carefully. She's the protégé of Madame DuBois' husband. She's driving everyone crazy on the fifth floor with her typing."

I hate politics, he thought. I hate whiney women. But then he realized, Diana hadn't whined. She had demanded.

At six o'clock his assistant put a cup of coffee in front of him. "See you tomorrow, Florian."

He took his coffee and lit a Gitanes. Looking at his agenda for the next day, he saw each hour was filled. The envelope that Diana had left was on top of his piles of reports. Glancing at his watch and realizing he was late, he slapped the films on the light box behind his desk.

The first group was taken within an hour of Diana's arrival at the hospital. Florian shook his head at the bone fragments from her hip and leg. The spine was untouched. Then he looked at those taken the week before. The fissures and the metal binding her bones together made a series of rivers and roads on the map of her body. He began reading her report.

The phone interrupted. He felt ice from the receiver even before saying hello.

"Where are you?"

"I'm here, Marie-Laure. You called me," he said to his wife.

"We're already late. Father will be furious."

"Go on without me. I'll catch up."

"You need to change. I told you this morning it was formal."

She probably had, but he had turned her off as she recited her list of his failings to her, her family and her interests.

"I can't leave my patients."

"You're a therapist, not a doctor." The phone was slammed down so hard Florian's ear echoed. He returned to Diana's report. He decided everything depended on nerve damage.

When the therapist approached Diana's door, he heard typing. He hesitated, then knocked.

"Come in." Diana's wheelchair was next to a table that held an IBM Executive typewriter. She wheeled around. He sat on the corner of her bed.

"What are you writing?" he asked.

"My memories of the riots," she said. "Isn't this too late for therapy?"

"Yes. I am on my way home, but I wanted to check some things."

"I'm all yours," she said.

For the next ten minutes Florian Boucher pushed, tugged, and manipulated Diana's legs. When she wasn't

95

looking he reached for a pin concealed in his lapel.

"Ouch, take it easy."

He smiled. "That ouch just made my job a whole lot easier."

Florian never had a patient like Diana. She was waiting when he unlocked the therapy department door each morning. She did every exercise he gave her and then did them more than he told her. "You can overdo," he said.

"Prove it," she said.

He tried to limit her time in the therapy room and twice had an orderly wheel her back to her room. She bitched all the way. The nurses called to ask if he had given her "homework." They'd found her exercising on the floor.

"I'll walk by Christmas," Diana told Florian, Maurice, Solange, the sisters and Jim when he called. "I'll be back to work by the first of the year."

"I've never seen a patient with her determination," Florian said to Solange as he passed her table in the employee canteen. Solange indicated he should sit. She was finishing *poulet provençal*. He had the same, and he spread the sauce over the rice, then speared a black olive.

"Diana is not your average anything," Solange said.

November 1, the day commemorating the dead, Diana went from wheelchair to walker. She could see a cemetery filled with yellow and white chrysanthemums from her window. She picked at her dinner in the fading light.

Once or twice a week Florian stopped by on his way out of the hospital. I am checking, he told himself, on whether she has overdone the exercises. They often chatted for an hour or so before he left. That night he wanted to congratulate her on her progress. The metal walker stood where the wheelchair normally rested. She wore jeans and a BU sweatshirt.

"I'm sick of hospital food." She threw her fork on the floor. He retrieved it.

Forgetting he and Marie-Laure had theater tickets he said, "There's a great restaurant around the corner. Maybe I can free you for a couple of hours."

He did. Diana didn't even fight the idea that she could only go in the wheelchair. Florian didn't remind her that she'd vowed never to sit in it again after taking her first few steps.

They drank champagne to celebrate her progress and then ordered *moules marinières*. The waiter brought the shell fish in a large metal pan with four legs. It stood in the middle of the table about twelve inches from the tablecloth. They ate silently, shells piling up around them. Diana eyed his salad. Roughage was something she could never eat again.

"When can I give up the walker? And the braces?" Diana asked. A little mussel juice she'd sucked from its shell ran down her chin. She wiped it off with the linen napkin.

"You just graduated to the walker," Florian said.

"I repeat the question."

"With anyone else I'd say a year to never. With you, I refuse to guess." He reached for another mussel.

"Today the wheelchair, tomorrow the crutches, next week the braces."

December 15th, Diana walked into the city room. No one expected her. No one noticed her at first. The type-writers drowned out the tap of her crutches.

Then Colette glanced up. "Oh, my God," she screamed. She stood so fast she knocked her chair over.

Maurice and Bernard rushed from their offices. Someone ran out for a bottle of champagne.

"When did you get out of the hospital?" Bernard asked.

"An hour ago. I need to ask Maurice when I can get back to work." Diana added, "The crutches are temporary," when she saw him look at them.

In Maurice's office, Diana rested the crutches against his desk. She used the arms of the chair to lower herself into the seat.

"You are in pain," Maurice said.

"I can live with it. I need to get back to work."

"I'm not sure you are ready."

"Maurice, you can protest. We'll fight. I'll win. Let's skip the middle step."

"I give up now. Start next Wednesday."

"How about January 2nd?" Maurice frowned at Diana who continued, "I want to go home for Christmas. If Jim sees me, he'll know I'm OK."

"January second it is. Has anyone ever told you that you are impossible?"

"Hundreds of times." She used her arms to lift herself from the chair.

Diana let herself into her apartment. She had not seen it since the accident. Her landlady had dusted it. Mail was piled on the table although Solange had taken the important things to the hospital weekly. There was the electricity bill, an alumni newsletter and an envelope with Jane's tight handwriting.

Diana tore the envelope open. The white dove looked familiar. She opened it. Underneath the words, "Shit on the whole thing," her old roommate had written, "We're making a baby."

Winter 1969: Boston

Lights from Beth Israel's windows cast eerie shadows through the snowstorm. Inside a second storm raged.

"Nathan, I'm going to pretend I didn't hear that. Now leave me alone." Jane was the color of the sheet. Kate, wrapped papoose-like in a pink blanket, slept in a bassinet within reach of her mother. Jane barely had the energy to look at her father-in-law and she wished he was somewhere that she didn't have to look at him.

"Two hundred thousand is a lot of money, Jane. You can find another husband. Free my son." The doctor loomed next to the bed, the cigar David had given him in his hand. He waved it.

Her teeth clenched. She wanted to sleep, to escape. If she'd watched this scene in a movie, she wouldn't have believed it. In all her childhood fantasies of cruel parents strengthening the ties between her and her beloved, she never expected to run into the real thing. She had expected a marriage like her parents had. Poor David. "Let me tell you something, Nathan. My commitment to David and my daughter isn't for sale."

"Everything is for sale. It depends on the price." When he couldn't find an ashtray, he snubbed out his cigar in the bottom of a cup as David and Lucille walked in.

The older woman scooped up the baby. "She's so beautiful."

Jane didn't think her daughter beautiful. She had huge cheeks, no hair and was red. However, she was healthy.

"She's a girl. We need a son, and now that is impossible," Nathan said. "If you had kept yourself under control until you were set up, you might have had a son, boy. Now . . ."

David reddened. "I love my daughter. And just because Janie shouldn't have any more . . ."

Nathan shot from the chair where he'd perched. "You stupid fool," he yelled. When he spoke next his voice was low, controlled, more frightening than when he raised his voice. "First you marry some flibbertigibbet, get her knocked up and now she can't even give you a son."

Lucille tried to calm her husband by placing her hand on his arm as he paced by her chair. He threw it off. She returned Kate to the bassinet. "It's all right, dear," she said. "It took the cab almost an hour to drive the mile over here, what with the roads and everything. Our nerves." No one listened.

"The Johnson name will die out. Who'll carry on our practice?"

David said, "Kate could be a doctor."

"Women don't belong in medicine," Dr. Johnson said.

"Remember Dr. June Clarke, dear," Lucille said.

Her husband turned around and looked at her, his eyes narrowing to slits. He pointed his finger. "That proves my theory. She and her natural childbirth. Fathers in the delivery room. Crazy ideas. Crazy woman." He turned back to Jane. "You couldn't even get her as a tax deduction." Kate had been born two minutes after midnight on January 1st, the second baby born in the city. She also lost the gifts given to the first.

"Oh dear," Lucille sighed. No one heard.

"David, you're ruining your life. If you ask me, you . . ." Nathan said.

"No one did," David said. He stood between Jane and his parents, his hand holding his wife's.

Tears of exhaustion and frustration rolled down Jane's cheeks. She'd thought a baby would mellow Nathan, another misconception in a long series.

David said, "You've upset Janie. I suggest you leave." He opened the door. When neither parent budged, he picked up their coats and his mother's purse and herded them into the corridor. He followed.

Jane waited five minutes, ten, twenty. When David reappeared he was shaking.

"I'm sorry, Janie."

"You aren't responsible for your father." She was so tired. She had been in labor thirty-two hours and then had a cesarean. They couldn't save her womb. She wanted to sleep. David's next statement banished sleep.

"He's cut us off. We're on our own."

"We'll do it somehow, Hon," Jane said. Then tears overtook her. David held his wife.

"Of course we will," David said.

Neither had any idea how.

On a Sunday night in mid-February, Jane stepped between the baby tub and the Didee Dee diaper container to fill the tub with bubbles. A loud squeak startled her. She'd stepped on Kate's rubber duck. It had fallen between the claw feet of the tub. She tossed it into the tub. The force of the faucet pushed it under the suds.

She almost always took showers, but Kate was asleep, and David was going to the library. All Sunday she had been fantasizing about this bath.

Dropping her jeans into the hamper, she sank into the water, letting its warmth pull the exhaustion from her body. "How come," she said to the rubber duck who had resurfaced, "only fairy tales end with 'and they lived happily ever after'?"

She held her breath and ducked under the water. When she came up she said, "Cinderella never had to quiet an infant so her prince could study." She picked up the duck and looked into its blue eyes. He had long painted lashes.

Reaching for the dish detergent she doused her hair. "Rapunzel could afford shampoo."

"So, duck, even if my husband is the most beautiful and smartest man I've ever met, there are no fairy tales for a girl named Jane in the Kingdom of Harvard."

Outside, another snowstorm made work the next day doubtful. Because JRP didn't pay for snow days, Jane mentally juggled her budget.

A knock on the bathroom door interrupted her math. "What are you doing in there? I have to go," David said.

Jane quit the luxury of the water. Wrapping herself in her robe, she brushed past her husband who carried a textbook. David had renamed the bathroom the reading room.

In the living room, Kate slept on her stomach in her playpen that doubled as a crib. She curled her legs under her, pointing her bottom in the air. A pacifier rocked against her lips every few seconds. Some instinct had programmed itself into Kate's little brain saying, "Mommy can't handle colic." The week Jane returned to work, Kate decided to sleep through the night. Jane's day began at 6:00 a.m. and didn't end until midnight with Kate's last feeding.

The Card

★ ★ ★ ★ ★

A nap came into Jane's life, a gift from her boss Lucy. She'd found her assistant staring, just staring, at her typewriter two weeks after she had returned to work.

"Thinking?"

Jane looked up. The question was too hard to answer. Tears ran down her face, first a few at a time, then rivers. She tried sniffing them back.

Lucy, good at bulldozing her way through problems, stood, her arms at her sides. She waited until Jane calmed. "What's wrong?" Lucy handed her the extra handkerchief she always carried. It was embroidered with LLF in navy thread.

Jane spit out her list of burdens finishing with, "I know you shouldn't bring your personal life to the office."

"You're exhausted. It affects everything you do."

"But there's nothing I can cut out."

Lucy swallowed the name of a good divorce lawyer. "How easily can you fall asleep?"

"Anytime, anywhere. The other night I was so tired I took the T. I slept through my stop and went all the way to Riverside." She looked up at Lucy, who really wasn't tall if three inches from her heels and three inches of her hair were deducted.

"Tomorrow bring a pillow and a blanket. When I go to lunch, unplug the phone in my office, lock the door and sleep." Before Jane could protest she added, "Go wash your face, then correct these proofs."

On nights after especially trying days, Lucy would give Jane a ride—allegedly on the way to a friend's house in Brookline. Jane knew better than to have accused her of any maternal instincts, because Lucy would have pooh-poohed them.

103

By late March the weather warmed enough to allow an occasional crocus to poke through the soot-stained snow. Holding hands became a commandment for couples on Park Drive, but not for David and Jane—who hadn't resumed love making.

David seldom went to bed until after Jane was asleep. April Fools' night he crept in after she'd just shut her eyes. She'd been reading, *Portnoy's Complaint*, whose angst kept her awake. She needed to stay awake until Kate's last feeding. Feeling David's weight on the mattress, she snuggled up to him, spoon style, and put her hand in the peach fuzz on his chest.

"I'm tired." He removed her hand.

Jane sat up. She wore a seersucker nightdress. The apartment had two temperatures, too hot and boiling. "David we haven't made love since October."

"So?"

"Tomorrow?"

"We'll see. Don't press me."

Within seconds his breath came in regular little puffs. Jane put her hands behind her head wondering what she was doing wrong.

A week later David initiated sex. The act was too quick to be called making love. Unsatisfied, Jane tried to seduce him the next night. "Men should be the aggressors," he told her. "You're never satisfied."

A latent drop of survival whispered to her "transference," but she wondered what had happened to the nights where they'd spent hours exploring each other's bodies.

"I've a special assignment for you," Lucy said in early June. She looked over the granny glasses perched low on her nose.

"Get your baby and go to the Rose Garden. Scout out a photo for that new biology book." As Jane left Lucy added, "And don't come back until tomorrow."

"I'm not sure it wasn't an excuse to give me the afternoon off, but I wasn't going to argue," Jane said as she and Bridget reached one of the bridges crisscrossing the Muddy River. Cecil and Kate were in a double carriage that Bridget had bought when she started babysitting Kate.

The two women walked along in companionable silence. Long grassy embankments magnetically drew not just mothers with small children but college students. On a day as perfect as that one, students were everywhere.

Suddenly Bridget frowned. "Look Jane, over there." She kept pointing to things to their right. She babbled about the baby's supper. Jane felt herded.

"You're acting weird," Jane said.

"Sun shock—after the winter," Bridget said. "Here's the garden." She pointed to a gate.

"That's not the entrance. It's locked," Jane said.

"Let's break in anyway. Won't that be fun?" Bridget asked.

"No."

"I think I'm going to be sick. Let's go home," Bridget said.

"I'll run into the garden real quick then we'll . . ." Jane never finished her sentence. David sat on a blanket with a woman. The royal blue and yellow plaid registered in Jane's brain as she watched him rub suntan oil on her back. The woman held her curly carrot hair up so he could massage the oil into her neck.

"Oh, Jane, I'm sorry," Bridget said.

"What should I do?"

"Let's go home. It'll give you time to think." Bridget led Jane home and deposited both babies with a neighbor. Jane sat motionless in Bridget's kitchen as she boiled water for tea.

"It may be nothing," Bridget said.

"You didn't think so back there." Jane's voice was a monotone.

Bridget measured tea leaves into the pot which she'd forgotten to prewarm. "I don't think David saw us. Pretend nothing happened."

David had seen them. When Jane got home he was waiting. "Why were you spying on me?" he demanded.

"What were you doing with another woman?"

"We were studying. Don't make more of it than it is. Now what were you doing there?"

"Working. I had to check out the Rose Garden for a photo, and—Jesus, Mary, and Joseph! I didn't get it done." Not only was her marriage coming apart; she'd failed her boss. Jane tried to define the fear swirling through her. Definition might make it manageable. "David, do you want a divorce?"

"Why would I want a divorce? Come on. I'll walk back over with you. It's not safe for you to go alone."

Jane didn't want to go back. The blanket and the warm expression on David's face, an expression that neither she nor Kate could generate, bothered her. As they walked to the Rose Garden she asked, "Why did you marry me?"

"Because I wanted you as my wife, dummy."

"Did you love me?" Jane felt the question was safer in the past tense.

He took his wife in his arms. "Let's pretend today didn't happen. You're my wife. Marriage is for life."

"Forgive and forget," Bridget told Jane. Jane tried, the forgiving being easier.

The Card

The plaid blanket affair, as Jane thought of it, accomplished one thing. They both tried harder, but like a weed cut back instead of dug out, it waited to bloom at a later date.

David helped Jane with chores. She was so appreciative that he relaxed under her praise.

During the summer, Bridget, Nigel and Cecil went home to England. The Johnsons stayed on in their apartment. David worked nights in a lab at the Med school and cared for Kate during the day. Jane began to think of themselves as an imitation family. Sometimes she wondered about the woman on the royal blue and yellow plaid blanket.

Maggie Maguire lay on her bed. Often she was described as having the map of Ireland on her face, a phrase that annoyed her. Christina Andretti was never described as having the map of Italy on her face.

The white lace curtain fluttered in the light breeze that did little to reduce the heat. The two other beds in the room were neatly made with rose chenille bedspreads. The color matched the roses in the wallpaper. The flowers were so profuse they hid the three crucifixes, one over each of the three beds.

Maggie fingered her rosary, praying not for forgiveness for her affair with David Johnson but for recovery. She had not seen David since the last day of classes almost a month before. The leaden pain each morning weighed a little less this past week. "I will know God has forgiven me when I stop hurting," she said to herself.

Her brother called from downstairs. "Maggie, come watch Neil Armstrong walk on the moon." She wondered what David was doing.

★ ★ ★ ★ ★

"Get me some ice cream, Janie, please," David said after Huntley and Brinkley signed off. Jane shut off the TV set. Kate was teething and had whimpered throughout the "That's one small step for man. . . ."

"Don't tell me there's no Santa Claus." Mary Andrews, standing behind her son-in-law, put her arms around him. He stiffened then melted into her. "I believe in Santa. Kate should too."

"It's a fantasy," he said.

"A little fantasy never hurt," Mary said.

Paul Andrews sat at the kitchen table peeling apples. He dropped the last piece in the bowl. "Come on, David. Let's chop wood. It's useless to try to convince my wife there's no Santa." He kissed her and said, "Besides I can't stand listening one more time to Nat King Cole sing about roasting chestnuts."

Mary changed the record as the men put on boots and heavy jackets. "Rudolf, the red nose reindeer, had a very shiny nose, and if you ever saw it you would even . . ."

"Say it glows," Jane sang as she came in with Kate on her hip. Mary reached for her granddaughter. The baby grabbed for the dish of apples.

Mary gave her a slice.

Christmas Eve in her childhood bed, David held Jane. "Is your mother always this crazy at Christmas?" The first two years of their marriage, the couple had gone to Philadelphia, where Christmas was formal. Jane snuggled in his arms. It seemed strange to be in this bed with a man. Her high school pennant hung over her dresser. "Yes."

David kissed her. Freed from all pressures, the couple

made love nightly. Unlike other nights it involved more than a couple of kisses, a breast squeeze and chuga, chuga, chuga.

Jane snuggled under the quilt her grandmother had made from scraps of her childhood dresses. When she touched her husband, his muscles no longer had the tension she was used to feeling. Her last thought as she fell asleep, *It's working. Finally.*

"We should have just bought the baby wrapping paper," Paul looked at Kate sitting in the midst of destruction. She showed no interest in the smocked dresses that Mary had made or the hand knitted maroon sweater with Harvard in white. Even the rag doll had given away to her absolute fascination with the gift wrap. She shook it, tasted it, threw it and crawled in it.

The smell of roasting turkey and baking pies filtered through to the library. A fire blazed. "The Little Drummer Boy" was going pa rum pum pum pum on the record player.

David wore the fisherman sweater Mary had knitted him. When he'd opened it he said, "No one ever made something for me." Throughout the day he chanted the names of the different stitches, like a mantra, "Double honey comb, cable."

"David, if you want to call your parents, it's all right," Mary said clearing the last of the mince pie from the table.

He shrugged.

"I'm sure your mother would like it," Mary said.

"Leave the boy alone," Paul said. "Women!" He winked at his son-in-law.

While the women did dishes and Paul napped on the library couch, David went to the hall phone. He shook his

head and went upstairs to lie down. He picked up a hema-
tology text. Then he went back to the hall and dialed his
parents' number. When the maid answered, he asked for his
mother. "Don't say it's me."

"Merry Christmas, Mother," he said when Lucille said
hello.

"Oh, David." Her voice glowed. "How's the baby?
Merry Christ . . ."

"David, this is your father. Don't call again until you
come to your senses." The phone clicked in his ear. Senses
and leaving Janie were the same thing.

David put on Paul's red plaid hunting jacket hanging by
the door. The door shutting was drowned out by Bing
Crosby's, "I'm Dreaming of a White Christmas."

Jane saw her husband out the window over the sink
where she scrubbed the turkey pan. His hands were in his
pocket. He kicked at the snow, his shoulders hunched.

"Something's wrong," she said.

"Go to him." Mary took the Brillo pad from her
daughter.

Jane slipped on her mother's coat and boots, which were
closest. She ran through the softly falling snow until she
found her husband. He was sitting with his back against an
oak tree.

He reached out to her. She rocked him while he cried.

The young Johnsons had planned to return to Boston the
day after Christmas. Instead David decided to stay until
New Year's Day. He did it day by day, saying each
morning, "Maybe one more day won't hurt." By New
Year's Day no "one more day" was possible. Classes were
starting, and JRP was reopening the next morning.

Paul and Mary drove them to Boston, saying that with

Kate, the baby paraphernalia and the presents it was too much to manage on the bus. "Besides driving you into Hartford isn't that much different," Paul said. The traffic was light because they left before noon while the rest of the world nursed hangovers.

As Paul and David unloaded the car and Mary settled the baby, Jane checked the mail. The box was full of after-Christmas publicity. She threw it out. Then a white envelope with a Paris postmark caught her eye. When she opened it, the same white dove flew across his blue paper sky that she had mailed to Diana the year before.

The third message said, "I'm going to cross the Sahara."

1970:
Paris and Algeria

"Fuck you." Diana sprang from bed and reached for her horse blanket robe.

"You just did," Florian Boucher said. He half smiled in the way that usually made Diana do exactly as he wanted. He reached for her. She pulled away. "Don't be upset," he said.

Diana walked to the window. One shutter was closed. Through the other, Sacre Coeur shimmered pink in the evening rain. Wind rattled the casements. She hugged herself, keeping the damp out, her anger in.

Florian came up behind her, turning her toward him. She noticed how his cock, small compared to minutes before, wobbled. *Weebles wobble but they don't fall down. Cocks fall down. London Bridge falls down. Love falls down,* she thought.

He moved in to nibble her neck. "I love you."

She shoved him away. "Not enough."

"I handled it badly," he said.

Telling me two minutes after orgasm that Marie-Laure is pregnant, is handling it badly, she thought. Her robe opened at the neck showing her breasts. She closed it, no longer wanting him to see her breasts. "I know I shouldn't be

112

angry that you sleep with your wife." *But I am,* she thought.

"But you are," he said, reading her thoughts yet another time. "Would you believe I did not enjoy it?"

"No." She never liked being the other woman. Part of the reason was ethics. More importantly, she wanted to be first in her lover's life.

Her eye caught the remnants of dinner, the empty wine glasses. They'd both spoken about how the candlelight colored the white walls ruby when they toasted themselves with the Nouveau Beaujolais. Florian had taken his napkin to wipe a crumb from Diana's lips, then replaced it with a kiss.

She saw the giant pillows where they sat for hours talking about everything, except the taboo subject—his marriage.

"I want to marry you," he'd told her after they'd made love the first time. He had stopped by her apartment two months after she'd left the hospital to see how she was getting along.

She knew from hospital gossip that his marriage had problems. "I'll let you work it out," she'd said. Well, he had. "You'd better go."

His tongue felt soft against her neck. He smelled of sex.

"Sometimes you scare me." He shivered.

Diana concentrated on the rain. Her vagina twitched in memory of his tongue. His face was reflected in the mirror. She loved how his eyes twitched in amusement. Except tonight. His eyes looked worried. "It's over," she said.

"I don't want to end it." He got back into bed pulling the mint green duvet to his chin.

"Do you think I do?" When he said nothing she continued, "No matter what we do, I'll hurt. You won't pay the price to make our couple work."

"We could continue like this."

"That price is too high for me. Please. Get dressed and go. Don't come back."

"Diana, turn around. Look at me."

"Just do as I ask." *Please,* she thought, *before I change my mind.* She could see him in her mirror as he pulled on his shoes.

He stuffed his tie in his pocket.

"Leave my key," she said.

It tapped against the marble tabletop at the entrance of the apartment. Then the door shut.

Diana locked the door. Putting on her flannel nightgown she got into bed. As she listened to the rain, she said, "I'm right. The affair was wrong." Being right didn't make her feel less empty. She turned out the light. Her leg hit the wet spot on the sheet. She punched her pillow and watched Sacre Coeur shimmering in the rain through her window.

In a different room filled with street noises, Diana, naked on the bed, aimed her body at a feeble breeze coming through the window. She'd have washed her face, but it meant walking down three floors. Water only went as far as the fourth floor of the hotel. Her room was on the seventh. If she had thought Paris had felt strange at first, it was nothing compared to the strangeness of Algiers.

She wondered what to do next. Her plane had been late. She had missed the departure of the geological mission that she'd been assigned to cover. The phone rang.

"Hello."

"How would you like dinner?" Maurice asked.

"When did you get in?"

"I just registered. Meet you in the lobby in ten minutes. By the way, the office left me a message besides yours.

There are problems at Nanterre again. Do you know anyone to call?"

Diana rattled off names and numbers. "Maybe they aren't still valid, but it's a start."

"You are not begging me to fly to Paris and cover it?"

Diana shuddered. "I'll stick with this story if I can get transportation, thank you very much."

Maurice laughed. "Good. I do not want to tell your father a second time that you might die. He gets so upset."

Maurice waited in the lobby. He kissed both her cheeks. "There is a little bistro near here, if it is still in business. Algiers is no longer the European city I knew in my youth."

Outside the hotel, donkeys, bicycles and old Renaults clogged the street. Women, completely draped in black, scuttled by.

"How do they stand it in the heat?" Diana asked.

"They probably wonder how you stand those pants."

"I'd rather wear shorts."

"Do not. It is not allowed for a woman."

"Why are the men staring at me? Is it my limp?"

"Arab men like big women. Stop frowning. I did not call you fat. A Rubens model, like you, is sexy." They walked in silence. Men continued to turn and stare. "Keep your eyes down. Do not make eye contact." After they walked still further, Maurice said, "I almost regret I did not send a man to cover the mission."

Diana hit him on the arm.

To enter the bistro they had to push aside chains of brown beads. A small man, placing unmatched silverware on checkered tablecloths, looked twice at Maurice before dropping the spoons. The two men exchanged kisses.

"Diana, this is Omar. Omar, meet Jim Bourque's daughter."

115

Omar bowed deeply and kissed her hand. "I am honored to have Monsieur Bourque's daughter in my establishment. How is your father?"

"Fine." She wished she knew who this man was.

Omar didn't usher them to seats, he swept them, pulling out each unmatched chair with a flourish. When he clapped his hands, an old woman, unveiled, appeared. "Bring couscous. Still love couscous?" Maurice nodded. Omar grabbed a third chair, turned it backwards and swung his leg over it. "When you first walked in I thought you had replaced Solange, since you Christians take one wife at a time."

"I cannot imagine replacing Solange, but in the unusual circumstance I might, Diana would be my next choice. She has the mind of her father in a beautiful body."

Diana blushed. She looked at the round metal trays, etched in elaborate designs hanging on the walls as she settled in to listen.

The woman returned with three glasses. "A toast to the old days." Omar raised his glass. The three swallowed deeply. The drink tasted fruity. More important to Diana, it tasted cold.

The old woman returned with a large wooden bowl of lamb, chicken and sausage. She then brought a bowl filled with carrots, onions and cabbage in tomato sauce, and a third with something that looked like yellow grits.

"This is your first time to eat couscous, no?" Omar asked. Diana nodded. "Let me show you." He piled the grits on her plate, selected meats then added vegetables and some sauce. He had a little bowl of something garnet and he took a tablespoon full.

"Gentle with that for her first time," Maurice said.

The spoon hung in mid air. Then Omar reduced the

amount of garnet stuff to about 10 percent and mixed it into Diana's couscous.

She dipped her fork into it. She held up her thumbs in approval. As she ate she listened to Omar and Maurice reminisce.

"Now we can laugh," Maurice said three servings of couscous later. "Then we were so frightened we could have messed our pants. Remember Omar, the boat? How we paid those fishermen for their clothes?"

Omar shoveled a piece of lamb into his mouth. "Remember? I couldn't forget. We never did learn if that periscope was Axis or us."

"Diana, we had hundreds of guns smuggled from Morocco on board," Maurice said. "Thank God, whoever they were did not think we were worth bothering with."

Sounds like a John Wayne movie, Diana thought. Maurice and Omar looked like such normal middle-aged men. They were, she decided, but they'd been caught in an extraordinary time. That her father had been with them was a shock. Except for the reason for her mother's breakdown she thought he had no secrets from her.

"Enough of the past," Maurice wiped his mouth. "This girl of Jim's is a heroine, too. She fought in our riots."

"An acorn never falls far from the tree," Omar said. He clapped his hands again and the old woman appeared with three glasses filled with a steaming green liquid, the sweetest mint tea Diana ever would taste.

"I'm giving her only safe assignments now."

"Like crossing the Sahara," Diana said.

Omar roared. His belly jiggled.

"Does SATT still run?" Maurice asked.

"The buses stopped when the French left. Private enterprise has taken over. Remember Petit Louis?"

"Is he still alive? I thought a jealous husband would have shot him long ago."

"Alive and owner of an old SATT bus. Runs it across the Sahara whenever he has enough passengers. Can you wait?" Omar disappeared before either could say yes or no and returned before they finished their tea. He was not alone.

Petit Louis' name was descriptive only if height were the criteria. His girth matched his length. Diana had found her transportation.

Although she'd showered less than twenty minutes before, sweat soaked the cloth between Diana's backpack and her skin. She arrived in the lobby at the same moment Petit Louis rolled in. He didn't ordinarily pick up passengers, but for Jim Bourque's daughter he said that he would have driven to another country. His armpits were encircled with stains.

The battleship gray bus, which belonged in an antique car museum, blocked traffic outside the hotel.

"Get that heap outta here," an Arab yelled. His head was swathed in cloth.

Petit Louis helped Diana aboard. "You're in first class." When Diana took the first seat in the bus he said, "No, no, no. First class is in back." He pointed to the wooden barrier where baggage was stored. Diana chose the first seat behind the barrier. It was lumpier than the second class place.

Other passengers waited at Petit Louis' garage. One, an overweight, under-haired man in a business suit, tie and shirt, paced back and forth. "You're late," he said, when Petit Louis hopped down, avoiding the oil puddle by the door.

"I'm never late," Petit Louis said. "My bus leaves when I say it does."

"You told me ten. It's noon," the man said.

"I said if you were here at ten you wouldn't miss the bus, Herr Burger. Good news. You haven't." He wiggled his eyebrows. A couple, also waiting, laughed.

"Miss Bourque meet Judith and Walter Tyler. They're my regulars. Every two years they come with me to Ghana."

The man, at least six feet four, shook hands.

"I'm curious. Why go so often?" Diana asked.

"We're anthropologists with a long-term research project," Walter said.

"And we only travel with Petit Louis," Janet said. Like her husband she had a Midwestern accent.

Herr Burger harrumphed.

Suddenly a VW Beetle careened into the garage, stopping an inch from the bus. Two men jumped out of each door. "Hans!" Petit Louis cried.

"See, Wolfgang," the taller of the two said, "I told you he'd be here. If he says ten I know noon is the earliest he'll start and even that's iffy." Under his breath Herr Burger muttered, "What a way to run a business."

"Who's the pretty new lady?" Hans asked.

"Diana Bourque." She stuck her hand out.

"Hans Bucholi of Stuttgart." He gave her hand a firm pump. "This is my friend Wolfgang Huober."

"This the latest car you're taking to sell?" Petit Louis walked around the Bug.

"*Ja.*" Hans turned to Diana. "We caravan behind Petit Louis to help him when this thing breaks down." He pointed to the bus.

"Who helps who?" Petit Louis demanded.

Diana had held many assumptions about the Sahara. All were wrong. She'd pictured miles and miles of the same terrain. There were flat lands, dunes and even mountains. The sand itself changed from fine yellow to gray gravel and back again.

She thought the desert would be deserted. They met a man on a camel, a group riding in a truck, so many nomads she stopped counting, and stragglers. A second truck joined their small caravan.

Diana pictured an oasis as a watering hole with tents and palms. She was right about the palms, but most of the oases were small towns with orchards. They found hotels—not four-star, but comfortable and clean. When they didn't reach an oasis they slept in tents. When the sun disappeared it took the heat, leaving clearer air than Diana ever remembered breathing.

"The stars are brighter than neon signs," she said to Hans. They sat outside their tents, huddled in sleeping bags, gathering warmth from the fire. It was the fourth night of their trip. Petit Louis stood over them with the coffee pot. Diana held her cup up. The coffee steamed in the frigid air.

"Ride with me tomorrow?" Hans asked Diana.

Emily Post never wrote instructions for desert dating with temperatures of one hundred ten degrees. So they teased one another. They shared knowledge.

"Did you know Targui nomads never uncover their mouths even to eat and drink?" Hans asked.

"Makes kissing hard," Diana said. Her feet were on the dashboard. She ignored Maurice's advice against shorts. Petit Louis had clucked. She had painted flowers on her braces, which she still needed to walk any distance. The metal felt hot against her skin.

Diana asked Hans, "Do you remember World War II?"

"Not a lot until the bombings. I remember the Americans coming. They gave me peanut butter. I ate so much I made myself sick." He patted her leg. It was so sweat-covered that his hand slipped off. "Damn." Hans had seen the bus veer off the road and sink into the sand. He pulled over. He and Diana jumped out.

Petit Louis and the passengers were already out of the bus. "I've blown a tire," he said.

"We're dug in deep." Walter kicked the sand away from the top of the tire. Herr Burger muttered about delays and deadlines. "Muttering doesn't change tires," Walter said in German.

Petit Louis opened the back of the bus. He had tires, an extra engine, carburetor, a ten-gallon drum of water, another forty gallons of gas and tools. He rattled tools until he found the jack. None of the men could get the jack to work in the soft sand.

"Unload the bus," Petit Louis said. Everyone but Herr Burger stripped the bus including the seats. They jacked the bus up but not enough. "We'll have to lift it. Judith, Diana, when we get the back up, shove the trunk under it."

The trunk came from the truck that had joined the caravan. Groaning, the men lifted the bus high enough for the women to push the trunk under the fender. Petit Louis shoveled sand. Once the tire was clear, he changed it quickly.

"How do *ve* get out of the sand?" Herr Burger asked.

"You lie under the wheel," Petit Louis said. Herr Burger stomped off. He sat in the limited shade cast by the contents of the bus.

Hans and Wolfgang pulled chicken wire from their Bug and rolled it under the wheels as Petit Louis hoisted himself into the bus. The spinning wheels created a sand fountain.

The bus lurched forward then stalled. Walter picked up the chicken wire and put it in front of the wheels again. Petit Louis inched the vehicle forward a little more. Six repetitions and they were back on the road. Everyone except Herr Burger cheered.

An hour later they arrived in a small town with three streets surrounded with white-domed buildings. A mosque was in the middle of town.

Petit Louis pulled up in front of a building marked *hôtel* in French and Arabic. "Everyone take shower. You all stink." To Diana he said, "Cover your legs." Then he looked at Hans. "Stay away from the room of Diana. I'm her father here. I won't have her defiled while she's in my care."

Diana and Hans looked at each other. She thought the little fat man was kidding. He wasn't. She wanted to be angry, but although she found Petit Louis' protectiveness funny in a strange way, she also felt cared for.

"Why did you let me ride with him?" she asked Petit Louis as Hans registered.

"American women are different, so I gave you some liberty. But I protect your father's honor."

"Can I at least take her for a walk? For dinner?" Hans asked with a half smile. Petit Louis thought about it before agreeing.

"Well meaning counts for something," Hans said to Diana before they separated to shower.

Water trickled out of the hand held nozzle washing sand and Diana's stickiness away. She used only a little shampoo hoping she would have enough water to rinse it. The hotel had no electricity. Diana ran a comb through her hair. She slipped on pants and a T-shirt. When she heard a knock, she opened her door.

"I'd better stay in the hall in case Père Louis is on patrol," Hans said.

Diana grabbed a shawl against the night air. The town was large enough for two restaurants. They chose the smaller. A woman, completely shrouded, showed them a seat. She spoke no French, German or English. They spoke no Arabic or any dialect.

Hans pantomimed eating. The woman led them to a back shed where pots bubbled over an open fire. Hans pointed to what he thought might taste good. The woman shooed them back to the restaurant. Within minutes she appeared with their chosen food.

Diana dipped her spoon into the assortment of lamb, gravy and vegetables, highly spiced and good. "I don't suppose I stand a chance of wine?"

Hans raised an eyebrow. "We should be able to get something non-alcoholic." He indicated he wanted to drink and she returned with a single glass of tea. Diana made the same motion, and the woman brought a second.

"I want to make love to you. Despite Petit Louis."

Diana, who hadn't slept with anyone since Florian, missed sex. She found masturbation a poor substitute. "I'd like you to, but we reach the geological site tomorrow." Neither would have gone against Petit Louis' sudden *in loco parentis* behavior. The pleasure wasn't worth the offence.

"Can I see you in Paris?"

She searched through her bag and wrote down her address and phone number.

Logs snapped in the fireplace, then shifted, creating a tantrum of sparks. Most of its heat was drawn up the chimney. Diana stared at Sacre Coeur through the rain.

Hans rolled over in bed and reached for her. "Come

back to bed, *Schatzie*. It's cold." She let him draw her in.

Rubbing her hands, he said, "It would be warmer if you would shut the blinds."

"Then I couldn't see Sacre Coeur or the roofs." Another tiny seed of resentment that she felt on most of Hans' visits grew inside her. She knew she could ignore it or water it. Lately she'd been nourishing it.

Diana spent the nights before his every-other-weekend visits cleaning like she never cleaned for herself. She went to Stuttgart once a month. When he jumped up to do the dishes in Stuttgart immediately after dinner it didn't bother her. In Paris it made her itchy, but she wasn't sure what to scratch.

Diana tried forcing dishwashing politics out of her mind. Yet this was only Saturday night, and she could hardly wait to reclaim her space. Hans had fallen asleep next to her. She tried counting his good traits.

That weekend, as all weekends as he was leaving, he asked, "When are we going to get married?"

"Well not until we spend some time in the States."

"That's a B+ answer. Better than your D- excuse of last week."

When they weren't together, she'd go days without thinking of him. Sometimes she saw something and thought, *I must tell Hans about this.* Sometimes she'd drop him a note telling him about this or that. Mostly she went on about her life with Hans as a weekend interruption.

Solange listened to Diana flip flop back and forth. The two women had just seen *Gone with the Wind* in the original version with French subtitles. They were seated in the Café Noir a block from the cinema, each with a tisane in front of them. Diana's was mint, Solange's was verbena.

The waiter swept the corner already closed to trade.

"Tell me what you think, really think," Diana said.

Solange pushed her hair behind her ear. She redid her scarf, pulling the cloth end through a ring forming a silk bow. "You may not like what I am going to say. I think you are a woman to have lovers, not husbands. Hans wants a normal wife. This is not a good combination."

"You don't think I could be a normal wife?"

Solange put her hands around her glass cup and leaned toward Diana. "I think you are an exceptional young woman who wants adventure and to run a newspaper. In this world there may be two or three exceptional men that could cope with that." Her eyes twinkled. "Unfortunately for you, I am married to one of them. No, the rest of the male species will try and stop you. They will kill your spirit."

Diana said nothing.

"*Chérie,* you do not agree? I have hurt your feelings?"

Diana shook her head. "Fiddle-de-dee. I'll think about it tomorrow." She signaled the waiter to bring the check.

Winter 1973:
Stuttgart, Germany

Kate rolled on the rug. Gray shag fibers stuck to her coveralls. "Watch out for the undertow," she said to Tiger Lion, not seeing a living room overlooking an apple orchard or the gray weather of a typical German winter day.

Her imagination took her to a sunny beach with blue ocean and gentle waves. Tiger Lion's blue mane and stripes matched the color of the sea. She loved him. He walked on two legs and always protected her, especially when Daddy yelled at Mommy.

Even if Mommy couldn't see Tiger Lion, she talked to him. "Good night, Kate. Good night, Tiger Lion," she'd whisper so Daddy wouldn't hear. Daddy wanted Kate to stop all those "stupid flights of fantasy." The only time Kate had flown was to Germany. She had asked if the plane was named fantasy. Daddy said no, it was a TWA 727.

Kate thought grownups talked funny—like last summer when they lived with Grammy. When they arrived she'd looked at Kate and said, "You've grown a foot."

"No, I only have two," Kate had said.

Last summer was fun. Daddy was someplace called OCS. O is for Oscar, C is for Cookie Monster and S is for Sesame Street. Kate loved Grampy's farm where Mommy had been a little girl. Mommy let her play with her favorite doll, Do-Ann. She had brown yarn hair and brown button eyes. Grammy had made it for Mommy when she was a little girl like herself.

There was lots of room at Grammy and Grampy's. And stairs. No one yelled if she ran up and down. In fact, everyone seemed happy she made noise instead of telling her to have more self-discipline.

Mommy let Kate crawl in her big brass bed, mornings, and they went on lots of picnics. Kate learned to swim in a pond and they picked strawberries and blueberries. For two weeks everyone went to a beach in Maine with lots of sand. After that they went on a plane to live with Daddy again. People now called him Captain Johnson.

At first everyone in her kindergarten sounded funny, but she now understood the new words. Mommy and Daddy knew some of them too, but Kate knew them better. When she and Mommy talked them, he'd say, "Speak English."

Mommy and Daddy fought about her school 'cause Daddy wanted her to go to the base kindergarten. Mommy wanted Kate to go near where they lived. And they fought because Mommy didn't go to a place called The Wives' Club as much as she should, and because she wanted to live in a place called "on the economy." Whenever they fought, Tiger Lion held her real tight.

Mommy didn't go to work anymore like in Boston. Kate loved that lots. Tiger Lion did too.

"What are you doing, love bug?" Jane peeked out of the larger of the two bedrooms where she was sewing a new red corduroy jumper for Kate.

Kate told her about the gray couch being the parking lot and pointed to the waves. "I made a sand castle next to the water. It's real cold."

Jane saw Kate's blocks piled up under the table. She walked over to it hunkering down to her daughter's level. She dipped her hand into "the water."

"You're right; it is cold." She glanced out the window. "Look, Kate—it's snowing."

Kate bounced on the 'parking lot' as Jane pulled the sheer curtain with its lightly woven flower pattern, so the child could see. Then Jane went back to her sewing.

"Someone is here," Kate called. Instead of the dingle of the doorbell, an envelope fell through the mail slot. Jane opened it and saw the familiar white dove. Above her 1970 message, "Things are getting better," was scribbled, "If you want to see me, open the door."

"Diana?" Jane shrieked, throwing it open. Diana leaned against the wall. The women jumped up and down, hugging. "What are you doing here?"

"Since I lost the card for a couple of years, I thought I'd return it in person. Actually, I'd filed it under H for holiday not C for card nor J for Jane."

"I can't believe you came to Stuttgart just to deliver a card?" Jane took Diana's cape and overnight case.

"There was a second reason. I went to an old lover's wedding."

"How did you get my address?" Jane asked. "I'd been meaning to send it to you."

"A good reporter can trace down anyone. Also I called your Mom. She says she loves you and look for a package."

"Diana, what a surprise." The women jumped. They hadn't heard David come in.

"I didn't expect you until the morning." Looking at her husband's face, Jane saw only whiteness. His hands shook.

"My parents were killed this morning," he said.

Diana spoke first, "I'm so sorry, David. Kate, show me

your room." She disappeared, Kate's little hand hidden by hers.

When Jane tried to touch her husband, he pulled away. "What happened?"

"They were driving to some charity breakfast. Father had a heart attack, and the car went into a truck. He died instantly, Mother in the ambulance." He swallowed several times. "My flight's in three hours."

"I'll come with you." *The guilt he must be feeling,* she thought, but she had no idea how to comfort him.

"No!"

"I belong with you."

"Stay with Kate. How fast can you get me packed?"

In five minutes David's duffel bag was ready. "I'll drive you."

"I don't want you driving in the snow."

"But I'll be stranded."

Reaching in his pocket he pulled out his wallet and gave her a hundred Deutsche marks. "Shop in the village." He kissed Jane on the cheek. "I don't know when I'll be back, Janie. I love you." The door slammed behind him.

Diana pushed her head out of Kate's door. "Coast clear?"

Jane nodded.

Diana eased out. "Let's have tea and talk." She rummaged in cabinets until she found what she needed. She took peeks at her friend who had sat down at a round table. There was a blood red amaryllis in full bloom in the middle. "How are you feeling?"

Jane bit her knuckle. "Sorry for David. Mad at him. Guilty 'cause I'm mad." She sighed. "I'm even guiltier that I'm glad I won't have to see Nathan ever again, but I feel sorry about Lucille." She sighed. "Damn Nathan for never making a move towards David."

There was silence while Diana put out milk and sugar. She stirred the leaves in the pot and poured the liquid. Wisps of steam floated above the cups. When she sat down, she said, "Tell you what. I've a week's vacation. I'll stay with you and Kate. OK?"

Jane chuckled. "More than OK. It's absolutely, fantastically fabulous."

That night Jane made meatloaf and baked potatoes. As the two women did dishes they sang "Little Bunny Fou Fou" with Kate. When Diana dug up imaginary field mice before shkloncking them on the head with her fist, Kate was reduced to fits of giggles.

"Is she asleep?" Diana asked as Jane later tiptoed from the child's bedroom.

"Almost." The two women had changed into pajamas. "You still have Dr. Denton's," Jane said.

"Jim sends me a pair every Christmas."

Jane brought out a package of Oreos.

"God, I haven't had Oreos since I left the States. Or after we left BU, either." Diana pulled apart the two chocolate halves and licked the white center frosting just as Kate would have done.

Jane usually left the radio tuned to the Armed Forces Network. It had provided background music for the women all day. They had jitterbugged to "Rock Around the Clock" and twisted to Chubby Checker.

A Beatles medley was interrupted. "This is Staff Sergeant Mike Flaherty, with a special announcement. The Supreme Court has returned the Roe vs. Wade verdict. Abortions will be legal for women during the first trimester. More news on the hour. And now here's Blood, Sweat and

The Card

Tears singing 'I Didn't Know What Time It Was.' "

"My God, I don't believe it." Diana thought of Shirley Bates, two floors down in the dormitory their freshman year. She'd had an illegal abortion. The ambulance attendants arrived too late. Diana never remembered seeing as much blood.

Jane said, "I couldn't even buy birth control stuff legally when David and I were dating."

Both sat quietly. Jane broke the silence. "I can't have more children."

"I never can have any at all. Part of having my body broken."

"I didn't know."

"Most of the time it doesn't bother me. Does it bother you?" Diana asked.

"I'd like to have the choice. You know I almost aborted Kate?"

Diana's eyes widened. "Because of your marriage?"

Jane shook her head no. "It was right after Bobby Kennedy died. I just thought we were bringing her into such a terrible world. I wasn't sure it was fair."

They were silent.

Jane picked an imaginary piece of lint from her sweater. "Funny how things change. At one time I wanted tons of kids. Now I can't imagine having another in this situation." Then before Diana could say anything she asked, "What do you think of the ruling?"

"Necessary."

They played catch up, massaging the small details of their personal lives that they had shared with no one else. "God, I've missed you," Diana said. "What a wonderful day."

Jane looked at her watch. "Wonderful two days. It's four

131

in the morning. I'll make up the couch."

"Too much work. Just give me a pillow and a blanket."

Kate, like most four-year-olds, cared not that the adults had gone to sleep three hours before she bounced out of bed. She climbed on a chair to get Rice Krispies and fell. Diana and Jane reached her at the same second.

"Tiger Lion hit his head, too," Kate sobbed rubbing her own.

"Hug Tiger Lion. I'll hug Kate." Having been briefed on the blue-maned animal, Diana hugged enough air to satisfy the child.

The fall was the only non-wonderful event that day. They went for a walk in the snow after kindergarten. It was too fluffy for snowmen but wonderful for making angels. They went to bed at the same time Kate did.

Again, Kate was the first one up and hopped into her mother's bed. Jane gathered her in under the thick eiderdown. Diana walked by on her way from the bathroom. "Can I come in, too?"

Jane switched on AFN to listen to the weather.

The announcer said, "We'll repeat Richard Nixon's historic address to the nation made last night at eight p.m. eastern standard time."

"Nixon before breakfast. Yuck!" Jane said.

"Hail to the Chief" played. "Good evening. I have asked for this radio and television time tonight for the purpose of announcing that today we have concluded an agreement to end the war and bring peace with honor in Vietnam and Southeast Asia."

Diana and Jane let out a whoop. They jumped up dancing around the bed. Kate, not knowing what was being celebrated, danced between them.

132

"Wow! It's over! But what's this shit about peace with honor. We were shmuckled," Diana said.

"Do you remember how Fred once said Nixon should just say we won and then leave?" Jane asked. "That's what the crumb bag did."

Diana nodded. "How can that bastard expect anyone to believe this honor crap?"

They hung onto each word. The announcer said, "President Nixon talked with former President Johnson shortly before Johnson's death."

"I didn't know he died. Shut the radio off for a day and the world changes," Jane said.

The week disappeared in laughter and talk, especially talk. Diana paid for a taxi to take Jane and Kate to the base. The duty guard at the entrance of Kelley Barracks accepted without question they were really sisters.

"I was all set to say you took after father's family," Jane said as they entered the Stars & Stripes bookstore where they loaded up on *Life*, *The National Enquirer*, *Redbook* and other magazines Diana had not seen since leaving the States.

Coming indoors out of the cold, the smell of wet woolen clothing permeated the air. They had left muddy prints and their boots outside the door.

"It's my *Kehrwoche* this week anyway," Jane said. "I'll wash down the stairs now." Before the suds reached the top of her pail, the phone rang.

"Hi Janie, I'm flying back at the end of the week."

"How are you?"

"It was really grim," David said. "I still need to clean out my father's office."

Jane carried the phone to the couch. Sitting down, she tucked one leg under her. "How are your brothers?"

"I didn't call them. Father disowned them."

She didn't say, *but he disowned you too.*

"But your mother . . ."

". . . Would have wanted what he wanted."

Overseas rates were too high to argue.

David sat in his father's office. Cardboard containers surrounded him. He had refused all help in packing up his father's things. Patient records had been turned over to the hospital administrator. A lawyer was dealing with probate.

On the wall, among framed diplomas and certificates, there were two photos of his father shaking hands. One was with a smiling Dwight D. Eisenhower, the other with a glowering Nixon.

There were no photos on the desk. David flipped through the leather agenda. The handwriting was not his father's.

Probably Nurse Opal kept it. Nathan had called her Nurse Opal for the thirty years they'd worked together. She had been reduced to tears at the sight of the cardboard cartons and had left the room. Now under control, she spoke softly on the phone, but he could not make out the words. He didn't really care.

His father had left her a bequest of thirty thousand dollars for the house in Florida that she had talked about buying when she retired. The will stipulated that was the only thing she could use the money for. *So like his father,* he thought, *controlling everything, even after death.*

David opened the left hand desk drawer. The desk was an antique, ornately carved. Despite the detailed work, no dust hid in the crevices. The smell of lemon oil hung fresh around him. When he opened the right hand drawer he found a safe.

"Nurse Opal?"

Her stockings rustled as her thighs scraped together. "Yes?"

"Can you open this?"

Her lavender smell overpowered the lemon oil. She twiddled the lock. On top were prescription pads. "I'll take these," she said and left.

He opened a box filled with report cards from Phillips Academy Andover for him and Owen, and from Choate for Nathan, Jr. He found the certificate that he'd won in *The Boston Globe* Science Fair. He had dropped coffee on it. The stain was still there. He picked up the medal Nathan, Jr. won as Junior State Golf Champion in 1956.

David debated calling his brothers. He had no idea where either of them were. Information had no listing in California for Owen. The Swedish consulate refused to help. Thumbing through his father's address book, he found only his own address. He had never given it to his father.

Three manila folders were labeled, David, Nathan, Jr., and Owen. Each contained instructions to the law firm, Firth, Fitch & Mackham, cutting his brothers, but not him, out of the will.

In his folder there were two letters written to Nixon asking that David be assigned anywhere but Vietnam along with Xerox copies of a check made out to Nixon's reelection campaign for $100,000. A third piece of paper was a response from Nixon that started "Dear Nathan." He wet the signature with a drop of spit. It blurred.

David picked up the agenda and threw it against the wall. It bounced off Nixon's photo, hit the Harvard diploma which crashed to the floor. Glass sprayed everywhere. Nurse Opal ran in.

"I'll finish tomorrow. Please clean this up." David bolted from the office. Outside the medical building he leaned against the wall.

"Are you all right?" A female voice spoke. David looked up to see a beautiful redhead, her eyes full of concern.

"Maggie?"

"David?"

Together they asked, "What are you doing here?"

"I practice with Dr. Peterson," Maggie said.

"I was cleaning out my father's office."

"I didn't know he was your father. My condolences."

David stared at Maggie. The unruly carrot hair had been tamed into a Sassoon cut. Proper makeup metamorphosed her pale blue eyes into sapphires. Between her familiar freckles, she exuded confidence.

"Do you have time to have dinner with me?"

She agreed. She chose the restaurant, Chez René.

The waiter brought their *champignons en croûte*. As Maggie picked up her fork, he said, "Come home with me tonight."

Maggie put down her fork. A mushroom dangled from it. "Why would I want to do that?"

David, taken back by her response, wanted to say, "Because I hate being alone in my parents' house." Instead he said, "For old times' sake."

Maggie reached for the vase with a pink tulip in full bloom. Some florist must have forced it. It was too early for tulips. She laughed.

"We had such good times together. Remember the hamburgers and fries in the café when I spilled ketchup on you. Then we went to George's room."

Maggie remembered that as soon as he had come, he had been so afraid someone would see them, that her own Catholic guilt had been increased ten fold.

"And remember that bone we used for the anatomy exam. We blindfolded ourselves and kept feeling it. Then we felt each other?"

Maggie remembered David throwing the bone across the room when she had outscored him on the test.

"And remember those sunny afternoons on the Fenway?"

Maggie remembered Jane's expression when she saw them.

"David," she said patting his hand, "no way."

"You're rejecting me?"

"Yes."

"Bitch. You pay for dinner." He threw down his napkin and got up.

"No problem," Maggie said. She smiled as she picked up her fork to finish the mushroom. God had finally forgiven her.

Spring 1973:
Paris

"I'll never understand how you persuaded David to let you come." Diana grabbed Jane's suitcase, plopping it on a baggage cart. Her hair was pushed in a loose bun on her head. Half had fallen out.

They wove through the crowd of Paris-Est. Jane looked to the end of the cavernous building at the light at the end of the platform. The train next to her let out a gust of steam. "I'm in the middle of an impressionist painting," she said.

"My God, how I've been taking Paris for granted. Ho hum Notre Dame. The Eiffel Tower, so what. Now I'll see it through fresh eyes." They walked under the departure board as it clickity-clacked new information.

"The car is across the street. Maurice and Solange loaned it to us." Diana put the luggage over a torn spot in the back seat of a faded blue Renault. The friends jumped in. The L-shaped gear shift thrust itself out of the middle of a dash covered with flowered blue and pink contact paper. Diana forced her way into traffic.

"We use the aim-and-pray driving method here." She slammed on her brakes at the window level red light. A man with two cameras around his neck hung on the traffic island. Jane and Diana waved at him as he snapped their photo.

Diana kept a running commentary as they crossed the city. Jane's head swiveled side-to-side.

"I want to see it all," Jane said.

"Difficult in four days, but we'll do our best." Diana took a corner on almost two wheels. "Maurice gave me time off on the condition we eat there one night. Solange's dinners are something the average tourists miss, poor dears."

Careening around another corner into a small side street, Diana angled the Renault between two cars on a two-foot sidewalk. An old woman, dressed totally in black and stooped, had just finished washing the sidewalk where the car landed. She carried her pail and bucket into her apartment.

The passenger's door faced a brick wall with less than an inch of air between the door and wall. "Climb out my side," Diana said. Jane tried maneuvering, but got stuck between the gear shift and the brake. When Diana stopped laughing, she helped haul Jane out.

The first floor shutters of Diana's building were closed against the late afternoon sun. They walked through a hall into a plant-filled courtyard and up the back stairs.

Jane put down her case in the entrance hall. The furniture was hodgepodge. Books littered the room. Paintings of all styles, from photographic to weird, littered the walls. "This is from Stein meets Toklas," she said flopping in a chair after removing a pile of newspapers. "I love it. It's so you." She squiggled in the seat. "Pardon me while I scratch. I kept going to the toilet on the train to scratch."

"Sounds like an infection."

"I thought it might be a yeast thing. I usually get one after I've had antibiotics. But that's not the case."

"Maybe it's crabs. I assume you're faithful to David."
Jane gave her an of-course look.

"And he to you?"

Jane didn't answer. Diana didn't pursue it. About ten minutes later, while Diana made tea and they chatted about Kate, Jane asked, "How would I know?"

"Know what?"

"About crabs."

"Look, I guess. Pull down your pants. This is my retribution for the day you met David."

Jane slipped off her jeans and white cotton bikini underpants in one motion. Diana closed her shutters before she knelt down.

"You're crawling with them. So where are you staying tonight?"

Jane started crying.

"Oh, Jesus-Mary-Joseph, I'm sorry, honey. I was just joking, trying to lighten things up." She walked in circles then said, "Seriously, let's go to the pharmacy and get you something."

The phone rang. "*Allo,* Bourque. Maurice? What's up? . . . Yes, Jane's here . . . There's no one? . . . Russian embassy? . . . No, I can't. I've got kinda an emergency here."

Jane mouthed, "It's OK. Go."

Diana put her hand over the receiver. "Shit! A Russian plane crashed at the Paris Air Show and Maurice is short staffed."

"Tell me where the pharmacy is. I'll work it out."

"They never teach you how to buy medicine for venereal problems in French courses. They just teach you to go to window forty-two to buy a ticket for Lyon." She put the phone back to her mouth. "I don't care if there's no one else, Maurice. There's something Jane and I have to do

140

first, and then I'll go. Take it or leave it. Should I try Viktor when I get there? Anyway, I'll tell you what happened, but you write it . . . No, don't worry."

After she hung up she scurried around looking for her pad and pencil. "I have to get the Russian reaction, which will be 'no comment.' " She threw them, her keys and wallet into a large cloth bag. "There's a pharmacy real close."

They ran down the stairs. Diana did a U-turn heading the wrong way down a one-way street.

"I could have done it, really," Jane said.

"Let me tell you what happened to me when I got crabs. I went to a druggist, and I didn't know the right French word. I had just moved here to this flat after I broke up with Hans. I went into this store and asked, *'Avez-vous un medi-cament?'* That was a stupid question. Of course he had med-icine. Since I didn't know the word I scratched my pubic region with three quick motions. He looked blankly at me. I wanted to pour one of his little bottles over his head, but in-stead I scratched my crotch again while looking distressed. Then I ran my fingers over my crotch like I was a bug, pre-tended to pour medicine on my pubis, then sighed with re-lief. The druggist looked at me and in perfect English said, 'Oh, you have crabs.' "

Diana angled the car onto the sidewalk and hopped out. She was back in less then five minutes with a small white bag.

Jane picked it up. "Listen, go to work. I'm OK."

"Really?" Diana's face said she didn't believe her.

"If I'm old enough to have crabs, I'm big enough to take care of them myself. I can't thank you enough for this much help."

Diana put her hand over Jane's. "It's normal. I'll be as

141

quick as I can."

When Jane reached Diana's apartment, she realized she had no key. If Jane watched TV, she did needlework. If she listened to someone on the telephone, she doodled on a paper. An hour sitting on the stairs with no book, no handicraft and an itching crotch was too much. Things she didn't want to think about invaded her mind.

She headed for a café between the pharmacy and Diana's place. She ordered coffee. As she stirred in a brown sugar cube, she watched a businessman with a glass of wine argue with two other men who stood at the counter sipping beer. A television showed a rerun of Dr. Welby, only Robert Young spoke French.

She wondered what would happen if she went up to the man with the wine and asked him why men cheated on wives? She asked herself what she could do differently. "Maybe the problem isn't me. Maybe I've been living in a dream world," she whispered to herself. After nursing the coffee for an hour, she walked back. Diana was there. Jane went to the bathroom with the medicine.

Diana was puttering around the kitchen when Jane came out. "We can talk about it or not, whatever makes you feel better."

Jane stared at her hands. Diana said nothing even after Jane said, "I thought David was cheating on me again. Probably my message of the card this year will be, 'My marriage sucks.'"

Summer 1974:
Norway and Florida

Olaf refilled Diana's beer glass from the pitcher on the table. He rested his arm on her chair and ran one finger up and down her upper arm. Reflected light from the setting sun blocked her view of the statues, a stone forest of humanity. A clock struck midnight.

"I've had enough," she said.

"No, you haven't," he said.

"You're trying to get me drunk." The beer had made her just woozy enough to make her less sure of herself. "I'm going to the toilet." She narrowly missed a waitress with a tray of beer balanced on her shoulder. A man came up to her. Trying to focus her eyes she said, "I don't speak Norwegian."

"English?" He was very blond, very handsome, an escapee from a Norwegian stereotype book. Olaf came up to them, said something to the man, who shrugged and disappeared.

"Let's go to my place." Olaf was also blond and equally beautiful with a face tanned from months at sea. They'd met on his whaling ship while she researched an article on whales.

Olaf hadn't made fun of her as she cried watching the

giant creatures die, but he had tried to make her from the beginning of the voyage. In Oslo, at the outdoor café in Frogner Park, he was still trying.

"What did you think of the three-foot whale's penis?" He leaned her against a statue of a man and woman kissing and put his lips on hers. "Mine feels as big."

"Good God, I hope not," she said. "How far is your place, anyway?"

Olaf nuzzled her. "I hope I can wait. If it were winter when no one was around, we could do it next to that statue." He pointed to a stone couple copulating for eternity.

"If it were winter you'd shrivel."

Diana surrendered the rental car keys without argument. They rode with his hand on her thigh and hers on his. He lived near the park in a brown Victorian style house. Lilacs filled the small front yard. Across the street was another large house with six red candles on the doorstep.

"Morton's having a party. That's what the candles mean. Any other time I'd go in, but tonight . . ." He leered. Diana smiled.

The lock clicked and Olaf swung his door open. The furniture was simple pine. Crystal candle holders picked up the tones of a colorful rug. Dried flowers hung from the ceiling. "I know it's feminine. My wife decorated before she decided it wasn't any fun being married to a whaling captain."

He kissed Diana's lips and neck. "You smell musky and taste like beer." He didn't tell her of the American woman he'd slept with who used strawberry douche, and whose vagina reminded him of fruit salad.

Diana was big even compared to Norwegian women. The top of her head came to his eyebrow. He pulled her into the bedroom. A bed covered three quarters of the floor space. Diana sank into the thick duvet on the bed. He lay next to her.

With one hand he unbuttoned her blouse. Her tight jeans proved troublesome. Unzipping them was easy, but he needed both hands to tug them over her hips. He tugged several times.

Diana, thinking of Erica Jong's zipless fuck, giggled and pushed him away. She lifted her ass into the air to free herself.

He ran his fingers around her nipples. "You're beautiful," he said. It wasn't a line.

"So are Norwegian women." Her words slurred only slightly.

"Remember we were Vikings. We only captured the best looking women. Now shush."

They climaxed, not together, but one after another. Diana rolled into a little ball and fell asleep. Olaf pulled the duvet over her.

The sun streaming through the window hurt Diana's eyes. "What time is it?" she asked.

"Three a.m. How do you feel?"

As Diana sat up, the room revolved. "I'm still a little drunk."

"You've only slept about an hour."

"You haven't slept?"

"I napped. I never sleep much."

Diana lay back down, and they both drifted into sleep. When she woke again her head hurt. Coffee smells assaulted her nostrils. Olaf appeared carrying a tray with lilacs, hard rolls, an orange and a cup of coffee in a blue metal mug. He'd put a doily under everything.

No one had ever given her breakfast in bed. The smell of the orange, coffee and lilacs made her want to throw up. As a reporter Diana could be direct. With a new lover, especially one who was thoughtful, she found it impossible.

"You have an over hang?" he asked.

"Hangover." She slid under the covers. "I think I want to die."

Olaf opened the door to the armoire that ran the width of one wall. It was blue with white doors. A red flower had been stenciled in the center of each door. Clothes were folded neatly on the shelves.

He found a plastic bag and rolled a joint. "Before you eat, try this."

She took a drag and passed it to him. The grass was top grade. Her muscles relaxed. "I feel better."

"Good. After I feed you, I want to make love to you again."

They spent the day making love, talking and snoozing. They woke ravenous. "I need a shower as well as food," Diana said, "Lots and lots of food."

Olaf's shower was small and without a curtain. He climbed in after her. There was a drain in the bathroom floor to catch spilled water. They spilled a lot. Diana took a handful of bubbles and made an epaulet on his shoulders. She saluted.

"*Mon capitaine.* Your friend's saluting, too," she said covering his penis with bubbles.

"He's too stupid to know he's exhausted. Amazing when we've been drunk or stoned for almost twenty-four hours," he said. "Do you get high often?"

"Rarely. I can't remember the last time, but being decadent for twenty-four hours every few years is OK. Listen, can we stop at my hotel before we eat?"

They walked, hand-in-hand, the several blocks to the hotel located near the palace. Half of Oslo was out walking. Unlike Frankfurt, Paris and other capitals, Oslo was small. Few buildings were over five stories. Most had gardens.

"I love the light. It's almost nine at night but it's bright as noon," she said.

"Think of December and January when we live like moles," Olaf said as they entered the hotel lobby. To the left, in an alcove, the tables were ready for breakfast. The clerk gave Diana her key. It could have anchored a boat. He also gave her ten slips of paper all saying, "Call Maurice."

"My rival?"

"My boss. Please make the call for me." She gave the clerk Maurice's home number. They waited until the clerk nodded toward the phone cabin.

"Hi, Maurice, what's up?" She had pencil and paper ready for her next assignment.

"Bill Reed called," Maurice said.

"Bill Reed? My dad's editor?"

"The same. Now sit down."

She sat. "What's up?"

"Jim has had a heart attack. He is at Tampa General. He did not want you to know, but Monsieur Reed felt you should."

The pencil clattered to the floor. "Maurice, I want to go home."

"I have had you booked on several flights from Oslo to New York, but we could not find you. However, if you take the ten-thirty to London there is a connecting flight to New York in the morning. Would you like me to meet you in London? New York? Or would you rather Solange?"

"I'll be fine."

Olaf asked only what he could do—then he did it. In the

passport control line, he handed her a paper with his phone number. "Call me when you know something. I want this to be the beginning not the end." Then he kissed her on the forehead. No one watching would have an inkling that they'd shared seven orgasms within the past twenty-one hours.

Diana parked under a palm. She felt filthy. She was filthy. She'd been traveling almost a full day, the last leg in a rental car with marginal air conditioning. The Buick seemed huge after Maurice's Renault. *I'm a foreigner in my own country,* she thought locking the door.

Icy air greeted her as the automatic doors opened into Tampa General's lobby. Grey-haired people mulled around, sitting in chairs, browsing in the gift shop. She faced the reception desk.

"Mr. James Bourque," she said to the candy striper behind the desk.

"ICU, only immediate family." The girl snapped her gum. Long bangs fell over her pimpled face, hiding one eye.

"I'm his daughter. Is that immediate enough?"

The girl handed a white cardboard pass marked ICU and Bourque printed in crayon underneath. "Fifth floor. Then hang a left as you get off the elevator."

Intensive Care was marked on a door between a lounge and a nurse's station. Monitors surrounded the desk. Diana wondered which heartbeat belonged to her father. A nurse, sitting behind the desk, worked on a chart.

"Hi, I'm Jim Bourque's daughter."

The woman looked up and smiled. She was in her early thirties and spoke with a Midwestern accent. "You're supposed to be in France."

"How did you know?"

"Your father has told everyone about his foreign correspondent daughter."

Diana brushed tears from her eyes. "My father didn't know I was coming. I'm afraid I'll scare him."

The nurse nodded. "He's stable, but you're right. We don't want to shake him up." Her nametag said, Sandy O'Hara. "I'll go in with you as soon as someone comes back to cover. Wanta wash up first?"

"Do I look that grubby?"

Sandy pointed to the ladies' room.

The mirror showed a Diana with stringy hair and a smudge of dirt streaking her cheek. Her armpits were soaked. Digging through her bag she found an elastic hair tie and pins to push her hair into a ponytail. After washing her face, rivers of gray lined the sink.

Emerging, she saw a second nurse at the desk. Sandy led Diana through the corridor with small rooms on each side. There was one bed, no television, no chairs, no flowers in any of them. They paused at a door with a chart marked "Bourque" resting in a paper pocket tacked to the wood.

Jim lay on his back, his face to the window. The Venetian blinds were closed. Oxygen flowed through a tube in his nose. Round plastic discs were pasted to his chest.

"There's someone special here, Jim," Sandy said. He turned his head.

"Oh my God."

"Nope, just me." Diana was shocked by his paleness. He'd shrunk. Tears ran down his face. Her strong I-can-solve-anything father crying made her cry.

"OK, guys," Sandy said, reaching for Jim's pulse. "Cut the tear city. Stay calm." To Diana she said, "You've got seven minutes, two more than normal."

"What are you doing here?"

"A little bird told me you decided to hang out at Tampa General."

"Rat fink more likely. Was it Reed?"

"Can't remember. But when you're better, I'm going to give you hell for not telling me."

"And what could you've done? You don't have a medical degree."

"I could be here."

Jim's love for his only child registered on the monitor.

Diana kept her eye on it. "What's happening? Truth."

"I've got bacon and eggs clogging my arteries. They'll operate tomorrow," he said.

She took her father's hand as a small, thin man came through the door.

"Dr. Sharma, my daughter," Jim said.

The doctor nodded then whisked out his stethoscope to listen to Jim's chest. "Ms. Bourque if you come with me, I'll explain what we plan to do. Is that fine with you, Mr. Bourque?" Jim nodded.

As they left Jim said, "Glad you're here, Kid."

In the intensive care lounge, the doctor poured coffee into two paper cups. Diana sipped hers. After French espresso, it tasted like flavored water.

"He needs a triple bypass. Do you understand what that means?"

Diana told him that she'd watched the operation in a Paris Hospital. She'd been fascinated. The patient, a SNCF driver, had survived.

Diana didn't ask to watch Dr. Sharma draw his knife down her father's chest. The next morning, fresh after ten hours sleep, she waited in the ICU lounge. She knew it would take several hours.

"Want company?"

She looked up.

Bill Reed sat down. "I'm covering the waiting room for the staff. You look wonderful. It's been years since I've seen you."

"Thanks. I didn't tell Jim who squealed."

"He'd only be half pissed."

They took turns getting coffee for Bill, Coke for Diana.

"Time is divided into seconds, minutes, hours, etc. Anyone who ever sat in ICU waiting for an operation to finish knows seconds take an eternity," Bill said.

Diana nodded. She paced. She sat down. She turned on the television. She shut it off.

"Want to take a walk?" Bill asked.

"No, I want to make him well."

"When your father got back from Paris after you were beaten, we went to a bar after putting the paper to bed. 'I just want to make her well, Bill. To rock her like she was a baby, to rock health into her . . .' Those were his very words. I didn't know what to say to him. I don't know what to say to you." He swallowed several times.

A woman, flanked by two grown men, sat in the waiting room with them. "What will I do if he dies?" the woman said. "I can't even write a check."

"We'll show you, Ma," the bigger one said.

Dr. Sharma, dressed in green from his surgical cap to his green booties over his shoes, came in. His surgical mask hung around his neck. "Ms. Bourque, come with me."

"I'm a friend. May I come?" Bill asked.

"If Ms. Bourque doesn't mind."

Diana was struck by Bill's grateful look when she agreed. Dr. Sharma led them from conference room to conference

151

room. All were occupied. Someone was sobbing when Dr. Sharma opened one door. Finally she could stand it no longer.

"Dr Sharma!" Diana's voice was three times normal volume.

He stopped.

"Is my father alive?"

"He's fine," the doctor said.

Bill enveloped a crying Diana into his arms.

"When you stop crying you can see him."

The post-operative room was soft green. The walls were green, the sheets were green. Even the nurses were green from the reflection of the low lights. Each patient had his own nurse monitoring everything. Monitors beeped. Booted feet made padding sounds. Dr. Sharma and the nurse exchanged nods.

Jim slept on the third bed to the right of the entrance, a green shower cap covering his head. Dr. Sharma, after exchanging nods with the nurse, whipped the sheet off him, leaving him stark naked. Staples ran up his leg where the veins had been transferred to the chest cavity. Blood ran freely through them in their new location, feeding Jim's heart.

Diana looked at her father. His skin around the incisions was bright yellow. He looked tiny and old. This was the man who once had swung her onto his shoulders so she could watch a parade. He had been invulnerable then. He looked delicate.

"I've seen from whence I came," Diana said to Bill as they shared a drink at the Hilton bar. "Until I saw him naked, I never thought of him as a sexual being. He must have had women in his life, but he never brought them home."

"Maybe the paper was wife enough for him. I really don't know. Diana, I know you idealize him, but he's more human than you think."

"Well now that he's weak, I'm coming to work for the paper. He can't stop me."

"He never intended anything else."

Before entering Jim's room the next morning, she steeled herself for the pathetic old man she'd seen the day before in the recovery room. She opened the door. The bed was empty. For a minute she thought he'd died.

Then a voice behind her said, "So shut the door." Jim sat in a chair. Next to him an IV bottle dripped a clear liquid into his veins.

"You bastard," she said.

"I am, you know."

As Jim recuperated, Diana often saw the advantage of patricide. No one would ever accuse him of being a good patient.

Diana's note on The Card to Jane six months later said, "I'm home. At last."

1975:
Germany and Italy

Dog paddling around the pool with Kate, Jane half watched, half listened to Chantal Lowell.

"Ace of spades, we have to gin. You're going to beat me. I just know it," Chantal said. Her voice was breathy, Jackie Kennedy-ish. Jane watched Chantal draw a king and discard it, ruining her run.

The glass table top where Chantal played with Alice Matthews was too small to allow for drinks and cards. The general's wife placed her lemonade next to her wicker chair. The ice had melted. Chlorine smells hung heavily in the stagnant air.

The pool area was deserted. Most officers had combined the Fourth of July weekend with leave to go to Garmish's cool mountain air.

Besides Chantal and Mrs. General Matthews, only the Johnsons and the lifeguard were in the pool area. The waiter sought refuge from the heat in the clubhouse and checked from time to time to see if anyone needed anything.

Sounds of traffic came from behind the hedge hiding the pool from the main road. This was an American holiday. The Germans went about their normal workaday routine.

Chantal had whispered to Jane as they'd changed into

bathing suits she didn't want to play gin, she'd rather drink one. "Damn Paul. He forbids me drinking when I dance attendance on Mrs. Old Wrinkly Neck. I'll be glad when he gets a new assignment."

While the general's wife pondered her next move, Jane saw Chantal eye David. Had he responded, she might have confirmed her suspicions they were having an affair, but he continued his laps up and down the pool. The Johnsons, like Chantal, spent so much of June as refugees from the heat at the Bad Cannstatt Officer's Club pool they were all golden brown.

Dirk, Chantal's son, was home. Only Kate had been disappointed. Jane thought if he'd been there he'd be running around screaming like a banshee, his bathing trunks falling down. Chantal called him gluteus minimus, predicting he'd grow up to a bumless wonder not able to fill out a pair of slacks. The lifeguard would have yelled at him for splashing too much. Mrs. Matthews would have clucked. Jane would have ended up caring for him, although she'd found with a hug and diversion, he was somewhat controllable.

Kate dived through her mother's legs. As Jane caught her and threw her in the air, David swam to them.

"Let me show you something, Katie," he said as he reached for a snorkel on the lip of the pool.

Jane floated on a raft where she continued watching Chantal peek at her tummy over her cards and check her reflection in the glass doors. Chantal had shared more secrets than Jane wanted to know. She knew an IUD kept Dirk an only child, after Paul flushed Chantal's birth control pills. He'd complained a couple of times she felt hard against his prick. "Thank God, men are so stupid," Chantal had said.

Chantal's geometrically cut black hair gave her a Eurasian appearance bordering on the exotic. Jane was tired of

155

Chantal's constant references to her mother, a French war bride and daughter of a very impoverished Count, and her General father.

"Gin," Alice Matthews said.

"I just haven't had any good cards all day. And you've played super well, Alice," Chantal said.

Liar, Jane thought, *you threw the good ones away.*

David gave Kate back to Jane. He swam to the edge of the pool and splashed Chantal.

"Come on in," David called.

"Ooooooooooh David, you're so mean," Chantal said.

"Go ahead, dear," Mrs. Matthews said. "Sitting here with an old lady isn't as much fun as a good swim." Although Alice Matthews was only fifty, her stocky figure, wrinkles and cork screw gray hair added years. On her way into the clubhouse, she dipped her toe into the pool.

Chantal wore a white bikini with red polka dots. A little red ribbon gathered the lace trim. She dove in the water. "Let's race to the shallow end and back to the diving board," she said to David.

Jane knew Chantal had placed first in the 1967 Ohio State Swimming Championship when her father had been stationed at Wright Pat. She watched her let David stay just enough ahead to win with a great deal of effort. Holding onto the side, Chantal let her body float onto his, wrapping her legs around his waist.

"You're really good," David said. He glanced at Jane who waved at them.

"Not as good as you," she heard Chantal say as she swung her body out of the pool. As she reached for David, he pulled her back in. They wrestled until the lifeguard blew his whistle.

Let 'em drown, Jane thought.

★ ★ ★ ★ ★

"Do Austrian cows moo in Austrian?" Dirk asked.

"Don't be silly," Chantal said.

"It's not silly," Dirk stamped his foot, a warning of another tantrum, making four since leaving Stuttgart that morning.

The Johnsons and Lowells were driving to Italy for holidays. They'd stopped to picnic in a field somewhere in Austria. They had parked their two Beetles at the edge of a pasture where five cows browsed. One poked her head through the fence, so close to where they had spread their blanket that Jane moved the picnic basket.

"German cows say mooooorrst. I want wurst," Kate said.

"French cows say meeeeeeese, I want cheese," Jane said. She cut two pieces of cheese and gave one to each child. "Listen, I want both of you to run and run until you get all the wiggles out." The kids took off, their shouts drowning out a bird singing in the large oak tree at the edge of the pasture.

"Nice going," Paul said. "She should be a child shrink. Right, David?"

David shrugged and stretched out on the army blanket Jane kept in the car for sudden picnics. Chantal sat beside him.

"Chantal, can Dirk ride with us?" Jane asked. Because the Johnson's Beetle had followed the Lowells', Jane had seen Chantal turn several times to hit Dirk.

"He's been awful. Sure you want him?" Paul asked.

"He'll be better with Kate," Chantal said.

The kids' voices could be heard laughing. Jane checked on them. A small stream tumbled over large rocks. Dirk and Kate balanced on one, poking pebbles with a stick.

"Take your shoes off," Jane said before rejoining the

others. She slit a *brötchen,* wet her finger to pick up crumbs that fell on the tablecloth. Resting against a tree, she alternated bites of sausage and *brötchen* as she watched a cumulus Abraham Lincoln face break apart slowly.

She looked at her husband, his eyes closed and on the verge of sleep brought on by fresh air, warm sun and six hours behind the wheel. He refused to ride when Jane drove. Even when Jane kept the car for the day, David would drive to the base, pull up in front of the infirmary and hop out. Then Jane would slide over behind the wheel.

"I'm bored." Chantal stood up.

Paul pulled her back to the blanket. "Dirk's attention span is longer than my wife's, and his is only thirty seconds on a good day."

"Let's go for a walk," Chantal whined.

"I'd rather nap." Paul rolled onto his stomach, pillowing his head with his arms.

"I'll go," David said.

The two disappeared down a path that ran along a fence, separating the field from the cow pastures. At the end of the fence was a wood.

Jane watched the couple disappear. *I hope I'm wrong,* she thought.

The couples found an almost hotel in an almost village on Lake Como. It was a postcard scene with the Alps reflected in the water. With the arrival of the Johnson/Lowell clans, the local population increased to nine families. The house was identifiable as a hotel only because a sign said so.

If Paul hadn't pulled over to stretch his legs after a particularly harrowing series of curves, they'd have missed it. They were almost at the foot of the mountain. Lake Como rested below the next curve. Paul walked up to the Johnson car and said, "I'm exhausted. I'd forgotten Italian drivers all pretend they're driving chase scenes in James Bond movies."

Both the children slept in the back seat of the Johnson car. Their faces were flushed in the late evening sun. Dirk, a mouth breather because of his adenoids, made little snores. David and Jane got out of their car and shut their doors softly to not disturb the children. Jane spotted the village of six houses, a hotel and church off a narrow road.

"Let's take a look. For tonight anyway," Paul said, spotting it, too.

The owner, dressed in a T-shirt and dirty pants, greeted them. Several children of various ages peeked from behind their father. The hotel lobby doubled as a kitchen with a tiled fireplace and a table. The wife, a rotund woman with dark hair pulled unsuccessfully into a bun, cooked dinner on a wood burning black stove. A baby munched on a bone.

"I don't think so," David said.

"Let's look, at least. Think of driving more," Paul said.

The owner ushered them to the top floor via an outside staircase. A balcony almost overlooked Lake Como. A jut in the hotel, forming the wall of a chicken yard, blocked the lake's view. Four scraggly hens picked in the dirt.

There were three rooms and a bath. The bathroom was larger than the small bedroom which was filled by two child-sized cots. The bathroom, however, had the largest tub any of them had even seen.

The bedroom furniture was oak. "The mattress is firm." Jane tested the bed. "The rooms are spotless."

"How much?" Paul asked in Italian.

"Forty-two dollars American," the man said.

"Too much for a night." Paul indicated they should leave.

"A week," the man said.

"For all of us," Paul said firmly.

"You hava cigarettes?" the owner asked.

David produced a carton of Winstons bought for such an occasion.

The men shook hands.

"Guys, I suggest we use this place as a base. We won't find anything cheaper," Paul said. The others agreed.

The vacation started out as almost fun. For Dirk and Kate there was no almost. They played with the local children, roaming the village with an unknown freedom.

Mama Mancini, who fried pizza dough and sprinkled sugar on it and made pots of stews and sauces, added Dirk and Kate to her brood. She hugged all the kids a lot, but Dirk seemed to be constantly in her arms. When the adults went exploring, the children stayed with her.

"Did you notice, Dirk hasn't had a tantrum since we got here?" Paul asked as they drove to a market in the next town. They arrived at the stands before anyone could answer. Chantal, spying leather pocketbooks, jumped out as soon as the car stopped.

The nearest villages were ten to twenty times bigger, which meant they were still tiny. To get to any, it was necessary to drive up or down an Alp. Two had restaurants, where the Johnsons and Lowells would eat, famished from spending the day outside and smelling the odors from Mama Mancini's kitchen. The children ate at the hotel.

No one wanted to go sightseeing. Relaxing on the beach during the day, eating out at night, then going back to the hotel was enough.

The second night Chantal suggested they play Mau Mau, men against women. It became a nightly ritual, the four of them sitting cross-legged on the bed. The couples kept a running score. As the first week wore on, cheating became as much a part of the game as the rules.

"I've a great way to signal each other which suit we want," Chantal said. "Whatever letter starts a sentence, means the suit you want. Like if you say, 'Did you hear Dirk,' it's diamonds."

"Can I borrow a handkerchief," Jane said.

"Clubs. Have you seen my sweater?"

"Hearts. That's brilliant. The guys will never figure it out."

Since the girls never used the same sentence twice, the men had no idea they were signaling. The women took a fast lead. The men tried fiddling with the score, until Jane and Chantal checked the figures.

One week and two days into the vacation, as they were ready to go to bed, Chantal said, "Wait a minute. We're playing with two decks of cards, but it looks like half a deck is missing." She slurred her words a little. They'd emptied two bottles of wine made by Signor Mancini.

"The wine is affecting your eyes, Chantal," David said.

Chantal stood up. "You guys have hidden cards."

Jane looked under the bed but found nothing. Chantal patted David's shirt pocket. She found two jokers.

"Sixty points. Add it to their score," she squealed. "What else have you got?" She reached down the elastic waist band of his shorts.

"Chantal!" Paul yelled.

"Keep your hands out of my husband's pants." Jane didn't yell, but spoke quietly, pronouncing each syllable carefully.

"Search Paul if you want," Chantal said. "You can even have Paul for the night." She put her arms around David's neck.

He took them off and handed one arm to Paul, "I think your wife has had a little too much to drink. Maybe you'd better put her to bed."

Chantal looked back and stuck out her tongue as Paul led her off. The door clicked behind them. Jane gathered up the cards that were on the bed. She threw them across the room.

"Are you sleeping with Chantal?"

David sighed. "Why is it you always think I'm sleeping around? No, don't answer that. Chantal is a spoiled brat."

Jane pulled her suitcase from under the bed. "I'm leaving with Kate."

"I forbid it."

"Forbid it? I'm your wife, not your child." Her voice was so soft he had to strain to hear. She threw Kate's and her clothes into the suitcase.

"Be rational."

"I am rational. I'm calm. I'm leaving. You can come or stay."

"It's midnight. Let's go to bed. We can go at dawn, if you want."

Jane thought about driving twelve hours when she was so tired, driving on mountain curves, searching for signs. It wasn't what she wanted. She wasn't sure she would ever have what she wanted.

She took the alarm clock and set it for five. Before she went to sleep she said, "David, I think you've mistaken my gentleness for weakness."

David sat at the kitchen table looking at brochures. "How about skiing for Christmas, Janie?"

She sat on the floor with Kate reading *Reddy Fox*, a book from her childhood that her mother had sent. Outside, rain pounded against the windows. With the fog it was impossible to see the orchard. She felt the same way about the future.

Jane wore her new diamond ring that David had bought on a getaway weekend in Amsterdam. The month before they had gone to Paris. She had a new Beetle, giving her daily freedom. She'd suggested he was throwing money at their problems.

He had looked hurt and said, "You struggled with me, Janie. Now I want you to have it easier."

Jane had been half thinking of the story and half thinking about how her father had taught her to open a new book carefully, unfolding one page at a time and pressing it open. Once when she was angry at him, she had torn the title page of one of his books into scraps. Terrified, she flushed the pieces down the toilet. In the middle of the night she had gotten up to flush again.

Since their vacation with the Lowells, she'd thought a lot about revenge. In a telephone call, Diana had suggested the Great-Balls-of-Fire trick.

"What is that?" Jane had asked.

Diana took a sip of her Coke. Jane could hear the ice clink in the glass. "Simple. Rinse David's shorts in pure Clorox. Let 'em dry. When he puts 'em on, his body sweat will mix with the chlorine and Great Balls of Fire."

Jane had filed it under fantasy revenge.

"Mommy, you're daydreaming. Tell me what Reddy does next," Kate shook her mother's arm.

"I'm sorry." She finished the chapter, which was only a paragraph more, then joined David in looking at the brochures.

"I prefer St. Anton," David said. "Garmish has too many military." He began talking about how much fun last year's ski trip was. How he had never gone on a vacation with his own family, having been sent to ski camps and summer camps while his parents went other places.

In the past Jane would have felt sorry for him. Now she felt like they were a family cut from a magazine, where nothing is out of place on the surface, but everything is a mess behind the scenes. Before she could comment the phone rang.

David took it. "I'll be right there, Paul."

To Jane's quizzical look he said, "Chantal overdosed on sleeping pills."

"I'll get the landlady to stay with Kate. Don't say no. Paul will need someone to sit with him." She ran to the closet, grabbed her coat and threw David's to him. "Katie, come quickly. You're going downstairs."

Except for Paul, the emergency waiting room was empty. He had his head in his hands. The chairs were army issue. Stale cigarette smoke hung in the air. David patted Paul on the back as he went into the treatment area.

Jane sat next to Paul. "What happened?" She had only seen the Lowells at Officers' Club events since they'd left Italy, except for a talk with Paul when he'd come by her apartment to talk about his marriage. She had told him she had no answers. She didn't even know the questions.

Jane put her hand on his shoulder and waited. Paul began pacing.

"Our neighbor had Dirk for the afternoon. When she brought him home, the door was unlocked but everything was dark. She found Chantal in bed. She'd messed herself. Mary thought she might be drunk because there was a bottle of Vodka, but then she saw the pills. Thank God, we were so close to the hospital."

"Did she leave a note?"

"I found this in her pocketbook." He pulled out a piece of lined paper. A lollipop was stuck to it.

Jane read, " 'I don't want to live without you.' Were you separating?"

"No."

They were both silent.

An hour later David came out. "She's stable. We've pumped her stomach."

"Can I go in?" No muscle in Paul's body had relaxed as he looked at David.

"Yes, but she's asleep."

They waited until Paul came out. "Let's take you out to eat. We can talk."

They went to a small restaurant in Möhringen. They ordered pork chops with hot potato salad and a green salad, then pushed the food around their plates.

"I suggest you send her home. She needs counseling. There's no one here I have faith in," David said. "I'm not sure she really wanted to die. She only took four pills."

"Is there something I could have done differently? I've been faithful."

"Man, I don't have those answers," David said.

Paul didn't send Chantal home. A week after leaving the hospital, she slit her wrists. It may not have been a sincere attempt, because she did it five minutes before Paul was due home. Unfortunately, he had been caught in traffic and arrived home only minutes after she died.

As Jane packed for the skiing trip to St. Anton, she took a moment to send The Card to Diana. Her message to Diana was, "Kate made a drawing for you." She enclosed a red Santa Claus on skis. She couldn't summarize the past year. She wasn't sure what lay ahead.

1976:
Florida

Cubist stained glass windows portrayed surreal saints. Colored hues beamed through the windows by a relentless Florida sun, turning the light pine paneling from beige to unordered rainbows. Statues, hacked from wood in tortured poses, were as surreal as the saints in the glass.

Mary Bourque's closed casket sat in the center of the altar. Both were buried by flowers. Their scent was overpowering. Bouquets had been sent from the paper's employees, neighbors, Governor Askew, congressmen, the two state senators, candidates for all those jobs, along with every local and aspiring politician, business leaders and heads of charities.

But the three hundred and six people who sent the flowers and crammed themselves in the pews hadn't come to mourn Mary Bourque. They couldn't mourn a person they'd never met. They'd come for Jim.

The few people that had known her sat in the front pew. Each was lost in thoughts that made more sense than the priest's words. "Beloved wife of James, beloved mother of Diana . . ." the priest droned. Jim Bourque squeezed one of Diana's hands. Olaf held the other.

Diana thought, *she wasn't my beloved mother*. The woman

166

in the slate-colored coffin was a stranger. She'd heard a staff member say at the wake the night before, "I thought the boss's wife died years ago."

When she'd heard that, she'd wanted to say, "My mother may have died at fifty-six, but she stopped living long before." What Diana did say over and over was, "Thank you for coming," until she felt like recording it on a cassette.

She thought of the poor nurse who found Mary clutching her rosary in the chair where she'd been tied for years. It had taken the nurse a few minutes to realize that she was the only one alive in the room.

Olaf glanced at Diana. When he decided she was fine, he slipped into his own thoughts about the Mass, his first. The church where he grew up had been built in 802 and was as austere as the services. Old wood carried a dry smell, not of rot but of sweet autumn leaves combined with caramelized sugar. Notre Dame's incense and flowers jarred his olfactory nerves. He wished he were in Norway, not running interference for Jim and Diana against the troop of curiosity seekers and alienated relatives.

"Peace be with you," the priest said.

"And also with you," the congregation responded.

The exchange echoed and re-echoed above the hum of the air conditioning, bringing Olaf's mind back to the Mass.

Diana's Aunt Theresa grabbed Olaf's hand and murmured the words while ignoring his eyes. A heavy woman, ample of chest, Theresa O'Rourke Flannagan had bustled into the funeral home during the wake. She had been followed by her husband, six children, their mates and their children. After glaring at Jim she turned to Diana and said, "You look like your mother."

Diana, until that moment, hadn't known she had an

aunt, uncle or cousins. As the evening progressed, she was happy she hadn't. When Theresa demanded, "Open the coffin. I want to see my sister," the murmurs in the funeral home had stopped.

Olaf had herded her aside to talk with the undertaker. Before he could arrange for Theresa to view the body after visiting hours, he needed Jim's agreement. He gave it, but his sister-in-law demanded he be with her. Diana didn't want to see her mother a second time but she wanted to be near her father if he needed her. Olaf insisted on being with Diana for the same reason. The four of them stood quietly as the undertaker removed the flowers and lifted the lid. It had creaked.

"She's changed. I wouldn't have known her. Are you sure it's really Mary?" Theresa had asked.

Jim spit out his words. "If you had visited her when she was alive you wouldn't be surprised."

Diana said to Jim, "Peace be with you" and thought how any loss she felt was for what might have been. More than ever she wanted to know what drove the woman in the casket into the recesses of her mind. She still feared the same thing awaited her, more acutely this day than for a long time.

She still could not understand why her father, usually open about everything, locked this information away. They shared Diana's life. They shared a business. They shared a home. Then why wouldn't he share his marital history, especially since his daughter was part of it?

For Diana the Mass was strange. She hadn't known until the funeral that some of her family was Catholic. Her experience with the church was Saturday night dances at the parish house. They'd held the best sock hops in town.

When she'd been ten, she asked Jim why they didn't go

168

to church like her friends. He'd taken her to the Everglades. "This is where you find God—in nature, not in a building." They never discussed religion again. They talked about right and wrong, good and bad, love and hate, beauty, bigotry, prejudice, ethics, politics, Diana's problems—but never religion.

"Peace be with you," Jim said to his daughter. Could she ever feel peace, he wondered *if I keep my secrets from her. I am a weak man,* he thought. *I love her too much to let her know where I've failed.*

He began praying not to God, but to Mary O'Rourke-Bourque. He prayed for her forgiveness.

The Mary he saw wasn't the hag in the coffin. Although the undertaker had done what he could with her hair and makeup, the body was wizened, witch-like. The soft blue dress that Jim had bought for the burial was the same color as the one she had worn the first day he had seen her. He'd spent several hours shopping until he found the right one.

Since he had received the phone call from the rest home, he had been holding a silent dialogue with his wife . . .

Ah, Mary, I remember you running after your twin brothers, your wild auburn hair streaming behind you. They split up. You stood at the edge of scrub pine grove, your hands on your hips threatening them with hell if they didn't return.

"You get one, I'll get the other," I said coming up behind you. After we'd captured them, I fell in love as only a twenty-year-old man should. But in my case, I shouldn't have.

You had no time for love, what with caring for the twins, your sisters, and your bitch of a mother. So our dates meant carrying clothes to the Laundromat or searching for the boys.

God, how your mother hated me. Alice Frances O'Brien-O'Rourke. On her deathbed she made you swear with one hand on the Bible and the other on the crucifix that all the O'Rourke children would enter the church.

Maybe I shouldn't have talked you into marrying me instead of Christ. I used every trick I could think of.

"You can serve God as my wife," I said.

"How do you know? You're not even Irish," you said.

"If you scratch an Irishman deep enough you'll find a Frenchman," I said. Your eyes grew so wide.

"Go on. You're pulling my leg." You used that phrase a lot. Maybe because I pulled your leg a lot. Trying to make you see things less seriously.

"The French settled Ireland. Take my name Bourque. The Irish changed it to Burke. All those fitz something or other were once fils. So, my lovely one, you're probably part French."

I was so full of myself back then. I had all the answers. Now I'm not sure I even know the questions.

Were you ever happy with me? Was I ever happy with you? I know you tried to keep your promise to your mother, no one wanted to be a priest or nun. It wasn't your fault.

When did you start to lose it? When the twins enlisted? When one was blown to smithereens in the Philippines? When the other was missing in action? When Fiona married the Protestant or Theresa left the convent? When I went overseas, the big time war correspondent? Or was it a little of one and some of another?

Does it matter? I came back to a stranger, not the bright-eyed girl I left in 1942. There wasn't much I could do. I needed months in a rehabilitation clinic after they dug shrapnel from my spine. I needed to confront my own demons.

"Peace be with you," John Freeman extended his gnarled fingers, interrupting Jim's memories.

"And also with you," Jim said to the old man before falling back into the past.

I remember my nurses walking through all the crumbled balls of yellow paper, my business plan for the paper. I cajoled John

Freedman into a loan. He gave it on instinct, not any guidelines. That was possible in 1946. Not now. John must be eighty-four, maybe more. The paper is their biggest account. That wouldn't have interested you.

Maybe Mary, if I'd been home more it would have been different. But I know I wasn't meant to be a family man. Too late for all of us. Still, we created something better than both of us in Diana.

You almost killed her, Mary and you didn't even know it. No state institution for you. You didn't know the difference. I did. At first I came weekly. You never acknowledged me. So I came monthly. I missed three times—twice when I was with Diana after the riots and once after my heart attack.

Forgive me, Mary, for my sins against you.

"Peace be with you," Bill Reed leaned over to say.

Peace was with Jim. This service was his final payment to the girl with the flying auburn hair. He felt no guilt at his joy in his freedom. He would never be free of his other guilt.

Jim Bourque looked at his daughter. Maybe he should tell her some of what happened. Not all. There were some things he could never tell her.

The organ began playing. The undertaker, a man with Clorox white hair, indicated they should leave. Jim took Diana's arm. Olaf took Aunt Theresa's arm. She bustled a bit.

Jim stopped at each pew to speak to people. Diana did the same. In the last row they both stopped. Maurice stepped out to embrace them both by kissing them on both cheeks.

"I would not miss being with you during this difficult time," he said. "Solange wanted to come but she is ill."

Jim invited him to ride in the limo to the cemetery.

* * * * *

The funeral and burial were over. Guests, except for Maurice and Bill Reed, had left the Bourque condo. Diana fired up the grill on the balcony to cook chicken. None of them had had a chance to eat. "The vultures took it all," Maurice said.

Diana in cutoff jeans, her blouse tied under her breasts, her hair in pigtails, looked more like a teenager than an assistant publisher, but her manner of directing supper preparations was adult. She assigned Maurice to lettuce washing, Olaf to making barbecue sauce and Jim to opening bottles and arranging the table.

Looking at the marina below, she saw a small yacht pull up. The skipper, dressed in white shorts and sailing cap, jumped off and tied his boat to the mooring. The setting sun cast pink shadows in the water. She took the chicken and brushed it with Olaf's sauce before putting it on the grill. A few drops fell on the charcoal and smoke flared. Ordinary events.

As they ate they talked about publishing. Diana put her hand on Olaf's to make him feel included.

"My daughter wants to buy a weekly paper. She's been nagging me all year," Jim said. "Down in Englewood. Run it independently." His face reflected his misgivings.

"The accountants approve. You're just lazy in your old age," Diana said. She wiped her fingers, sticky with sauce, on her paper napkin. Small bits stuck to her fingertips.

Maurice stretched. "Jim, look at the three of us. You've built your empire. I'm still working on mine. Now it's Diana's turn—trust her."

Jim opened another Budweiser for each of them. "You're saying I should give her wings." He tilted his glass pouring the liquid into it. "OK Diana, get the lawyers on it."

Olaf cleaned the kitchen while Diana and Jim drove Maurice to the airport for an 8:00 p.m. flight. Olaf had expected them back within an hour. He began to get worried as Johnny Carson teased Doc Severinsen. The closing credits were rolling as father and daughter walked in. Diana's face was puffy and Jim looked exhausted. Jim said he was going to bed.

Olaf lit a joint and offered it to her. "Are you OK?"

She refused it. "Maurice says Solange has cancer. I feel sad."

He said, "I understand."

"There's more. Jim told me everything about my mother."

Taking her hand, he led her into the bedroom. They made love, a gentle communication. Olaf fell asleep. Diana didn't. For the first time since she first saw her mother, she felt the madness in her veins was controlled. Her last thought before she fell asleep was, I think I'll write on The Card this year "I'm free, truly free."

1977:
Massachusetts

The ball cracked against the club, a clean breaking sound. Soaring into the blue sky it landed a respectable distance down the fairway. Jane watched, her hand shading her eyes. "Your lessons work, Tom," she said.

Dressed in burgundy pants and an Izod shirt, the golf pro swaggered to the markers. Holding the ball and tee as a single unit, he bent over, one leg slightly behind the other.

"Watch my follow through," he said. His swing was fluid, hundreds of muscles, tissues and ligaments at one with the club. His ball followed the path that Jane's took, passed it and landed near the green. They jumped into the cart.

As she addressed her ball, Tom said, "Wait." He put his arms around her, holding his hands over hers on the club. "Check where the head of the club is facing. You'd have shot it into the woods." He pressed into her. "Unless you want to make a detour."

Jane shivered. The pleasantness of the shiver shocked her. It was at least a month since she and David had made love. The murmurs of club women as the pro strolled by joggled around her mind. Virginia Grayson called him a walking stud. "Be good," she said.

"I am."

"That's not even original," she said.

Tom shrugged. "I'm sorry, I thought you might want to play a bit."

Ignoring him, Jane's next shot went to the green's edge. She scooched down, measuring the angle of the green with her club. "I'm doing this because I've seen others do it. I haven't the foggiest idea what I'm looking for."

Tom said, "You're checking the curve of the green." He leaned down beside her, his thigh against hers. "Your ball will break to the left of the little rise before the cup. Hit it hard enough to go over and in. Don't overshoot."

Jane overshot.

He brought the ball back to her. "Try again."

She did, but too gently.

"Again."

On her third try she sank her putt.

"You'd be good if you played more seriously," Tom said back at the pro shop. Jane leaned on the glass counter that displayed a variety of balls, gloves and tees. She uncapped her felt pen to write the check.

"It's a way to use my time," she said.

As he took the check, his hand lingered on hers. "If you change your mind, you know where to find me."

"I'm not apt to take the game more seriously," Jane said deliberately misunderstanding.

"I'm a better lover than golfer. And we both know I'm a great golfer."

"I'm not going to be a notch on your putter." Jane walked away thinking that was a retort that Diana would have made.

Besides an eighteen-hole golf course, the Lexington

175

Country Club offered members a health club, snack bar, cocktail lounge, gourmet restaurant, tennis and racquetball courts, as well as indoor and outdoor swimming pools. The members were doctors, dentists and executives, most of whom lived in the town that fired "The shot heard around the world."

Jane reached the pool too late to see Kate finish her synchronized swimming lesson. The area around the cement edge was fully landscaped with flowers. Several women sunned themselves, their oiled bodies glistening in the late morning sun. Jane spotted her daughter poised on the high diving board. The child was stick thin with long blond hair braided into a ponytail. Had she not been blond, her racial origins would be of question.

Kate dived, surfaced and climbed out of the pool. She ran to her mother. "Can we go to McDonald's?"

"How about the snack bar?" Jane wasn't anti-McDonald's. How could she not admire any place so consistently mediocre for billions of burgers? However, today she wanted a curried chicken salad, not a Big Mac. She wanted to be served by a waitress, not stand in line. "You can get a cheeseburger there," she said.

"Rock, scissors, paper?" Kate asked. "Winner chooses the restaurant."

Jane nodded. They raised their hands. "One, two, three," Jane's fist beat Kate's two-fingered scissors.

"Would you believe this was paper torn in half?" Kate asked.

"No."

"Two out of three?"

"No."

The Johnsons had lived in Lexington for a year. After leaving the army, David had deposited his wife and child with his in-laws. Without consulting Jane, he'd bought into the Lexington Women's Medical Center and purchased a four-bedroom, center chimney colonial dating from the late 1600s, for Jane to renovate. "You should be grateful I saved you looking at houses," he'd said.

The house had sixteen rabbit warren rooms. Jane looked at it with dismay the first time she saw it. Then she called an architect. While walls were torn down, fireplaces restored, wide board floors sanded and varnished, she researched fabrics and early New England folk art. She selected the right antiques from the Johnson storage and bought the rest.

"See, you did like doing it," David had said after their home warming party for the medical center staff. "And Grayson, he was astonished." David smirked. Grayson headed the medical center.

"It was more interesting than I thought it would be," she said. She still felt warm from Frank Grayson telling her it was a restoration more than a renovation. As a local history buff, his compliments meant a lot to her.

With the house done, Jane felt at sixes and sevens, as her grandmother used to say. Kate was always playing with Judy down the street, where they rode horses and pretended they were the $6 million children of the $6 million man and woman. Jane feared her time would drag even more after Kate went back to school.

The Johnsons were not fighting during this period. They weren't together enough to fight, for David was totally driven by his work. The day of Jane's golf lesson they planned a family night, the first in three weeks.

After the hamburger and curried chicken salad, Kate and Jane stopped for cream, blueberries and rock salt. David had promised to make ice cream.

For once David made it home on time. He came in singing, hugged his wife and tickled Kate. "Ice cream, homemade, tonight, as promised."

As they packed the rock salt around the cream cylinder, Jane said, "I can't believe we will get through an evening without an interruption." The phone rang.

"Please tell your husband Mrs. Pierpont's pains are five minutes apart," a voice from the answering service said. The name could have as easily been Falkenstrom, Doherty, Higgins. The result was the same. Jane passed the phone to her husband. She plugged in the ice cream machine and planned to eat it all.

In bed, a four poster with a canopy, Jane waited for David to come back. A breeze floated in the window. Jane turned the pages of *Yankee Magazine*. "This is boring," she said. A fly, which had escaped the screens, buzzed. Jane thought about her daily life. Bridge, golf, tennis, lunch and volunteering at the hospital were fine on a limited basis, but they did not make a life.

The radio was tuned to WERS, which played oldies. Peggy Lee sang, "Is That All There Is?" Jane floated in a semi-awake state. Come on Peggy, don't you start too, she said to herself as she fell asleep somewhere between the lyrics about the fire and the broken love affair.

When she woke, David's side of the bed was still neat. The wind had changed and she shivered under the light sheet. A lawn mower hummed outside. Drawing on her robe, she stood looking out the window, trying to decide her day.

The Johnson home sat on a five-acre lot facing woods. The landscaper waved at her from the back of the lawnmower. David had ordered a pool and tennis court for the backyard where it melted into the wood. Jane cancelled the order. She dreamed of a garden bursting with fresh corn and tomatoes. David, who ate to live rather than living to eat, had accused her of having a sharecropper mentality.

The phone rang twice. Mrs. O'Brien, the housekeeper, called from the foot of the stairs, "It's for you Mrs. J." Jane, already at the head of the stairs, ran to the kitchen phone.

"Jane, come back to work for me after Labor Day," a voice, instantly recognizable by the permanent rasp carved into vocal cords from years of smoking, said.

"You still don't waste time," Jane said. "How are you, Lucy?"

"I'd be a lot better if I had a decent assistant. How are you?"

"Wonderful, but I hadn't thought of working."

"Think about it. In fact, come in. We can think about it together. Over lunch."

Jane needed to go into town to buy Kate's school clothes. "Meet you at the office at 11:30?"

"Good. Then we'll eat at the English Tea Room," Lucy said.

Walking back into JRP's reception room, Jane saw the same Oriental rug under the same three Queen Anne chairs. The oak book case held an assortment of JRP publications, some of which she had promoted. Only the receptionist was different.

Lucy swept through the door separating the public and private areas of JRP, gathered Jane into her arms, then brushed her into the inner sanctum. The men were the same, but the women had been replaced with other women of a similar age and eagerness that Jane had known when she was there. The men shook her hand and asked about her husband and son and how she had liked living in Italy.

She didn't correct them.

Lucy's office had changed. Her drawing board and desks were in new positions. Her battered typewriter had been replaced by a word processor.

"Gets the cobwebs out to look at a different wall every few years," Lucy said. Her bleached blond hair was gray, but her beehive hairdo remained. When she showed Jane several layouts, Jane reached down and adjusted a piece of type that was slightly crooked. "Let's go eat. We can talk," Lucy said.

As the women walked through the Common and the Public Gardens, pleasant memories of lunches eaten from paper bags jogged Jane's memory. A swan boat, pedaled by a kid wearing a MIT T-shirt, floated under the footbridge. A duck, hoping for peanuts, circled the boat.

The English Tea Room on Newbury Street was between two galleries and under Second Chance Used Clothing. A Christian Dior worn once at the most was in its window. A full-size sculpted woman, her body twisted in unnatural contortions, was in one gallery window. She was painted with zodiac signs and wore antlers. A six-by-eight foot, peach and avocado painting was on plywood in the other.

To enter the Tea Room, patrons walked down ten stairs—not just into the restaurant but into the 1940s. The restaurant had dark tables and a stamped tin ceiling molded into intricate square patterns. For slightly over 40s' prices, a person could get a complete meal.

Neither the ambience nor the value was what made the restaurant beloved. It was the large salad with a vinegar/sugar/celery seed dressing dumped unceremoniously on tables by the waitress. The huge aluminum bowls stayed until diners ate their fill. Then, and only then, would the dish be moved to another table. When a dish was empty the waitress refilled it from a giant salad bowl in the center of the restaurant.

Jane, having eaten two servings of salad, broke a white roll streaked with strawberry jam as the waitress stood by the table. Lucy ordered pot roast, Jane, the lamb. "The menu hasn't changed one iota since the last time I was here," Jane said. "We had some good working lunches here."

"We can do it again. Come back to work," Lucy said. "I've had five assistants in as many years. They come out of a mold with a degree in their right hand, an engagement ring on their left. I listen about bridesmaids, bands and menus until I want to vomit. Try and talk about galleys, line art, market segmentation—their eyes glaze over as if I said something dirty."

"I thought with women's lib that didn't happen."

Lucy snorted. "Maybe they never heard of it. Or maybe those with career aspirations go on for MBAs and leave the honor of working for me to those who want an MRS. Our pay is terrible."

"Is that your idea of selling me a job?"

Lucy lit a cigarette that she stuck in a little plastic mouthpiece taken from a box marked Aquafresh. "I want you to negotiate yourself a good salary. Harrison will be a tightwad as usual. Old Yankee. Spends every nickel three times."

"I don't know, Lucy."

"What you don't know is that I'm retiring in two years. I've been told to groom my successor. When I mentioned you to Harrison, he liked the idea. Never forgot what you did with the Lobi book. Nothing has ever topped it."

Jane listened to Lucy promote the job as if it were a book. Memories faded in and out: reworking copy, rushing proofs back to a printer to keep scheduled production time, memories of full days.

David would hate her working again. He positively glowed when he bragged how she was a lady of leisure. And Kate? Lexington Academy, a private school, didn't get out until five. The bleakness of Jane's future—lunch, golf, shopping with women who brushed their lips against her cheek in greeting, then used the same lips to rip her apart behind her back, hovered in front of her.

"Will you at least talk to Harrison?" Lucy asked. She ran her fork over her plate, catching the last bit of gravy on the prongs.

Jane nodded. Lucy smirked.

The president's desk, an original Louis XVI table, its decoupage shepherds and shepherdesses protected with twentieth century glass, had been handed down by his wife's ancestors, whose portraits ran along a dark green felt wall. When Jane first saw this office, she'd felt intimidated. Now she warmly took Harrison Codrington's extended hand.

Despite his fifty years, he still owned a full head of hair thicker than most younger men's. When Jane had left JRP it was black. Now his sideburns and forelock were gray streaked.

"How nice to see you again, Jane. How is your daughter? Catherine, isn't it?"

Jane nodded. "We call her Kate. Growing."

What some might call Yankee charm was a card file with names of spouses, children and birthdays, and other information of importance to employees and vendors. Lucy had told Jane about it years ago, so his memory on her daughter's name did not surprise her. They exchanged the required formal courtesies while seating themselves.

Mrs. Palmer, his secretary, brought china cups and saucers, and tea in a silver tea pot. She served them as if it were a tea party, not a business meeting.

"Lucy is convinced you are the best person to succeed her. I could pretend I disagreed, but we both know how much I respect Lucy's opinions. I'm prepared to be very generous. Say seven thousand a year while she teaches you the ropes."

Jane didn't say how much she'd hate to see him be stingy. "The job is interesting. But seven thousand is really starvation wages, even for publishing."

"Well you do have a husband to support you, Jane." He rubbed his hands together, something both women knew he did when he was having a good time.

"If Gloria Steinem were dead, she'd spin in her grave, Sir. My husband's income doesn't change the value of my talent."

Codrington cringed. Lucy looked at him pointedly. Everyone in the room knew she was saying, "I've told you that JRP, Inc. is ripe for a discrimination suit from young women sidetracked into dead end jobs at a fraction of the pay males earn."

"Don't tell me you're a woman's libber, Jane. A pretty little thing like you."

Jane thought of rising to his comment about her looks, but let it go. "Women's lib has nothing to do with it. What would you offer me if I came in here with a beard?" Jane had checked with a headhunter who said the men in the firm were earning about twenty thousand. As a student, she had always been good in research.

"Besides a place in a sideshow?"

"You know what she means, Harrison," Lucy said.

"The same as I just offered you."

Jane wanted to say liar. "You were paying me seven thousand when I left. Anything I promoted did better than projections. Fifteen thousand and a percentage of sales over projection."

Lucy sucked in her breath. She earned fifteen thousand without percentages.

"A lot of things have changed: we're computerizing, you've been out of the work force."

"I've always learned quickly. Let's think about what I've done since I left. I was treasurer to the post nursery. I've learned German, adapted to another culture, handled the murky politics of an Officer's Wives Club. Transferable skills, Mr. Codrington."

"Ten thousand?"

"Twelve thousand five hundred, a raise to thirteen thousand in six months, annual reviews and a minimum of fifteen thousand when I take over Lucy's position."

"We'll shake."

"I'd like a written contract."

"No one has a written contract."

"A letter with your signature will be fine."

They shook hands. Codrington checked his wallet. "It's still there," he said.

"Keep it out," said Lucy. "I'm coming back to talk to you. I like the idea of percentages."

"Lucy, I am not surprised. Next time I negotiate with this little shark, I'll do it alone." Jane glanced back as they left. He was writing on a card. She bet it was Kate's name and a summary of the negotiations. She was right.

"I will not have my wife working!" David banged his hand down on the kitchen table next to a blue-grey ceramic pot filled with wildflowers. The flowers quivered.

Jane sat at the table, her fingers drumming against the wood. Kate slept upstairs. David paced in front of the fireplace where wood was stacked ready for the first fall fire. Jane picked up a spoon to stir her tea although she drank it black.

"I don't understand what's gotten into you. Most women would kill to be in your shoes. You can do anything you want."

"I want to work," Jane said. Until she dickered with Harrison, she had no idea how much. What had begun as a game had become serious.

"Our taxes can't take it."

"I want my own money," Jane remembered an earlier battle where David had expected her to list every expenditure she made, like his mother had done. He had shown her Lillian's book which included things like "Twenty-five cents, soda; fifty cents, flower (rose)."

David and Jane never reached the screaming stage because neither were screamers. But no matter what each said, the other didn't hear. It wasn't a matter of volume. The couple marked their territories as surely as dogs lifting their legs.

Jane returned to work.

David fired the housekeeper.

Jane rehired her.

He volunteered Jane for a new hospital committee. Jane found a replacement.

David came home for more dinners and complained about their quality. He found complicated recipes for her to try. She did. On weekends.

He refused to stop at the dry cleaner's, saying it was her job. She took his clothes to a dry cleaner in Boston, between the office and the train station.

During Thanksgiving vacation she located The Card in her desk drawer. She looked at it for a long time thinking for the right message. She rejected, "I love working again." "Merry Christmas" wasn't enough. "Kate is growing" or "David's practice is going well," were cop-outs. She bit the end of her pen as she always did when trying to write. Jane knew that Diana would accuse her of bullshitting at any of them. Finally she wrote, "1977. I'm tired of one-way streets." What she didn't write was that she had no idea what to do about it.

Summer 1978:
Argelès-sur-Mer, France

As Diana guffawed at Garp fighting off Mrs. Ralphie, the woman sitting next to her moved as far away as it is possible to do in a train. *"Excusez-moi, mais le livre est très drole,"* Diana said.

The woman nodded. Her expression said she was not convinced that she was next to an enthusiastic reader rather than a madwoman.

The train stopped at Carcassonne. Diana glanced up, remembering when she and Solange had explored the shops behind the medieval walls. God! She couldn't believe Solange had been dead a year. She shuddered, remembering Maurice's pain at the funeral—those devastating tears.

After Garp escaped Mrs. Ralphie, Diana's eyes closed. Her flight had been delayed twice, first at Kennedy then at de Gaulle where French workers staged a work slow down. She'd decided to take the train.

When the train pulled into Argelès-sur-Mer, Maurice bounded out the station door. He looked tanned and rested, nothing like the beaten man that had driven her to the airport after Solange's burial. They kissed on both cheeks.

After the air conditioned train, Diana felt slapped by the heat. By the time they reached the station, her clothes had glued themselves to her body. "I'm glad you guessed I wasn't flying into Perpignan. I tried calling, but you were out."

"I thought you might take the train when I heard about the strike." Maurice took Diana's backpack. "If I knew this is all you had for a two week holiday, I could have left the car at home." He led her to the parking lot on the other side of the station, where the faded blue Renault cooked in the sun.

"You still have it," Diana said. The door stuck. She reached in the window automatically to open it from the inside. The seats seared the flesh of the back of her legs. The dashboard was covered with the same floral contact paper she remembered from her first weeks in Paris when Solange drove her around. The woman's absence sat between them.

He pulled out the choke and jiggled the shift bar, feeling for reverse.

Diana stroked the dash. "I always loved borrowing this car, it was so . . . so . . ."

"Fun to drive?"

"I was thinking challenging. Every time I arrived some-place, I felt victorious." She saw palm trees out the window. The stucco houses on each side of the street were washed in sunlight.

"This is the village's only traffic light," he said turning at a bank. They passed a store selling beach balls, a *chacuterie* and a church. He turned into a road so narrow that opening both car doors would have been impossible. He pulled into a garage at the end of the street.

The front door of his house opened into a dark hallway

which was at least ten degrees cooler than the street. "Behind the curtain is where you wash anything, including laundry. The toilet is straight ahead."

After using the toilet, she joined him in a kitchen as bright as the hall was dark. The walls were covered with a yellow gingham. Matched curtains blew in a breeze. The screen-less windows opened onto the streets, but bars protected the room. In front of one window was a seat covered with floral pillows.

Maurice opened the half-sized refrigerator to pour Diana a Coke and himself some Evian. Diana drank half, then placed the cold glass against her forehead. She jumped as a German shepherd padded down the stairs.

"Meet Zola. A friend who works for UNICEF could not take him on his assignment, so he is with me for the summer. He is a terrible watch dog unless I am threatened by a pussy cat."

Zola offered Diana his food dish. When Maurice snapped his fingers, the dog settled in front of the fireplace that covered half the wall.

Maurice picked up her backpack. On the second floor he said, "This is where my father vowed never to set foot in this house again. I do not know why he and my grandfather fought. I just know we suddenly moved to Paris. I inherited the house from my aunt five years ago. We . . . modernized it with new windows and . . ." He shuddered.

Diana put her hand on his arm. She felt Solange everywhere—in the clay pig head cornice holding up a beam, and in the photograph of a fountain with a single leaf in the water.

Maurice turned abruptly to take Diana's bag up one more flight to where there were two bedrooms. The master room had three smoky blue walls and one white.

He opened the door to the smaller bedroom. "This one is yours."

Diana put the Coke she'd been carrying on the dresser. "How are you doing?"

"I have adjusted. I am trying to make new memories, like with you as my guest. Life is a tapestry we weave until we die. I just am missing a lot of yarn."

"I never knew you were trilingual," she said. When Maurice looked confused she said, "French, English and analogy. I'll help to create a new square inch of your tapestry."

Maurice smiled. "Now you must nap."

Before leaving, Maurice drew the shutters, darkening the room. Only after she was prone on the cool sheets did Diana hear voices wafting up from the street. As she fell asleep she thought about her new weekly newspaper and Olaf's ultimatum to marry him and move to Oslo.

A knock at the door woke her. Maurice came in with a wicker tray, a basket of croissants, jam and a bowl of tea. "Sleepy head, it is nine." Vivaldi's *Four Seasons* came from the speaker system in her bedroom.

"I slept two hours."

"More like fourteen. It is nine in the morning, not night. What do you want to do today?"

As she broke off a piece of croissant and spread it with some strawberry jam she said, "You decide. Part of a vacation is not making decisions."

Maurice took her on a tour of Argelès-sur-Mer, stopping to buy fresh tomatoes and fish for lunch. In the afternoon they biked to the beach. Unlike Sarasota's flat landscape, there were mountains in the background with medieval fortresses on strategic peaks. They repeated the routine the first four days.

Everything in town shut down between noon and three. The housewives, who gathered in the streets sitting, snapping beans, watching children and gossiping, disappeared. Diana and Maurice napped also.

On their fifth day, they sat at the kitchen table after the noon siesta. Noise on the street was just beginning as women placed their chairs in front of their doors. They could see out, but the women couldn't see in unless they pressed their faces against the bars.

He peeled a peach bought from a roadside stand before lunch. He cut it in quarters and popped one piece in Diana's mouth. "Listen to Tante Jeanne. She sounds like a duck."

At least eighty, Tante Jeanne ruled the other ladies. She walked with a cane which she converted into a weapon if a youngster were too fresh, but the same youngster, if good, might be given a chocolate from those stashed in her pocket. Maurice and Diana heard her say, "The American is beautiful but what would Solange say?"

"I don't think she's pretty. She's too big," Béatrice said. Younger than Tante Jeanne by twenty years, she took care of her granddaughter's twins. The twins were fighting over which one would sit in a wash basin.

Tante Jeanne rapped one of the boys with her cane. "Take turns. Do you think they share a bed?" Tante Jeanne chortled.

"Enough eavesdropping. Let me take you to Collioure this afternoon," Maurice said.

Diana changed into a sundress and combed her hair into a single French braid. She grabbed a straw hat.

"Give them something to talk about," he said in English grabbing her hand and opening the door. *"Bonjour, Tante Jeanne, bonjour, Tante Béatrice."*

191

The women nodded and commented on the heat.

The drive to Collioure wove up and down the mountains, but never did they lose sight of the sea. Turning into the village, Diana saw a château and a medieval church on each side of the harbor. There was a clock on the church tower that resembled a giant penis. Diana giggled.

"What?" Maurice asked. "I thought you would go ooooh, or aaaaah."

"I'm picturing a digital clock on the church," she said. He punched her arm, but not so hard it hurt.

They sat on the terrace of a small café that ran to the rocky beach. Bathers stretched out on straw mats, their oiled skin glistening.

The waiter brought two glasses of Banyuls then tore the receipt in half after Maurice paid him. The sun reflected through the liquid casting purple shadows on the white table. To their left, an artist dabbed almost the same color on his canvas.

They talked as they'd talked all week. She asked his advice about keeping a local flavor to her three weeklies. She told him about a press she'd seen demonstrated. He'd thought about buying the same one. When he saw her squint into the sun, he adjusted the striped umbrella to protect her eyes. "Must you return so soon?"

"Haven't you heard that guests and fish stink after three days?"

He sniffed. "It has been five. I do not smell anything." She picked up a straw left by the previous customer at their table and blew the paper cover at him.

Tired of sitting, he showed her the sea wall behind the church. As water crashed onto the rocks, he helped her over the slippery stones.

They wandered through shops and boutiques. In an art

gallery, Diana found a matched set of prints showing the château from the church and the church from the château. "Don't say it. It's airport art, but it captures the feeling of today," she said.

He pulled her braid. "I was going to say I have an exceptional idea for dinner, but I need to make a telephone call."

While he phoned, Diana went to the next shop to try on hats. Her nose and shoulders were rosy. Freckles popped out in record numbers.

Maurice returned. "Domininque says she has enough couscous for us. It is the best this side of Algiers. We must return to Argelès."

The café was two streets from Maurice's house. Tables spilled onto a square. A chubby woman, her eyebrows plucked to nothing and redrawn in an expression of perpetual surprise, rushed from the bar to kiss Maurice. She held his head in her two hands, pinching his cheeks before letting go.

"Dominique, meet Diana. She has come all the way from America for your couscous."

"You are a terrible liar," Dominique said, but she preened as she bustled to remove a reserved sign from a table under an oak. A vase with a single red rose anchored the paper covering the white linen. Their table was the only one with a flower.

When Diana seated herself, she noticed a blackboard outside the door of the café. In pink chalk was scrawled, "Wednesday, couscous, Reservations 24-hours in advance." When Diana pointed at the sign, Maurice turned to look and shrugged. "She adores me."

A lanky waiter brought a wooden bowl filled with lamb,

vegetables and couscous that he heaped on their plates. He poured them each a glass of wine, leaving the carafe on the table. He made another trip with rounds of sliced baguettes in a basket covered with a red checked linen napkin. In his care of Maurice and Diana, other diners were ignored. When Maurice suggested that he help them, he cocked his head in Dominique's direction.

For dessert the waiter brought *Poire Hélène,* espresso and two glasses of Banyuls.

A crowd gathered, filtering in two or three at a time. Some sat at the café's tables. Others carried chairs that they placed around the square. A band appeared. Men unloaded speakers from a truck.

"A street dance," Maurice said as the band began whining. It sounded like the instruments were fighting with each other.

A small balding man, holding a mike, gave directions to the circle of people around him. *"Un, deux, trois, un, deux, trois,"* he said moving his feet almost imperceptibly. Everyone held hands, their arms at their sides. When the beat shifted they lifted them.

Maurice pulled Diana into the circle. Quickly she was doing the three steps left and three steps right, raising and lowering her hands without missing a beat. Her sandals flopped, not like those of the local woman in red or blue espadrilles laced half up their calves.

When they sat, Dominique appeared with another Banyuls. "You like our Sardan dance, no?"

Diana said she did.

When the square had grown dark enough for spotlights to be turned on, the local band took a break. A man dressed in sky blue pants began playing records. The dancers pretended to be birds, flapping their arms, then rocked around the clock with Bill Haley. "Can you jitterbug or am I dating myself?" Maurice asked.

Diana grabbed his hand. "You want to jitterbug, I'll show you how it's done." They matched each other step for step. The DJ switched to a low sax playing "Strangers in the Night." Maurice pulled Diana into him, folding her hand against his chest. She went naturally.

She rested her head against his shoulder. When she lifted it, her lips brushed his. *Oh my God,* she thought. He'll think I did that on purpose. But then his lips were against hers, his tongue in her mouth. They stopped moving to the music.

"I think we should go home," he whispered in her ear. As he moved his body away from hers, he ran his hand down her arm to keep contact. As they turned the corner he leaned her against a house and kissed her. "I want you," he said.

"I want you, too." She was shocked she said that to her father's war buddy, her first mentor, Solange's husband. Poor Solange. Nothing else mattered as her hormones surged through her body. She wanted to see what he looked like totally naked, she wanted to touch his salt and pepper hairy chest that she'd seen each day at the beach.

At his door his hand shook as he battled the lock. They glanced at Tante Jeanne's closed shutters. Inside the hall he kissed her again and let his hand drift to her breast. He continued pecking at her. She responded in kind.

"My place or yours?" she asked.

"Mine." Upstairs he patted Zola and told him to go lie down.

He undid the zipper of her sundress. She wore no bra. She undid his shirt. He took off his slacks. Leaving their underpants on, they slid under the sheet. They caressed slowly, working their way down to their sexual organs, then shed their final clothing. He felt huge in her hand.

"I can't wait," he said.

As she spread her legs, he slipped into her. He came quickly. She didn't. He put his head between her legs until she stiffened and relaxed, letting out a long sigh. Zola sighed too.

"Wow," she said, "it's a good thing I don't have to write what I did on my summer vacation."

He was quiet beside her, his hands behind his head. Moonlight shone through the casement window. "Marry me?"

"Yes," Diana heard herself say.

"I know our ages are different, holidays are not for decisions, but we have a lot of . . . what did you say?"

"Yes."

"Without thinking?"

"Without thinking. It feels right."

They made love again. The clock struck midnight as they came together. Then the second clock set twelve seconds behind the first sounded its bells.

"Not bad for an old man," he said. He propped his head on one elbow and traced her left nipple with one finger.

"Maurice?"

"*Oui.*"

"When did you decide to propose?"

"This afternoon at the café. It suddenly hit me how right we were for each other. I thought how I wanted you to stay another week, but then I knew a week wasn't enough. After that I could barely keep my hands off you."

When she awoke the next morning, she thought she had dreamed it all, but then she saw Maurice's arm across her stomach and his head on her shoulder. She lay still until the women's gossip on the street below woke him.

"It's true," Tante Jeanne said. "Women mourn, men re-place."

Diana shuddered and rolled away from Maurice. "I can't replace Solange," she said aloud.

Maurice stirred. "I am not asking you to. I want to build something new with you. Now here is a more important question. Do you like making love in the morning?"

"Not 'til I go to the bathroom and brush my teeth."

"Hurry."

When Diana called Jim, and said, "Guess what?" he didn't. When she told him there was a long silence. Let him approve, Diana silently prayed, although she knew she was old enough to make her own decisions. The little girl part of her still wanted his approval.

"I can't think of any one better for you. Put Maurice on."

"He's listening on the half receiver."

Diana asked Jim to go to the top drawer of the desk and find The Card. "Write on it. 'If you want to be my matron of honor, call 011 33 66 72 35 87 fast.' Then can you Fed Ex it to Jane?"

Jim, Jane, Bill Reed and Kate were there in three days. This time no one fell going down the aisle.

Fall 1979:
Connecticut and Massachusetts

The plane taxied into sight and stopped. Men scurried to roll out a red carpet. Boston Mayor Kevin White, his hair combed to hide his bald spot, waited next to Senator Ted Kennedy on the tarmac. Pope John Paul II rushed down the stairs, then knelt to kiss the pavement.

"Germy," Paul Andrews said to his television. He sat in "his chair" the one that Mary and Jane had bought him fourteen Christmases ago. The fabric was ripped, but no one dared suggest throwing it out or having it recovered.

A commercial interrupted the program. A woman, dressed in leaves, zapped a thunder bolt through a corn field. "It's not nice to fool Mother Nature," she said to the ashes of the person who'd given her margarine in place of butter.

"I love that ad," Jane said. When a panty hose commercial started, she said, "You should've seen Mrs. O'Brien. I gave her the day off to go see the Pope say Mass on the Common. David calls her a church groupie."

"With the crowd, your poor housekeeper probably won't see him at all," Mary Andrews said.

"David loaned her his binoculars," Jane said. "She kept hugging them to her breast and thanking him."

The stove dinger danged. Mary left and returned with a plate of ranger cookies made with coconut, oatmeal, raisins and nuts, along with three glasses of cider that earlier that day had been pressed in the barn.

"Only time your mother makes these is when you're here. Or Kate." Paul reached for one.

"I wish Kate were here today," Mary said. "I never see enough of her."

After the Pope settled in for the night in the Cardinal's residence and the television had been shut off, Jane ran next door to visit old Mrs. Cotton taking half a dozen cookies with her.

Paul set the kitchen table. "Has she said anything to you?"

Mary tossed the salad. "Not a thing. But something's wrong. Mother's intuition."

He wiped some dust off the soup bowls. Each had a different flower. He put a violet at Jane's place and a lady slipper at his wife's. "You're worried."

"How can you tell?"

"Supper changed from beef goulash to corn chowder. You use corn chowder like Jewish mothers use chicken soup."

Mary threw him an *oh-go-on-with-you* look. "I wish she'd talk to me."

Jane came back in as Mary rummaged through the odds and ends drawer for her soup ladle. Paul put the rest of Saturday night's brown bread on the table. There were four rounds left.

Mary served the chowder. Corn floated in milky liquid. Just as they picked up their spoons, the phone rang.

Paul answered it. "It's for you, Jane."

Jane, after unclipping her earrings, put the phone to her ear.

"Hi, Jane. It's Stephanie. Sorry to bother you, but Kate came home with a temperature and complaining about her ear. I can handle it but thought you should know." It was Judy's mother.

"Thanks, Steph. Can I talk with her?"

"Hi, Mummy."

"Hi, Twerp. What's the matter?"

"I don't feel well."

"Want me to come home?"

There was silence.

"Tell you what. I'll finish dinner and start home."

"Really?" The eagerness in Kate's voice told Jane she'd been right. "I was hoping you'd say that."

Then why didn't you say it?, Jane thought, a thread of worry that Kate tried too hard to be good.

The drive took two hours. Stephanie had left the driveway light on. Before Jane could ring the bell, the door opened. Kate flew into her arms.

"Hot chocolate before you go?" Stephanie asked.

Jane felt Kate's forehead. It was warm, not burning. "Sure."

Watching Steph prepare the chocolate was like watching a play. Jane had thought her theatrical even before she'd seen her on a revived Boston Gas commercial.

At one time Jane hoped they might be friends, but Steph's frequent acts of generosity were never done without an audience. A pot of allspice bubbled on top of the wood burning stove, giving fragrance to her stage set.

"Poor Kate," Steph said. "She was so looking forward to gathering pine cones tomorrow." She flowed into her chair.

Jane pictured the girls traipsing after Steph, wearing her red woods-tramping cape and alpine hat. She claimed they kept hunters from mistaking her for a deer, but hunters were forbidden to shoot in the woods behind their houses. Jane's theory was that Stephanie thought she looked pretty in red. She did.

Jane finished her chocolate and carried her mug into the kitchen. "Kate, put your coat on. And just your shoes and socks." Kate wore her pink flannel nightdress with a turtle neck.

The Johnson house was dark when they drove in. Leaving the car in the driveway rather than the garage, Jane hustled Kate into the kitchen.

"OK, up to bed. I'll follow in a minute." By the time she checked the heat—68°—and picked up a bottle of baby aspirin, Kate had scooted upstairs. As she passed her bedroom door, which was slightly ajar, Jane heard a noise. *Damn cat,* she thought. Caramel loved jumping from the dresser to the top of the canopy. Because he clawed at the fabric, she tried to keep the door shut.

She flipped the light on, ready to catch the cat in the act. The canopy was fine. The bed was a mess but not from Caramel. Irene, a secretary from the Medical Center, pushed David aside and pulled the patchwork quilt over her bare chest.

"What are you doing?" Jane asked.

Realizing how stupid that question was, when anyone in their right mind would have known, she could neither control nor stop a giggle. Inner strength swelled through her, clearing her vision for the first time since her senior year at BU. "I'll give you five minutes to get dressed and out of my house," she said. Her voice was soft.

David jumped out of bed to look for his clothes. "Janie, I know this is upsetting."

"No, David, it's not upsetting. It's confirming. I thought you were catting around again."

"Irene doesn't have her car. I'll drive her home and be right back," he was feeling around for his clothes but keeping his eye on his wife.

"Perhaps you misunderstood. I said I wanted you out of my house in five minutes. I said nothing about coming back."

He had to lean forward to hear the words. He had his pants in his hand. A condom hung from his shriveled prick.

Jane noticed his pot belly for the first time. She wished him bald, fat and impotent.

Turned on her heel, she went to Kate's room. Her daughter lay on the lower bunk of her red metal bed.

"Rub my back please, Mummy?" Kate turned on her tummy cradling her head on folded arms. Willing her hands to stop shaking, Jane rubbed back and forth across the smooth skin.

She heard David's car start and the crunch of rocks under his tires as he pulled out. Kate fell asleep under her hands. Kissing her daughter, she shut off the lamp and tip-toed out.

Downstairs she locked the doors making sure the chains were on. Back upstairs she stripped her bed and threw sheets, quilt, pillows and spread out the window. Then she sat in the upholstered arm chair staring at the bed.

Within an hour David's car pulled into the yard. He used his key. The chain stopped him. "Jane!" he hollered.

"We've nothing to say," she said through the crack. "Talk to my lawyer." She didn't have one—yet.

"You don't mean it, Janie. You're just a little upset," he said.

"Don't tell me how I feel." She pushed the door, squeezing his fingers. He yelped. "This is my house, too. You can't keep me out." He went away, but was back in a

The Card

few minutes with a crowbar.

Jane grabbed the kitchen phone and dialed 911. "Help, my husband's trying to kill me," she screamed. The cruiser must have been in the neighborhood, for in less than ninety seconds two cops were behind David.

"Freeze," one said, his gun pulled. "Up against the house."

David dropped the crowbar, and put his hands over his head leaning on the house.

The younger cop patted David down. "No weapons."

Jane opened the door. "Thank God you're here."

"Calm down Janie," David said. All four people stood at the door. "She gets hysterical easily, Officer."

As he moved toward Jane she backed up fast. "Don't let him near me." The younger cop came between them. The old cop put his arm around David, guiding him away.

"We've had a little spat, Officer. You know how women are."

The older cop looked into the kitchen. "Can't live with 'em or without 'em. Listen Doc, my wife is one of your patients. Thinks you walk on water. Let's go to the cruiser, have a little talk." He raised his eyebrow at the younger man, a signal worked out in a family sensitivity training seminar under the heading, "Separate the fighting spouses."

As David walked to the car with the cop, Jane heard him ask, "Can you shut those lights off. The neighbors, you know." As the red and blue lights stopped flashing, Jane shut the door.

"My partner hates these cases," the young cop said.

Jane started shaking. The cop helped her to a chair. "Can I call somebody for you?"

"No, thanks."

There was a knock at the door.

"I need some things," David said. The older cop let him enter the kitchen and followed him upstairs. David came back with a night case, the cop still attached.

"We'll talk tomorrow, Janie when you feel better," David said.

As she opened her mouth, the young cop moved his hand as if to say, "Don't enflame the situation." She said nothing.

"You stay and get Mrs. Johnson locked in tight. I'll follow the Doc to the Sheraton. He's spending the night there."

"Don't try coming back tonight, Dr. Johnson," the young cop said. "We'll be checking the house regularly."

Gilbert Lothrop, Jr. formed his fingers into an upside down V. He tapped the index fingers together. He'd found Jane stationed at his office door when he arrived before eight. Now she sat on the other side of his oak desk, talking so fast he'd given up taking notes.

"Jane, Jane, Jane. You know most husbands have their little flings, but it isn't important compared to keeping the family together." He smoothed his moustache in three downward strokes with his index finger.

She bristled. "Not from time to time. Constantly."

"Begging your pardon, dear Jane, but a doctor doesn't have time to cheat constantly. Now . . ."

"Don't patronize me, Gilbert."

He leaned back in his chair. "You've had a nasty shock . . ."

"The shock was that I wasn't shocked." She leaned forward. Her chair was low, forcing her to look up at him. She wondered if he'd offer her a lollipop. She hadn't foreseen a fight with the person who everyone at the club said was such a good lawyer. "Except at his nerve for doing it in my bed."

Gilbert nodded. "Maybe that wasn't in the best taste, but think of your sweet little girl, what's the name, Katherine? Jane, Jane, Jane. You've such a comfortable life. Why you work is beyond me." He narrowed his eyes. "You aren't one of those women libbers are you?"

"Not yet." Jane stood, picking up her briefcase. Gilbert came around his desk and put his arm around her shoulders. She felt a pat, pat, pat against her upper arm, perfectly proper for a portly grandfather. She stiffened. He didn't notice.

"Take your time. I'm sure you don't want to give up that lovely home. Let David stew a bit then kiss and make up. Think about it."

"I've thought about it. I'm finding a lawyer who wants my case." She made sure the door slammed as she left.

As Jane barged onto the street she ran into the young cop from last night. He was in jeans, not his uniform. They picked up her briefcase, which had fallen and opened, scattering her papers on the sidewalk.

"Good morning. Feeling better?" he asked.

"No. I'm twice as mad. Patronizing old fool. I thought because he was town moderator . . ."

The cop glanced at where she'd come from. "Lothrop represents those who can do him good, not those who need it. He wouldn't cross Dr. Grayson or anyone at the Women's Center."

Jane nodded.

"A cup of coffee? By the way. My name's Andy Eaton."

"Jane Johnson."

"I know."

She glanced at her watch. She'd told Lucy she was

having a crisis and would explain when she got in.

They walked into the Pewter Pot, three doors down from Lothrop & Lothrop.

"Two coffees, two blueberry muffins," Andy said. "OK, Mrs. Johnson?"

She nodded. "It's Jane. I really want a divorce. Do you know a lawyer?"

The coffee came. She added milk and two sugars. Stirring it carefully she set the spoon next to the white ceramic mug. She didn't drink any, nor did she taste her muffin. Andy wolfed his down.

"Does your husband want a divorce?"

"I don't care what he wants."

"You are one feisty woman."

"Only practicing to be one."

"I've a friend in Woburn who's just setting up an office. Want me to drive you over there?"

"Please." She went for her wallet.

"Let me pay. I'm collecting $50 off my partner who said you and your husband would be lovey-dovey this morning." As they left, he picked up her muffin and ate it in two bites.

Andy and Jane found Tony Bertelli in jeans and a Suffolk Law School sweat-shirt. He put down a hammer and took three nails from his mouth before shaking hands. His diplomas rested on a chair. Half-empty cartons were scattered between stacks of law books. Parts of a bookcase awaited assembly. Andy explained why they were there.

Tony ushered her into his office area, cleared off two chairs and listened. He didn't lean back, he didn't pose his hands. Instead of assuming Jane was having a passing snit, he asked, "What do you want, really want?"

"David out of my life."

"No, I mean for money."

"I hadn't thought about it."

"Think."

Jane sat quietly a few minutes. "I want the money I spent putting him through medical school, half the value of our house and Kate's schooling paid through college and normal support for her. No alimony. I don't want to see him or have to talk to him."

"I'll ask for a restraining order in Cambridge Court this afternoon. We'll serve divorce papers in a couple of days. But, you're letting him off light."

"That's not important."

Tony got up to sit on the corner of his desk. "I won't drag it out. One thing that pisses me off about my fellow lawyers are all those delays. Let's hit him fast so you can get on with your life." He stuck out his hand. She took it.

She started to walk out but turned. "There's one thing else. The house is only in my name. There's no mortgage. He was afraid of a malpractice suit."

He rubbed his hands together. "Great ammunition."

They joined Andy, who was reading a sports page from *The Boston Globe*. It was rumpled from being used as packing material.

"How about lunch?" Tony asked. "To celebrate my first client."

Jane agreed if she could use the phone. It was still in its box.

Tony plugged it in and handed it to her.

Jane then called Lucy.

"David's called here every half hour. What's going on?" Lucy asked.

"I'm at my lawyer's. I'm getting a divorce."

"Hallelujah," Lucy said. "Take the rest of the day off."

★ ★ ★ ★ ★

Like the wolf in the *Three Little Pigs*, David came huffing
and puffing at Jane's fragile sanctuary. When she called the
police the next night, Andy and his partner arrived. She had
spent the afternoon packing David's personal things. The
cops carried them from the front hall to his car.

After they'd gone, she sat in her rocker in front of the
dying fire, tears running down her face. She cried for the
necessity of her actions.

The phone rang, their private number. She waited for
the answering machine to click on. The recorded message
ended with the beep. "How's it hanging, you guys?"

Jane leaped for the phone. "Diana!" She struggled to
make her voice normal.

It didn't fool Diana. "Level with me." They talked till
midnight.

After they hung up, Jane crawled into bed. As dawn
lightened the sky, a car pulling into the driveway woke her.
Before calling the police she looked out the window at a
Buick, not David's Mercedes. Running downstairs, she
threw open the door, running outside in her nightgown and
bare feet.

"I was in the neighborhood and thought I'd drop in."
Diana leaned against the fender. She yawned.

"New York is in the neighborhood?"

"Compared to Paris it is." When Diana had called
Maurice he not only agreed she should postpone her flight,
he insisted she go to Jane.

Three things brought Jane through her first few weeks—
work, Kate and Diana.

Work reinforced her self image as a competent person, at
least where her career was concerned. Unlike the negotia-

tions for her divorce where she had to wait, she could start and finish projects.

When Jane told Kate, she asked, "Do I have to choose sides like Lisa had to or are you guys going to be civilized like Peter's parents?"

"At least with so many of her friends from broken families, she doesn't stand out," Jane said to Diana after Kate had gone to her room. Diana wore a pair of slippers that looked like raccoons.

"Kate will be fine. She's a neat kid."

"Maybe it's a good thing David isn't here. She got a B in math."

"Getting a B in math is not a crime," Diana said.

Silliness became the rule when Diana was there, which was often, as she added Lexington to her Sarasota-Paris commute. They played football at Stop & Shop with toilet paper, ate popcorn after midnight and watched horror movies in Jane's bed. Even when Maurice flew in, he kept shaking his head and saying, "I do not believe this," but his face told the others that whatever "this" was, it was more than fine with him.

Despite uncertainty, Jane considered her life better. David did not. He fired Irene. Frank Grayson was furious. David listened to a lecture about women not wanting to come to a doctor who cheated on his wife.

"I'm giving Irene six months leave with pay," Grayson said. "And you will apologize to her. And I suggest you start winning your wife back."

David rented a furnished apartment on a short-term lease. He ate at the hospital and plotted his fight to get back into his house.

Round one was named the War of the Roses by the local

roses to Jane's house. Each night when Jane got back from
work, she sent them back. Finally Angelo said to the doctor,
"I'm making money, but it ain't doing you a bit of good."

Round two involved reinforcements.

Jane put down the Yahtzee dice to answer the bell. She,
Kate and Diana were on their championship game.

The Graysons stood there. Frank shifted his weight from
one boot to the other. Virginia adjusted the paisley scarf she
wore over her coat. "I know we should have called first, but
we saw the car and lights," Frank said.

Jane invited them inside. Diana stood up. "Meet my best
friend from college, Diana DuBois. Diana, Frank started
the medical center. Virginia is responsible for a lot of the
pro-women ideas I told you about."

"I hope we don't appear rude, but could we have a few
words with you, privately, Jane dear?" Virginia asked as
Kate took their coats.

In the living room Virginia sat on the edge of her chair
twisting her handkerchief. She always had a real handkerchief with her initials. Frank perched on the hassock in
front of his wife.

"I feel so strange, all the times we've been here. David
asked us to come by and see . . ." Frank said.

". . . If you could talk some sense into me." Jane could
imagine him saying, "Go see Janie. She'll listen to you."

"David's devastated. And there's Kate . . ."

As he talked, Jane walked to the window, her arms
crossed over her chest. Frank's monologue faded out as she
stared at the Graysons' Chrysler behind her Ford Escort.
She pulled down the window quilts against the night's chill.
She thought of different ways to handle them.

Going to Frank, she knelt in front of him, putting one

hand on his knee and reaching behind him for Virginia with her other hand. "I really appreciate your caring . . ."

Virginia grabbed the offered hand covering it with both of hers. "We do, we really do."

Jane felt the nervousness of the Graysons in the tightness of their bodies. "But there's nothing to be done. My marriage should have ended years ago and . . ."

Before she could say more, Diana swung open the door. She carried a tray with four mugs, a tea pot, spoons and ginger cookies. The smell of mint came from the pot.

"I listened to make sure I was interrupting. I'm a hopeless eavesdropper, you know."

Her truthfulness broke the tension. When the Graysons left, they promised to keep in touch.

Diana loaded the dishes in the dishwasher. "They won't for very long . . . keep in touch, that is." Jane knew she was right.

Round three involved Kate, who should have been a noncombatant.

The week after Christmas, Diana sat at the table going over a union contract. Maurice had brought it with him when he'd arrived for Christmas because she'd forgotten it in Paris. Her notebook, full of lists for each trip, lay open on the table. Between scrawls, check marks and cross outs, she was the only one who could read it, and sometimes even she couldn't decipher it.

She wore jeans, a sweater and the raccoon slippers. She left clothes, makeup and toothbrushes in Sarasota, Paris and Lexington. She could grab papers and her ticket and be wherever she was needed without packing.

Although it was after nine at night, Jane still wasn't home. She'd called, saying she needed to take one more press proof before a run for a promotion to be dropped the last day of the year. Kate was having a Big Mac with David.

The door opened and shut. Kate walked in. Instead of hugging Diana and sitting down for a long talk full of laughter, her "hi" was so soft Diana wasn't sure she heard it. Kate didn't hang up her jacket but went upstairs.

Diana wrote a question mark over clause 16B in the contract. She clicked the pen cover back on and followed Kate. The door was ajar and she could see the ten-year-old on her bed, her parka open but still on. Her boots were next to her bed.

"Hey, Brat, can I come in?" Diana asked.

Instead of the normal "sure thing," there was no answer. Diana poked her head around the door. Kate's lips trembled. "I've got big shoulders and lots of Kleenex," Diana said.

Kate rolled over, her back to the door, her stuffed panther in her arms. Her shoulders shuddered.

Diana sat on the bed, putting her hand on Kate's back. The child threw herself into Diana's arms sobbing. She rocked the little girl. When Kate quieted, she said, "I lied about the Kleenex, but you can use my sleeve."

Kate gave a nervous giggle and wiped her nose on her own sleeve.

"Wanta talk about it?"

"I don't know," Kate said.

"Sometimes when you share something it doesn't seem so bad after."

Kate sniffed. "Maybe, but you gotta promise not to tell Mummy."

Diana crossed her heart.

The next morning, when Jane had gone to work and Kate had gone to Judy's, Diana called David. "Meet me at the Pewter Pot at noon. It's important."

When she walked in, she saw him in the corner booth.

"You look good," he said.

"Thank you," she said. She resisted adding, "You don't."

"Do you want coffee? An omelet?" he asked, looking for a waitress.

"I'm not staying, David," she said. "You pull any more shit with Kate, and I'll go to the Graysons and tell 'em what a scumbag you're being. That kid is not a weapon for either of you. You don't put her in the middle."

"Stay out of my family's business."

"Look, you asshole, Jane and Kate *are* my business."

He glared at her. "I never understood why my wife liked you."

"It's called trust and loyalty. You should try it." She leaned down so her face was a few inches from his. "Listen up and listen good. I've got lots of connections because of the paper. If I can't get to you through the Graysons, perhaps you'd like to lose a hand. Or have your legs broken. I don't care what it takes. The first thing you do is tell Kate you were wrong about Jane fucking Andy Eaton. And you *never* pump that kid for information again."

"Bitch! Ball breaker!" He spat at her.

"Thank you. They could break those too." She turned without saying goodbye. *God, I'm good,* she thought. *I almost believed my own threats.*

Winter 1980:
Massachusetts

Spring, summer and fall came, and all Jane got from Tony were apologies that he hadn't kept his promise for a fast divorce. About every two weeks, he would call. "No progress. His attorney still won't talk to me." Finally, Tony invited Jane in for a strategy session. The date was Halloween.

As she entered his suite, his secretary put down *Modern Bride* magazine. A pile of wedding dresses had been cut out and sat on the corner of the desk. Seeing the girl's diamond, Jane swallowed the words, "Don't do it."

Tony bounded into the reception area. "How's my favorite first client?" As he led her into his office he said, "This could take years. His attorney won't discuss this case. We're doing another divorce together that we negotiate the hell out of, but bring up your name and he clams up."

Jane digested the information. "What do we do?"

Tony paced around the room where there was already a path of worn carpet. "Divorce in Massachusetts is a farce. The lawyers fight out an agreement. You get a court date. A witness lies, saying she saw the husband hit the wife. The judge clucks and approves the agreement." He waved his pencil like a baton, "I've an idea, but it's a risk."

She cocked her head.

"We go to court without an agreement. Let the judge decide."

"Can we do that?" she asked.

He nodded. "The only problem is that the judge might get mad and you'd lose everything. Can you live on your salary?"

"I'm living on it now."

"We need to prove David cheated on you. Seeing him and Irene in bed isn't enough. You need another witness, and without the agreement you can't have someone perjure themselves." He outlined his ideas.

At home Jane called a locksmith to break into David's roll top desk. She knew it was locked. She discovered that years ago, when searching for a stamp.

When the locksmith left, she opened each drawer, alternating left and right, working toward the middle. The first drawer was full of Visa, MasterCard, American Express, or Diner's Club receipts, but the motel charge slips Jane hoped to find weren't in the stack. There were slips from jewelry stores that didn't match any gift she'd received, but according to Tony that wouldn't be enough. There were tons of household bills, old golf scorecards and a dance program from Kate's dance recital.

In the middle drawer was a key that didn't fit any lock. Her parents had a similar desk. Jane felt for a secret compartment. She found it under a piece of felt. It snapped open, a jack-in-the-box without a clown. Seven letters without envelopes rested inside. All were signed Maxine.

Who was Maxine? The letters bore dates from January to June of last year. The handwriting was even. The *a*'s and *o*'s had extra loops and there were circles, not dots, over the *i*'s and *j*'s. She begged David to leave Jane and wrote, "I'll give you the son you deserve."

Jane threw David's letter opener across the room. It bounced off the wall and fell on the carpet.

Jane arrived at Tony's Saturday morning with a carton filled with papers from the desk. Tony grilled her for three hours about every woman David might have slept with.

"Sleep is a euphemism," she said. "Fucked, screwed, used—those are the words." She congratulated herself that she sounded more like Diana than the old Jane.

The session drained her, and she crawled into the bed at 8:30. The cat, Caramel, rested on top of the canopy, casting her shadow through the material onto the spread. She liked having the bed to herself without wondering whether David was really delivering babies or performing the act that created them. *I can eat popcorn, fart under the covers, do what I want,* she thought as she put out the light.

She floated in that pre-sleep contentment, warm in her navy floor length sweatshirt two sizes too big and toasted by an electric blanket. The doorbell jarred her from her cocoon. Stomping to the window she saw a car but didn't recognize it.

John Thompson, a doctor at the Women's Medical Center, stood at her door, his hat and coat in his hand. "I was on my way home, and thought I might stop to see if you need anything? Hard for you being alone and all."

Shit, Jane thought but said, "Thank you."

"May I come in for a cup of coffee?"

"I was in bed."

"I won't stay long."

Jane moved to let him in. She prepared herself for another why-don't-you-take-David-back talk. "I'm out of coffee."

"Tea will be fine."

Jane put the kettle on. "How's your wife?"

"Due any day."

As Jane stood on tip toe reaching for the tea canister, John came up behind her and put his arms around her. He bent to kiss her neck. "Do you remember dancing at the club two summers ago, and I told you how nice you felt in my arms?" His breath felt hot in her ear.

Jane twisted around. "Forget it, John," she started to say, but her words were pressed back into her mouth by his lips.

"I know you want me. How long since you've been fucked."

Jane brought her knee into his crotch. "Not long enough."

"Bitch," he gasped. As he grabbed himself, the doorbell rang. Jane slipped away.

Andy Eaton stood at the door, his hat pushed back so his curls stood at angles against his forehead. "Hi, Mrs. J. My partner and I saw a strange car in your drive. Thought we'd check on you and Kate. Hi, Dr. Thompson. How are you?"

John, having regained an upward position, said, "Fine." His voice was hoarse.

"Thanks for dropping the book off." She smiled in what she hoped radiated sweetness. "Give my best to your wife." *You bastard,* she thought.

"Right," John said, brushing past her.

After he'd gone, Andy said, "He hits on every single woman in town. I know his car and wanted to . . ." he stammered and blushed. "Maybe you didn't want to be interrupted."

"I did. Tea?"

He checked with his partner who wanted to nap in the cruiser. Coming back in, he found Jane stomping around slamming cupboard doors and dishes. "The nerve. I throw my husband out for cheating and he thinks I'll . . . I'll . . . words fail me."

Andy smiled. "You're attractive. Can't say I blame him for trying."

She patted his arm. Andy had checked her regularly to see if everything was all right. He'd even picked up Kate one day at school when Jane had to work late and no one else was around. On his night off he would drop in to play cards with Kate, Jane, Diana and Maurice, if the latter were there.

When he left he chucked her under the chin. "Remember to leave the garage light on if another bastard bothers you. I'll come in."

The marble walls of the Middlesex Court House ladies' room were impregnated with a urine smell. The frosted windowpane, protected by chicken wire, was permanently sealed. A cracked mirror hung above a cracked sink. The towel holder was empty.

"I can't believe it. Your piddling caused me to meet David, and you're still at it for our divorce." Jane avoided touching the sink. It was filthy.

"Consistency," Diana said, her hand holding the stall door closed as she pulled up her panty hose. She opened the door to see Jane take out her lipstick. "What are you doing?"

Jane showed her the lipstick.

Taking it from Jane, Diana put the cap on and dropped it in her bag. "You should look like you've suffered."

They found Tony pacing outside the ladies' room. He grabbed Jane by the elbow. "I almost called it off. Thought we had Judge Arsenault. Real ass. Refused a divorce the other day because a woman didn't have her wedding ring. Said only he had the right to tell her to take it off."

"Who do we have?"

"Shapiro. Wife is on the Committee Against Discrimination. Women's libber, trained him well."

Tony opened one of a double set of doors for them. Judge Shapiro sat on a platform behind a large desk. Paint, maybe grey, maybe dirty white, peeled from the walls. Five people in the gallery watched a woman testify about her missing husband.

Three more divorces were heard, each with almost identical testimony as if the plaintiffs and defendants were actors and actresses trying out for the same part. Jane wondered if these couples had big weddings. How many orgasms had they shared? How did they split their photos?

David and his attorney, John Hancock, slipped into court. John looked grey: grey hair, grey suit, grey tie. David had lost weight. He had shadows under his eyes. He kept straightening his shoulders.

Tony went up to the judge. "Your honor, I've tried repeatedly to negotiate a settlement for this divorce. The marriage has hopelessly broken down, but my honorable opponent kept avoiding me."

My marriage has broken down, Jane thought, *like a television or a dishwasher.* She saw the judge roll his eyes to the ceiling.

Hancock said to the judge, "Your honor, I refused to negotiate because my client wants a reconciliation."

"I hate cases like this," Judge Shapiro said. "Two intelligent people use my court to throw mud. But let's get it over with."

Hancock stood. "We want a continuance."

Shapiro picked up the document. "Your client was

219

served sixty-two weeks ago. Continuance denied."

Jane took the stand. Her voice shook. She felt David's eyes boring through her. As she gave preliminary information: name, age, date of birth, date of marriage, address, she gathered strength.

"Why do you want a divorce?" Tony asked as he had in the four practice sessions he'd put her through.

"Because my husband has had affairs with other women throughout our marriage." From there on she followed Tony's script, telling about her venereal problem.

"Don't say crabs unless you have to," he'd coached. She talked about the Maxine letters and finally finding David in bed with Irene.

Hancock cross-examined. "You could have written those letters yourself."

"It's not my handwriting."

"Or had a friend do it. I think you're jealous, Mrs. Johnson." He turned to Shapiro. "Despite years of false allegations of affairs he never had, my client wants to resume the family unit," he said.

"I'm not jealous," Jane said, but Hancock had walked away.

Diana testified about getting medicine for Jane in Paris. Hancock said she had no way of knowing how Jane had caught her problem. "She could have had a lover."

When she sat next to Tony, she whispered, "This isn't going to work."

"Once we call our witnesses it will. Don't worry," Tony said.

A red-headed woman took the stand. She carried a brown leather bag matching her brown leather boots. As she walked by David, he slumped into his chair.

Dr. Maggie Maguire Halloran not only promised, but

did tell the truth, the whole truth and nothing but the truth. When the judge asked her after she had finished if she were seeking revenge, she smiled at Shapiro and said, "I don't need to. I've got a good practice, a wonderful husband, a little girl. Let's say as a good Catholic, I am making a penance to Mrs. Johnson." Shapiro excused her.

During the lunch recess, Jane, Diana and Tony ate at a little lunchroom a block from the court house. As they played with their salads, Maggie entered. Jane signaled her to join them.

"Thank you," Jane said.

"I owed you," Maggie said. The discolored menu was encased in plastic. "Chili," she said to the waitress. "Also, I owed him."

"What I don't understand is how you knew about the divorce."

"Grapevine. I found out who your lawyer was," Maggie said.

"Maybe David's women should form a club," Diana said.

"With annual reunions and T-shirts," Maggie said.

Jane looked at Maggie. She found herself liking the woman from the plaid blanket.

As Tony paid the bill for them all, Maggie put her hand on Jane's. "I hope you can forgive me."

"I did. Long ago."

Irene testified after lunch, followed by Tony presenting bank statements, tax forms, house appraisals, lists of Jane's contribution to David's education. He asked for what Jane said she wanted.

Hancock broke in to say, "My client no longer contests the divorce. He does contest the settlement."

"So do I," said Shapiro.

Hancock and David smiled at each other. Tony sat up straight, and Jane mentally thought of how far her salary would stretch.

Then Shapiro said, "It's too small." The judge doubled what Jane had asked for.

The second they were free of the courtroom, Jane bolted into the ladies' room where she vomited.

Diana called from outside the stall. "You OK?"

Jane came out gasping. As Diana handed her a napkin she had stuffed in her bag at lunch, Jane said, "I'm throwing up my marriage."

"Poetic," Diana said. Jane wiped her face then cupped her hand, ran water in it and rinsed out her mouth. She looked at her watch.

"We need to get you to the airport."

"I can catch a flight tomorrow if you need me."

"I'll be fine," Jane said. As they left the courthouse the Salvation Army played "Silent Night" on the steps. The snow had stopped. The street lamps cast long shadows ahead of them as they walked to the car.

Two weeks later, Diana was in Paris; her turn to cross the ocean for time with Maurice. Jim would join them in two days' time. She had a long list of things to do for the holiday meal, one of which was not to buy boar meat from the boar hanging outside the butcher's.

The doorbell rang. The postman handed her the mail. He showed her the annual calendar, the purchase of which would improve chances of regular mail delivery. She saw a large envelope with Jane's writing. Although she wanted to hurry the postman she couldn't. He had to show her each photo on the calendar.

It can't be The Card, the envelope is too big. She was

wrong. Also, in the envelope was an 8 ½ x 11 photo of a brick townhouse. The windows were boarded up. On the back Jane had written in a black felt tip pen, "I've bought it and am renovating. My new address will be 82 Union Street, South End, Boston. Diana searched for the 1979 message. It said, "Living Well is the Best Revenge."

Spring 1981:
Florida

The screen went dead. "No!" Diana screamed. She looked at ten pages of figures she'd spent two hours entering onto the spreadsheet. Breathing deeply to regain control, she walked through the press room.

Half the desks were empty. Those who'd been writing stories instead of being out gathering them, stared at blank screens murmuring, "Thank God, I'd saved my stuff" or "Shit, I'll have to rewrite."

Diana marched into the computer room without knocking. The paint smelled fresh. A new VAX rested on its raised platform allowing air conditioning to flow under the computer, keeping it at the proper temperature. Flashing red lights winked at her. On a shelf over the VAX were a series of what looked like ten plastic cake dishes but held the guts of the paper instead of cake.

"What happened?" Her voice was soft.

Pete, the computer operator, said, "P-p-power surge. Had to b-be rebooted, Mrs. DuB-b-bois." Towering over her, he blushed, as he did whenever he was near her. "Your f-father wouldn't p-pay for the regulator that would have c-c-controlled it."

Diana nodded, turned and walked to Jim's office, not really prepared for another battle with the man who kept saying typewriters were good enough. As she entered he was packing up his briefcase. "I'm heading home, early, kid. I'm beat."

Had he not looked so tired, she'd have yelled about false economy. *Tomorrow,* she thought. "See you later. I'll probably be late," she said.

Back in her office, she re-entered data, this time saving every few minutes. She pressed a button. The cell accepted the salary figure, adjusted for raises, rippling all the numbers on the screen. A knock interrupted her.

"Hi Boss, got a minute?" Maria Ramez stuck her head in. She wore ripped jeans and a grubby T-shirt. Her face was dirty. "Check me out." She held out her arms. They were scarred. "Would I convince a pusher?"

"Not having inspected real track marks, I can only guess they look real." Diana shuddered thinking of Maria spending hours sticking pins into herself to give herself authenticity. "Be careful. Getting a story isn't worth getting killed." *God, I sound like an old fart,* Diana thought. *What I really want is to let Maria do these figures and go on the street in her place.*

"I'll be careful, Boss. Wanta be around to collect that Pulitzer."

Diana worked steadily for an hour, when another knock interrupted.

"Press is stuck again, Boss."

"Shit, Fred, not again." She saved her work then followed Fred into the press room. Normally she would have needed ear plugs. Silence greeted her. The press occupied three quarters of the room, dwarfing the people poking at it. When it ran, papers rolled off four times faster than off the old one, allowing her the increased production she needed for her new weeklies.

"Transfer everything to the old one." God bless Jim for insisting they keep it. Sometimes old technology was better. "How long?"

"We'll be about an hour late on the street. Folks will need a second cup of coffee to read us, tomorrow."

"Shit," Diana said. As soon as she was back in the office she called Germany.

"Dieter Holtzman."

In perfect German, when they told her he was busy, she said, "This is Diana DuBois and if he ever wants to do business with our paper again, he better get unbusy fast."

"How is the press?"

"Quiet. For the fifth time this year. The old one broke down once in five years and that was because someone dropped a wrench in it. I want a new one, Herr Holtzman."

She heard his intake of his breath. They battled for half an hour. Holtzman agreed to come in person with his best repairman.

"Tonight," Diana said.

"The next flight is tomorrow."

"I have three papers that I need to call and give them a recommendation on your equipment. If you want anything but a deal-killer, rent a plane." She slammed the receiver down. *Let him sweat,* she thought.

By midnight she gave up. She checked into the press room, now quiet. A light shone from the office at the back. She went in sat down and toyed with the desk marker saying, "Bill Reed, Editor-and-Assistant to God."

"Say something nice, it's been a bitch of a day," Diana said.

"Wanta get a drink?"

"Bill, you've such a way with words."

The bar was dark. Two other reporters sat at the bar. Diana patted one on the back as she walked by. "Nice coverage of the fire," she said.

A TV with no sound flickered over the bar. Magic Johnson dribbled a ball and passed it to Kareem, who nonchalantly dropped it in the basket.

Bill pointed to a corner table slightly bigger than a plate. Diana sat first.

"Whata y'all want, guys?" the bartender called from the spot where he dried glasses.

"Beer for me," Bill said.

"Kahlua sombrero. No, make that a wine spritzer. I'm driving and haven't eaten."

"Sub, Diana?" the bartender asked. There was a window cut between the bar and the sub shop next door.

"Fantastic. Italian cold cuts. The works—pickles, onion, hot peppers, especially pickles."

She was too tired to talk. She and Bill sat in a silence, neither feeling the urge to fill the void or even considering there was a void.

The bartender brought the drinks and sandwich. It was wrapped in wax paper which was soaked through with olive oil.

"Want half?" Diana asked Bill.

He nodded. She tore it in two. As they bit into them, the tomatoes, onions, pickles and part of the provolone oozed onto the table.

"Tomorrow will be better," Bill said halfway through his beer.

"God, I hope so." Too tired to focus her thoughts, she threw down a ten dollar bill. "It's on me. See ya first thing in the morning."

Pulling into her parking spot, she saw a light from their

227

living room window. Jim must have forgotten to shut it off. Not like the man, who when she was a child, said things like, "Wait till you grow up. I'll visit you and put on every light. I'll open the screen door and invite the bugs in, and put on your air conditioning then open every window in the house." *We all mellow,* she thought.

She glanced at her watch. Two in the morning, eight in Paris. Maurice would be between his paper and apartment. She wanted to call and bitch about her day. He couldn't make it better, but he'd say hmmmm in a way that spoke paragraphs of understanding. *Crazy life,* she thought, *me one week in Paris, and then he spends one in Florida then we have two weeks alone.*

In the elevator she thought about a feature on commuter marriages. Not on hers, on other people's. She'd been written up in *Fortune* as the southern Katherine Graham. They said Diana was the woman who did for local news what the *Washington Post* did for national. *Ms. had done a story on her but only after flip flopping.*

The elevator arrived on the third floor. As she reached for her key, she felt a wave of loss that it had been five years since she caught the scent of a story and tracked it down. "What does a football player do when he can no longer play football? But an athlete quits because of age. Reporters don't have age limitations. But I'm not a reporter, I'm a publisher." *Back to talking to myself,* she thought. She turned the key.

There was an unpleasant odor in the apartment, as if Jim had forgotten to flush the toilet. He lay on the couch. *Poor man,* she thought. "Hey, Jim. Better get to bed." His eyes stared at her without seeing.

At the wake, the neighbors told her how she'd screamed,

how she kept shaking her father. She remembered none of it. She refused the doctor's tranquilizer. "I need to feel this pain," she told him.

As Diana entered the church for the memorial service, flanked by Jane, Maurice, and Bill, a bum stood at the door. The funeral director pushed him away.

"Miss Diana, make him let me in," the man said. He wore a very greasy tie and a shirt that had not seen soap and water for a long time.

"He was one of my father's friends," Diana said. The director shrugged and stood aside. The man disappeared into the crowd.

Bill Reed said, "I think it's the largest funeral ever in Sarasota," as Jane and Maurice propelled her down to the front row. She saw the governor, and the secret service surrounding Vice President Bush. There were more newspaper people there than at the National Press Association's annual meeting. Every off duty cop and fireman stood, making four rows of blue shirts. Diana walked by them all with her back straight until the three of them reached the only empty seats.

People shared their memories of Jim.

A former drug addict told how Jim gave him back his life.

A man said that after he got of jail, Jim found him a job.

A hooker said Jim saved her from a pimp.

The head of the pressman's union said they never doubted his word in a negotiation.

Bill Reed got up and tried to tell of the early days, but he lost control. "I'm sorry," he sobbed. Maurice helped him to his seat before talking about their war experiences.

Then it was Diana's turn. She had not cried since the night she found Jim, holding herself together as a representative of all her father stood for, her last assignment for him. She mounted the three stairs to the pulpit. Her text had been placed there earlier by the funeral director.

"Some say I was born with ink, not blood in my body. Lord knows I had a different childhood, crawling around the floor of the city room when other kids played in sandboxes. I could say Jim taught me all I knew about getting a story but that would be a lie. He showed me how to teach myself. That's a greater gift.

"Some people might think he forced me into following in his footsteps. That's not true. He couldn't keep me out of them. He told me one time if I wanted to be a reporter he'd be thrilled, but if I wanted to be anything else, he'd be equally thrilled, but I had to be true to myself. I didn't realize it at the time, but he accepted me as me. Only as an adult did I realize how few people do that." Diana saw a glass of water and she swallowed half to keep the tears in check. She took a deep breath before she began again.

"Looking out in this church, I realize how many lives he touched. That is his memorial, you who were his friends, his coworkers, his fellow professionals. We have all lost a part of our lives. For me he was my father, my mother, my teacher, my editor, my publisher, but he was mostly my friend and confidant. No daughter can ask more."

She couldn't see. She felt Maurice's arm encircle her waist. She knew him by his smell.

"We thank you for coming," he said. They stood at the door of the church for what seemed like hours shaking hands.

Diana lost her energy. She went into the paper each morning, did what had to be done and went home. She threw out the couch where Jim died. She sat in her room for hours. Maurice went back to Paris, Jane back to Boston, but only after she told them repeatedly that she was fine.

"I'm not fine: I have to get a hold of myself," she said to her reflection in the mirror.

Jim's bedroom door stayed shut. She did not go into his bathroom, unready to face his razor, his shaving cream and his deodorant. She found the Gitanes Maurice had left. She lit one, then choked. "God, how can he stand these?" For the first time in her life, she felt totally without resources.

"Get your buns to the airport tomorrow morning at eleven. Kate and I are coming for April vacation," Jane said. Diana was at the gate as they deplaned, reaching for a lifeline that even Maurice had not been able to throw to her.

The next morning Kate appeared on the balcony, dressed in her bathing suit. She held a towel over her arm. "I don't want to be a snowbird anymore," she said.

Diana winced. She could see Jim in the empty chair saying, "Hope you snowbirds closed the door when you crossed the Mason-Dixon line. We don't want to let any of that cold air in."

Under Jane's not-so-gentle pushing Diana agreed to clear out Jim's things while Jane was there to help. First they drove to Piggly Wiggly for cartons. As long as they were there, Diana stocked up on bread, Coke and juice.

"Let's eat at Chin Ming's," she suggested. Lunch was followed by an afternoon movie, *An Officer and a Gentleman*, which brought them to dinner, an early bird special at The Crow's Nest. As they pulled into the parking lot, Diana said, "I've got a headache."

"I know what you're doing, and it won't work tomorrow," Jane said.

The next day, Kate told Diana she did not want to go to the Barnum and Bailey Circus Museum, the Tamiami Trail, shopping or anyplace else.

"Your mother told you to turn me down," Diana said.

"Of course she did. I'm spending the day at the pool while you guys clean out Jim's room. If you want to do any of that other stuff afterwards, I'm game." She draped her towel around her shoulders and blew a kiss.

For the first time since the memorial service, Diana opened Jim's bedroom door. Everything was dusty. His green shirt lay across a chair. A book about Watergate was open on the bed. As Diana started to turn away, Jane stopped her.

"For a little shit, you're pushy," Diana said.

They started with the dresser, folding underwear and dropping it in a carton to take to the Salvation Army. When Jane opened the top left drawer she found it crammed with snapshots, most of them black and white, the kind with pinking sheared edges. Toward the bottom were the colored ones.

Jane asked as she held up one, "Is this you?" A little girl with curls sat next to a ball half her size. A second had the same little girl in a young Jim's arms.

"I think so. I never saw them before." There were twenty-two photos of Diana's mother including the one she remembered from Jim's dresser. It was still in its silver filigree frame.

Jane sorted them on the bed. "Here are the ones from our graduation."

Diana dropped a last pair of socks into the box marked Wheaties. She looked over Jane's shoulder. "God, we look like such babies."

While Diana went over to Jim's desk, Jane folded Jim's

glasses and slipped them in their case. She opened his closet door. It ran one whole wall, but was only half filled with clothes thrown haphazardly on hangers. Shirts hung wrong side out. Shoes lay under the pants, not side-by-side. Jim, who hated ties, had three hanging from a rack meant for twenty. Each was a solid color: blue, brown, gray. There was a two-drawer file cabinet stuffed to the brim with unfiled papers.

"You want to do these?" Jane asked.

"Doesn't matter."

"I'll finish the clothes first. How you doing?" Between each activity she watched Diana's movements for what her friend wasn't saying.

Jane pulled down the cotton sweaters that were tossed on the shelf above the rod. Behind the sweaters was a shoe box. She needed to stand on tip toe to reach it. She inched it forward, but then as she pushed on one corner, it fell, spilling more photos, all Polaroids. Quickly she stuffed them back in the box and pushed it under the bed.

Diana caught her action out of the corner of her eye. "What's that?"

"Do you want to save any of his clothes as a memory or something?"

Diana shook her head. "I have his newspaper."

"Let's break for some ice tea. Why don't you go down and ask my sun bum if she wants some." As soon as Diana left, Jane grabbed the shoe box from were she'd stashed it and put it on her bed in the guest room. Closing the door she went to make the tea.

Jane, Kate and Diana sent out for pizza. The delivery boy shifted his feet, waiting for a tip. Diana searched for change, but she only had a twenty.

233

"I've got some change," Jane said. She went into her room and reached for her purse. Her hand knocked the shoe box onto the floor. The contents spilled on the rug.

Diana, who'd followed her, bent to pick up the Polaroids. "Oh my God!" her hand flew to her mouth. She shuffled through them.

Jane rushed to the living room and paid the delivery man, told Kate to watch TV and went back into the bedroom. She shut the door behind her.

Diana sat on the floor, her legs open like a five-year-old with the photos between them. She opened her mouth and shut it, saying nothing. Taking a handful of the photos she pushed them toward Jane.

Bill Reed stretched naked across Jim's bed. His finger was crooked as if saying come hither. A second photo had Jim and Bill arm in arm. Others showed a party with only male guests.

"This has nothing to do with you," Jane said.

"My father lied to me."

"No, he didn't. He just didn't tell you."

Diana kept looking at the photos, then shaking her head.

"Diana, think about it. That's not a thing he could easily tell you."

"I thought he trusted me," Diana said.

"I'm sure he did, but maybe . . ."

"Maybe, nothing. He's made a lie of our whole relationship." Diana got up. She began pacing, which was hard because there was limited floor space between the twin beds and dresser.

Jane watched a moment. "Bullshit! Did you tell Jim about all your lovers?"

"No, but they were all . . . all guys." They exchanged looks. Neither said the obvious.

"Diana, remember what you said in the eulogy about Jim accepting you as you," Jane said. "Would you do less for him?"

Diana ran her hand through her hair. "I'm going to ask Bill."

Jane raised an eyebrow.

"I am."

"What good would it do?"

"I'd know for sure."

"You already do," Jane whispered.

Diana punched her pillow. Her left side, right side, back and stomach were all equally uncomfortable. She took the zapper and put on the late show, then didn't watch it. She raised and lowered the air conditioning. She drank two glasses of water and peed four times.

The next morning she went to the paper. Bill Reed was in his office.

"How ya doing?" he asked as she walked in. "Jane helping you get the stuff cleared out?"

"It's hard Bill. What about you?"

He shrugged. "I miss him. We go back a long, long way."

"I realize that. More and more." He looked at her sharply. Before he could say anything else, she got up. "Can you handle stuff for a couple more days? I want to take some time while Jane's here."

Bill nodded. "Whatever you need, Diana, I'm here for you."

She was halfway across the city room toward her own office to do a quick check of messages. She stopped. Someone spoke to her, but she shook her head. She went back to Bill's office. He hadn't moved.

"It's OK, Bill." She turned around and went home to Jane and Kate.

Fall, Winter 1982:
Maine and Boston

Jane, flat on her back on scaffolding, swirled sand paint on the ceiling in rainbow-shaped strokes. "Lucy!" she called, "I dropped the roller."

Lucy, in painters' overalls, a cigarette dangling from her lips, came into the room to pick it up. Her hair had been cut short and swirled around her face like the new arcs on her ceiling. Her facial muscles had relaxed since retirement. Without high heels and severe suits, she had taken on a grandmotherly air that would have shocked her former JRP coworkers. "You just can't get good help these days," she said.

"Not at what you pay."

"A real Maine clambake and a week's vacation in my wonderful home is good pay in my book." Lucy returned to her own project. "And don't forget you have the satisfaction of helping a little old lady," she called from the other room.

"Hah!" Jane said. She glanced at her watch, worried about Kate and Andy on their way Down East. Traffic was always heavy on the New Hampshire and Maine turnpikes in late August. Stupid being a worry wart, she chided herself as she wiped her hands on her jeans that looked like a snowstorm from the paint drops. She heard Lucy start up her floor sander in the next room, drowning out the Bob Franke tape she'd been listening to.

Jane dipped the roller into the sand paint and made another swirl, content there were only two square feet to finish. The scaffolding would not have to be moved again, which Jane hated doing. She always feared that she'd set it up wrong, and she would crash to the floor.

She wrote her initials in the corner of one swirl. They were almost imperceptible. *If Michelangelo can sign the Sistine Chapel, I can sign Lucy's ceiling,* she thought.

Suddenly Kate was by the ladder. "YOU DIDN'T HEAR US CALL," she screamed. She dropped her backpack under one of the two ladders holding the scaffolding.

Jane slithered off the scaffolding, dropping to the floor.

"HOW'S YOUR BABY BROTHER?"

"ADORABLE." The sander stopped. "After Daddy and Alice left for the party, I got him up to play. He's got his first tooth."

Andy and Main Man, their Japanese Chin, followed Lucy into the room. Lucy was covered with dust spit out by the sander. "Help yourself to a beer. I'm going to get cleaned up," she said as Andy and the dog fought to kiss Jane.

Andy found the last free parking spot along the sea wall. He, Kate, Jane and Lucy piled out of his VW Bus leaving pants and pullovers piled on the seats for when the sun went down. In a state where people claimed to have three seasons—winter, July and August—Down Easters never went anywhere without being prepared for plunging temperatures.

The smell of salt hung in the air. On the beach about a hundred people mingled about, some sitting, others playing volley ball or talking. Only two hardy souls braved the cold water.

Steam escaped from a bunch of rocks piled waist high out of the reach of the tide. Long tables and benches were placed to the left of the rocks.

"Let's find a seat," Lucy herded them towards an empty spot at a table closest to the rocks. She waved to a man dressed in jeans and a T-shirt. It had the words, "First Unitarian Church Clambake—August 22, 1982" written on it, along with a cartoon of a lobster trying to escape a mob of chefs.

"That's Alexander, my minister. Very active in the sanctuary movement when he isn't playing chef," Lucy said.

He looked more like the devil rising from hell than a minister as he stood behind the steaming rocks. He loaded lobsters, clams, oysters, sea weed, chicken legs, hot dogs and ears of corn onto huge platters. The part of his face not covered by a gray beard was redder than the lobsters.

Waitresses, all members of Lucy's church, all wearing the same designed T-shirt as Alexander, put the platters on the red checkered table cloths. People swung their legs over the benches and began to eat.

Andy got them a pitcher of beer and a ginger ale for Kate. "Wow, all I can eat!" He reached for a square of johnnycake from one of the baskets placed between individual dishes of melted butter.

"All you can eat," Lucy said. She dismembered her lobster, sucking the juice out of its small legs. Bending the tail back until it snapped from the body, she used her finger to push the meat through the hole in the tail. She dipped it in her cup, swirling it in the melted butter, before putting it in her mouth. She closed her eyes. "Paradise."

Andy and Jane each took a clam, letting the meat slip

from the shell onto their tongues, while Kate slathered an ear of corn with butter. By the time the blueberry pie arrived, they all groaned, but each took a sliver.

Kate found some people her own age to hang out with. Lucy helped herself to a Styrofoam cup of coffee from a passing tray and lit a cigarette. "I really appreciate your help these last few weekends." She peered at Andy and Jane with the same look she used to interrogate printers and clerks. "So—are you guys getting married?"

"Yes," said Andy.

"No," said Jane.

The minister came up and put his hand on Lucy's shoulder. "Nice going, Lucy. Thanks to your publicity we raised somewhere over a thousand dollars." It was the only time Jane ever saw Lucy blush.

Side-by-side in a brass bed covered with a patchwork quilt, Jane and Andy cuddled. She felt she'd burst from having eaten too much. The muslin curtains blew almost straight in. The air smelled of the pine trees that surrounded the house.

Andy said, "I think we should get married."

"What?"

He repeated himself.

"Why?"

"We're almost a family," Andy said, "I'm with you and Kate more than I'm not. But no rush. Just don't say no."

That night Jane dreamed of their wedding. *It took place in a jail. Then she saw herself, a little old lady bent over with a hump on her back. She rang the bell of Andy's house in Lexington. A much older Andy, but still many years younger than her, opened the door. He took out his wallet and handed her a dollar. As he shut the door in the old Jane's face, another woman, younger than Andy, put her hand on his arm.*

"Who was that?" asked the younger woman.

"Just an old hag," he said.

Jane woke up. Andy slept next to her, one arm thrown across her chest. His face in repose looked like a teenager instead of a man in his mid twenties. The room was freezing. She lowered the window. Getting back into bed, she pulled the quilt over herself and made sure Andy was covered. He moved. She brushed his cheek with her lips before closing her eyes.

Jane rushed into her office. Anne, her new assistant, was typing on the computer. As she passed, Jane read the first line—"Dear Lisa, let me tell you about the guy I met last night . . ." Dropping the proofs on her own desk, she returned to Anne's.

"Traffic was miserable," she said. "Did you order the mailing lists?"

"I wasn't sure which ones," Anne placed her body so it hid the computer screen.

"The internal list?"

Anne shook her head. "I didn't know who to ask."

Jane indicated that her assistant should come in her office. Step-by-step she repeated the instructions and information exactly as she had before she'd left for vacation. No sooner had she finished, the phone rang. "I'll be right down," she said.

She walked past the closed office door of Martha Pringle Codrington, Chairman of the Board, into Harrison's office. The couple's divorce had everyone tiptoeing between the two.

Until the divorce, Martha had been chairman of the bored, dropping in only to have her husband take her to lunch. Somehow the publishing house had become part of their arsenal of weapons. The other board members, children and in-laws, split all votes, making stalemate the byword of company operations.

Harrison sat behind his desk. He indicated Jane should sit by a sweep of his hand. She thought he looked haggard.

"You look rested after your vacation. Nice tan. I feared Lucy would work you to death," he said.

"She sends her best." Jane perched on one of the two chairs, both antiques, not designed for relaxation.

Harrison pulled the report she'd left with him. "I read this over the Labor Day weekend." He flipped the pages with the careful columns of statistics. She saw he'd written several notes in the margin. "Nice job, but we can't do any of it. The board thinks it's too revolutionary."

A focus group to find out why sales are down isn't revolutionary, she wanted to say. Pringles and Codringtons were part of the American Revolution; the word, revolutionary shouldn't be considered negative. She didn't.

Harrison handed her the thick report. "Jane, you've got lots of good ideas, but they take you away from making brochures. Stick with brochures."

Andy watched Jane fume around her kitchen. He interjected phrases between her ramblings such as, "All corporations are political . . . don't take it personally . . . do you want to go out to eat . . . they don't appreciate you . . ."

Kate came in. "Mom, tell Dad I can't go out for the weekend. I'm sleeping over at Mary-Catherine's." Jane took the extension. "Hello, David."

"Alice and I have a party to go to and we wanted Kate to babysit."

"She has other plans."

"She could change them."

"This is a big thing with her friends," Jane said.

"I don't suppose you would consider taking little Nathan?"

"I don't suppose I would," she said.

"Do you think the rumors are true?" Anne asked. She wore her blue power suit, white blouse and blue tie. She was changing from her Nikes to her office shoes.

Jane had arrived at work with two Egg McMuffins. She wished her assistant was as businesslike in her work as she was in her appearance. Anne handed her *The Boston Globe*.

"Which rumors?" Jane once told Diana that JRP produced two products, text books and gossip. She only spread the word about one.

"That JRP is being sold," Anne said.

"Nothing has been said to management." Jane put an Egg McMuffin on Anne's desk and went into her office.

She heated water for a cup of tea and opened the newspaper. She ignored her normal pattern of glancing at the headlines, obituaries, *Doonesbury*, *Calvin & Hobbes* and Ellen Goodman. She smiled at Szep's latest cartoon of Reagan on her way to the business page. The lead article was that Reiner, Inc. was talking with the board of JRP. Since it was not a public corporation, the takeover fight would be within the family. There was a portrait of the first J. R. Pringle, who looked a lot like George Washington. Jane knew Frederick Reiner had a reputation for stripping the companies he bought.

"Why did you use this headline?" Martha Pringle Codrington stood in front of Jane's desk, waving the promotion for the new Lebenwitz Biology text.

Jane could smell the alcohol. "Because our test mailing showed it out-pulled the other headline three to one." She carefully avoided using the words, "My headline out-pulled yours three to one."

"I don't care. Use the other one."

Before Martha slammed the door, Jane caught Anne's face peering in. She wanted to say wipe that smirk off your face, but didn't. Instead she called the printer and ordered the mailing reprinted with the different headline. "Keep the old ones, until I tell you to junk them." She noted the conversation in her diary under 15 September.

Andy, Jane and Kate left the Charles Street Theater. They swung their joined hands as they headed for Brigham's for a soda. The evening was a celebration of Kate's making the Boston Latin School Declaiming Team. She'd failed on her first attempt.

"I've seen *Shear Madness* four times now, but that was the first time the hair dresser did it," Kate said. "I always try yelling for a different actor to be the murderer."

"That explains why my ear drum is still ringing," Andy said.

In bed afterwards, he and Jane cuddled. They hadn't made love, but they didn't always when Andy stayed over. "Did you set the alarm for five-fifteen?" he asked.

"Yes."

"Did you lock the door?"

"Yes."

"Do you think Kate had a good time?"

Jane's eyes were closed, and she was almost asleep, relaxed in the warmth of Andy's arms. "Yes."

"Marry me?"

Her eyes opened. "ANNdyyyy!!!"

"As long you were answering yes to so many questions, I thought . . ."

"She turned and kissed him on the nose. "You're wonderful, but I don't want to be married. If I did, it would be you."

"I'll take it as a maybe."

"Jane, come in here, please," Harrison said as she walked by his office. Jane walked in. He put his hand on his intercom. "Tea for both of us. Still take two sugars and lemon?"

The secretary deposited china cups and sterling spoons in front of them. The cups were decorated with rose buds and were rimmed in gold leaf.

Harrison prepared the tea from a silver service, using tongs to drop two sugar cubes into her cup. He left the lemon wedge on the side. He prepared his the same way.

They drank their tea in silence. She wondered what she had done wrong, because when he had good news he always got right to the point. He cleared his throat several times. "Would you tell me, Jane, please, why you reordered the promotion on the Lebenwitz book, and chose the one that did poorly in the tests." He held the 8 ½ x 11 self-mailer in his hand. On the desk were the printer's bills for both versions.

"Martha told me she preferred that one, regardless of the tests."

"Have we dropped the mailing?" He rolled the sheet up and held it against his chin as he swung his chair a little to the right and a little to the left. His voice was calm.

She shook her head no.

"What happened to the ones you'd already printed?"

She told him they were still at the printer's.

"Thank God for small favors," he said. "I'll take it from here."

She got up to leave. "You know, Harrison, this is the third time this year something like this has happened. I'm a very effective promotion manager. I make a terrible ping pong ball."

"I know, Jane. I am sorry," he said.

Twenty minutes later, Martha screamed into Jane's telephone, "How dare you go behind my back?"

Jane stormed into Martha's office. "I didn't go behind your back."

Martha tapped her pencil on the desk. She lost control of it, and it flipped behind her. She didn't retrieve it. "Harrison just told me he was pulling my copy. How did he know?"

"He discovered a double bill and asked me. I told him."

Before the older woman could say anything, Harrison walked in. "Martha, this is not Jane's fault. We need to talk."

Jane excused herself. When she left, she saw more people than normal finding things to do near Martha's door. No one would ask her what happened. They'd learned a long time ago she kept her own counsel.

"Why do you want to leave your present job?" the human resources director asked her. He wore a white shirt and black tie. His office was little bigger than a closet.

Jane's knees were jammed against his desk. There was no room to move her folding chair. Two days ago, a friend whom she knew from the New England Direct Marketing Association had called her to say Atlantic & Green needed a new promotion department head. The interview came about so fast on his recommendation, Jane hadn't had time to prepare a resume. She did have a portfolio with samples of different mailings.

The human resources director passed her on to two other people: the current head of promotion, an elf of a man, who never asked her a question. He told her about himself.

The other person was a woman, vice president in charge of something. Jane never learned her full title. The woman talked about how hard it had been to get her own promotion. "Younger women like you get all the benefits from my struggles."

Only the woman flipped through her portfolio. "That pulled 20 percent from our house list," Jane said.

"Interesting," said the vice president.

At the end of almost two hours she'd spoken less than two hundred words. She was directed back to the human resources office.

"We are definitely interested," the director said.

Three days later when Jane shuffled through her mail, there was an envelope from Atlantic & Green. Inside was thanks-but-no-thanks. *Shit,* she thought.

"I'll never find another job," she said to Andy. Kate was babysitting for her father. Andy had picked up Chinese food on his way in from Lexington, and they were surrounded by paper cartons.

"It's only one interview. Consider it practice."

Jane hemmed through the beef and snow pea pods and hawed through the fried rice. She barely ate. He picked two pea pods from her plate with his chopsticks without her noticing.

Andy listened as he ate. He listened as he cleared the table and listened as he did the dishes. Drying his hands on the dishtowel, he walked up behind her and put his arms around her and kissed the top of her head. Almost in a whisper he said, "Why don't you call and ask Lucy if she thinks you're marketable."

"Of course, you're marketable," Lucy said when Jane talked to her an hour later.

"What should I put on my resume?" Jane asked.

"How the hell should I know? I worked in the same place for forty-five years."

The telephone interrupted Jane going over Anne's copy and layout. It was not only good, it was a day ahead of schedule.

"Hi, honey. Dad and I wanted to know when you'll be down for Thanksgiving," Mary Andrews asked.

"Andy's working till midnight Wednesday. Then we'll leave. There'll be less traffic then."

"You staying all weekend?" Mary asked.

"We're coming back Saturday. Andy, Kate and I are officially joining the Unitarian Church on Sunday."

"Good place for a wedding."

"I'm not marrying Andy. He's too young."

Jane's father, who had been listening in on the extension said, "Since women live longer than men, means he'd be around to nurse you."

"Stop it you guys."

"He's a good one. Don't let him get away," her mother said. "But we won't bring it up again."

Till the next time, she thought as she picked up her pencil to make one tiny change in Anne's copy.

Jane continued working at her desk. Outside a light snow fell, frosting her windows. Everyone else had left, but she needed to tally sales by page from the last catalogue before laying out the next one.

Kate called to say that Alice had phoned in a panic, because she needed to go shopping and the au pair was too ill to sit. Jane felt annoyed. David's and Alice's devotion to Kate's company was often in direct relation to their need for a babysitter.

"I'll catch the train. Andy will run me in tomorrow for school," Kate said. Before hanging up she added, "I left a note for Barbara or Julie to walk Main Man if you're not home." They were Jane's tenants, but the two apartments were often as one, with shared meals and lots of borrowings of whatevers.

It was nine when she shoved her things away. There was a knock on her half opened door. She jumped. "I thought I was alone," Jane said when she saw Harrison in the doorway.

He had on his Chesterfield coat. It always looked as if he'd picked it up from the cleaners an hour before. He carried his briefcase and hat in his hand. "I was preparing board reports. I thought you'd forgotten to shut off your lights. Heading home?"

"I thought I'd get something to eat. Kate is at her dad's."

"Could a lonely old man buy you dinner?"

They walked to Dini's, about three hundred yards from the office. The restaurant was usually empty at that time of night, but when they arrived, Christmas shoppers, surrounded by their packages, filled most of the tables.

The waitress, who knew them both well, found a table for them ahead of several other couples. "They had a reservation," she lied.

Neither wanted a cocktail. Both ordered scrod. Harrison requested a Bishop Riesling to go with the fish.

"How is Kate?"

"Doing well. I'm lucky she is at Boston Latin School."

"I think it's as good as Phillips Andover." He had sent his three sons to the exclusive school that was so out of Jane's range. Had she thought, she could have had a private school clause in her divorce agreement. No matter. Kate was getting a first class education. She looked at Harrison, who had lowered his eyes. She wondered if he were thinking of his youngest who had been killed in a crash three years before.

"I should be at a committee meeting tonight, but work lately is too much. Still, I'm sure Reagan will be re-elected without me."

Jane didn't say, "Not if I can help it."

He paid the bill in cash. As they left the restaurant, he tipped his hat, and said, "Thank you. I eat alone too many nights. It was nice to have intelligent company."

Jane had twenty-two bottles of alcohol lined up on her office bookcase—scotch, whiskey, bourbon and champagne—all gifts from vendors. There was an empty white carton that had held one of the two gifts she did appreciate more than the alcohol—a strawberry cheesecake. She'd shared it with the staff. The other gift she liked was a box of meat including four filet mignons, six lamb chops, six pork chops and a roast beef.

She had reported every gift to Harrison, who wanted to limit gifts to a value of twenty-five dollars. "I'll take most of the meat to Rosie's Place," she told him.

He said she could keep it if she wanted.

"No, I'll do Rosie's. It'll be my Christmas good deed this year."

She did scoop out the four filet mignons before going to the women's shelter. That and the champagne would be wonderful for New Year's dinner with Andy and her tenants. Kate would be at David and Alice's, babysitting Nathan. On the way home from Rosie's Place she wondered why her vendors couldn't come up with more imaginative business gifts.

She still hadn't rid herself of last's year's bottles or the year's before. Then she had a flash. Each time she left the office she put a bottle or two in her case. She gave them to the first wino she passed. "Merry Christmas," she would say to their bleary, astonished stares.

She received a registered letter asking her to sell the two hundred shares of JRP stock she'd been given as a bonus. "I'm not taking ten thousand dollars to be out of a job the next day," she said to Andy. "Besides compared to the family's stock, my shares don't count."

"If the Codringtons don't stop fighting, you'll be out anyway," he said.

Main Man slept on the couch. Kate spread the Christmas decorations in front of the still bare Christmas tree. Jane sat at the counter. In front of her was the book, *What Color Is My Parachute?* None of its resume ideas inspired her. Her notes on her yellow legal pad were minimal—her name, address, telephone, then the word objective. After that there were question marks. She got up to get The Card.

Seeing it, Kate asked, "What's your message this year?"

"My job's in jeopardy, or I'm not getting married."

"Choose the first one. I still have hopes you'll get sensible about Andy," Kate said.

Jane followed Kate's suggestion. On a note she typed to be put in with The Card, "It's still better than if I were still married and doing lunch and bridge all the time." The Card was getting too crowded for long messages.

1983:
Florida

Diana stood by the gate watching Eastern Airline Flight 438 from New York taxi to a stop. As the passengers emerged, they held their faces to the sun. Most were snowbirds, carrying winter coats.

She examined each businessman in a suit. Finally, the next to the last person off the plane was Maurice. Usually he landed in Miami and caught a commuter flight across the state, but last night he'd called to say he'd be late because he needed to stop in New York.

As always he grabbed her as if it had been months instead of only two weeks since they'd seen each another. She buried her nose in his sweater, inhaling the odor of his sweat, cigarettes and cologne. He kissed her, his tongue seeking hers.

An old woman clucked disapprovingly. Her friend frowned.

Diana saw them exchange looks as she broke from his embrace. *"As-tu quelques valises?"* she asked, knowing he kept duplicates of everything in both places.

"Pas du tout, chérie, pourquoi?" He shook his head, not used to her asking stupid questions.

Before she could answer, the older of the two women

said, "What do you expect? They're French."

Maurice's face broke into a smile, the wrinkles from the corner of his eyes almost touching the corner of his mouth. He understood.

As they headed to the car she asked, "Hungry?"

"Oui, pour toi," he said.

They made love as soon as they arrived at Diana's. "God, I missed you," she said, her head resting on his shoulder. She picked at his chest hair, twirling the gray around her fingertips.

She felt his restlessness under her hand. Rolling over, she handed him the Gitanes he'd dropped on the night stand as he stripped. The lighter she had given him for Christmas two years ago had fallen to the floor, and she patted under the bed until she found it. He cupped his hand to light his cigarette. "Sometimes I think the cigarette is more important for you than the sex."

"Only after." He fell asleep within minutes of stubbing it out in the ash tray unused since his last visit. He did not wake when she dressed to go to the paper the next morning.

She left the room dark. Normally she slept with the curtains wide open. Maurice, after years of closing shutters, found light distracting. She knew she could always enjoy the sun coming up over the Gulf when he wasn't there.

When she arrived home that night, she smelled fish grilling as soon as she opened the door. Although the winter sun had set an hour before, she could see her husband, wearing an apron, from a lamp he must have moved onto the balcony. She watched him brush a sauce onto the fish and heard some sizzle as it hit the hot coals.

He looked up and saw her. "Hi, beautiful." He ushered her to a deck chair and took off her shoes. Rubbing her feet, they both felt her relax under his hands.

As her eyes closed, he poured her a glass of Rivesaltes Muscat. The amber liquid slid down her throat. "I didn't know we had any," she said.

"I brought it with me, and a bottle of Banyuls—we'll save it for another meal."

Diana looked at the table. He had made a red pepper mousse as a starter. He brushed garlic oil onto a piece of toast, then, spreading the mousse, he fed her the first bite.

As Diana did the dishes, Maurice put Chopin on the stereo. He sat on the couch and read the *Sarasota Journal*. "Good story on the bank fraud," he called through the sliding window between the kitchen and living room.

Diana's face appeared in the window then disappeared. "Check the article on alternative uses for the schools," she said loud enough to be heard over the music.

Maurice read it. "One of the new reporters?"

"They're both going to be great." She wiped out the sink, appreciating that Maurice was not only a good cook, but that he cleaned up after himself. Hanging up her dish towel she curled up next to him.

"Let us talk," he said.

"About what."

"Us?"

She felt a surge of panic. "Aren't you happy?"

He leaned over to kiss her forehead. "I had an interesting call right before I left Paris. International Media wants to buy me out."

"They're based in New York."

"That's why I stopped on my way here."

"What would you do?" she asked.

"I thought I might just live full time with my wife."

"Share a continent? What a concept."

★ ★ ★ ★ ★

The deal came together faster than Maurice and Diana dreamed possible. By April he'd rented his Paris apartment and had moved to Florida.

He tried being a house husband. "You said you always wanted a male wife," he reminded her as she looked at her burned blouse. She had said nothing about the sweater that had been reduced to the size of a Barbie doll's. *On-the-job training,* she thought. However, his meals were works of art. She gained five pounds in March.

They started jogging in the mornings before Diana left for work. When they got back he made her coffee and breakfast. She would eat on the balcony, and read the paper, circling things she wanted to tell her staff. Moments like that made her feel as if God were in his heaven, all was right with the world.

On June 15th Diana met with her accountants at their offices. The secretaries and the rest of their staff had left. They sat in the conference room around the teak table.

"You're spending too much," the older said. He had worked with Jim since the seventies. The younger was his son. They looked more like brothers, the father more tanned and fit than the son.

"Accountants always say that," Diana said.

The younger removed his glasses. "The cost of your health insurance is going up. There've been too many claims. The amortization of the computer and press are dragging your balance line almost into the red. Had you not bought . . ."

". . . That last paper," she finished. They had been against the purchase, but it had been on sale in a market that had no other papers.

"You've angered too many advertisers."

"Those stories need to be written. If businesses cheat the . . ."

"You lost over one hundred fifty thousand dollars in ad revenue."

"But we boosted circulation."

"If you can't get more regional ads with the figures, it doesn't matter."

When she dragged herself home well after ten, Maurice greeted her with, "Where have you been? Dinner is ruined."

The argument ended with her promising to call. He promised not to take her delays personally.

Two days later he bought her a car phone. "That way I do not have to worry, and you do not have to look for a telephone." She did not tell him that his reasonableness annoyed her. Had it made sense to her, she might have said something.

If mornings were ideal, nights were often tense between them. She needed time to unwind. Maurice, who had been alone most of the day, wanted to talk. Understanding that didn't alleviate it. Diana found herself sitting in the car twenty minutes before entering the apartment. If he noticed the car outside, he'd come down. She imagined a cat pouncing on a mouse.

An idea came to her on her drive to work when she passed two men with golf clubs in the back. As soon as she arrived in her office she called Sven, her neighbor.

"Can you do me a favor?" she asked. "Take Maurice golfing or something with you. Anywhere. Just get him out of the apartment. Often."

The first of July Diana came home late. The apartment was dark. Maurice had driven to Miami with Sven to pick up the neighbor's granddaughter.

Diana threw her briefcase on the chair, as she always did, before turning on the light. It was a habitual action. It crashed to the floor. Maurice had rearranged the furniture that had been in the same place since Jim had first moved in.

Diana was shocked at how much Maurice's constant presence disturbed her. Thinking it would get better, she grew more uncomfortable when it increased. She felt stupid complaining about hearing him cough in the morning, finding his brush in place of hers or having to readjust the shower nozzle. It sounded even more stupid complaining that she had to eat a wonderful meal he had spent the afternoon preparing, although she might not be hungry. When she told Bill Reed, he said, "He's in your territory full time, that's the problem."

She called Maurice, "Meet me after work for a drink."

They found a cocktail lounge. She chose one where she'd never been, neutral territory.

It was dark, but she could make out one other couple seated and talking with their heads almost touching. The couple didn't notice them as they walked by. A folk singer, strumming a beat up guitar, nodded at them.

Diana ordered a Kahlua sombrero. He had a whisky. At the table next to the bar, he picked up happy hour munchies: meatballs, stuffed mushrooms, and a potato skin heaped with sour cream and bacon bits for Diana.

She thought he would say how amusing he found eating potato skins, as he always did, but the expression on her face stopped him. It was more than the green light reflected from the jar and candle in the center of the table. Instead he put the plates down, sat, and looked at her waiting.

"I love you, but . . ." she said.

256

". . . But we will drive each other crazy." He reached for her hand. "I have not enough to do, you have too much. Despite all the time I spent, spend, in your flat, I still feel as if it is yours, not ours. Maybe we should look for a home that is ours. No more my things and your things, just our things."

The real estate agent marched them through six houses the next Saturday. Efficient and in her mid forties, she kept trying to speak French.

He took her hand and kissed it. In English, but with an accent six times heavier than normal, he said, "When you speak French you are a very sexy woman, but not as sexy as when you use your own language. Your English has the taste of southern honey." The woman shut her eyes and swayed. Maurice winked at Diana.

The seventh home they entered, Diana and Maurice, gave each other a *this-is-it* look. Part of the Florida room contained a small swimming pool. The four bedrooms allowed them each to have an office plus a den.

The landscaping was perfect with masses of flowers and several large palm trees shaded the house. The backyard was hidden on two sides from the neighbors' views by walls of bushes. The lawn ran to the canal leading into the Gulf. It even had a small dock. Across the canal was flat land with cactus and palms.

"That's protected land. They'll never build on it," the agent said and walked away to let them talk.

"I can fish for our dinner," Maurice said.

"You hate fishing," Diana said.

Maurice took a month to find the furnishings. After he scouted out what he liked, he took Diana to give her approval or disapproval. With the exception of the desk for her office, she agreed to everything. "This is fun," she said. "You do the work, I get the benefits."

They moved the last Saturday in September. By eight in the morning the temperature was 105°. The humidity was ninety-five percent.

The movers knocked at the door. Maurice pointed out what was going and what wasn't. Despite the couple's pledge to have only things in common, neither could imagine parting with books, records, photos or paintings.

Replacing appliances that still worked well seemed equally stupid, and there were many pots and pans that Maurice said he needed to prepare this or that dish. "I didn't ship them from Paris to throw them out."

"Fine with me," she said.

The Salvation Army arrived at the same time to cart away the things that they weren't keeping. Deserting the confusion, Diana drove to Dunkin' Donuts for blueberry muffins and coffee for the work crew and themselves before going to the new house.

When she turned the key in their new door, the significance hit her. This was their first home as a couple. Her husband was already standing in the middle of the empty living room. She put the bag on the counter. "Where are the movers?" she asked.

"They are arranging their truck. They should arrive any minute." He took a muffin and handed her another. As one, they sank crossed legged on their new kitchen floor. The bell rang. The movers had arrived with the delivery men.

"Put it here," she said to the blond carrying one end of the couch. His hair was shoulder length. He wore shorts and a sleeveless undershirt. Sweat poured from his body.

"Not there, *chérie*." Maurice took a paper out of his

pocket. It was a floor plan. Everything that was arriving was marked as to where it should go. Used to taking charge, Diana watched as her new home was set up around her. Her job was to get out of the way.

Finally they were alone. Diana started to unpack her new dishes and put them in the closet. Maurice took them and put them in the dishwasher.

"They're fine," she snapped.

"They are full of microbes," he said. He was as sweaty as the workmen and oozed a masculine odor that only could come from physical work.

Diana put sheets and towels in the linen closet. Maurice took the blue set, not the flowered ones she planned to use, and made up their new bed. She finished before he did, found a hammer and nails and banged a nail into the living room wall to hang her large abstract over the couch.

"Be careful of the wall, *chérie*," Maurice called from the bedroom.

"Blow it out your saddle bags," she screamed.

Maurice, looking puzzled, came from the bedroom. "What is wrong?"

"I don't know."

He sat on the couch and pulled her down next to him. "Maybe it is the heat." The air conditioning had not caught up with all the hot air that slunk in with the movers and delivery men. She shook her head. "I know," he said. "Let us leave everything, and take a swim in our wonderful new pool."

"Do you know where our suits are?"

"Why do we need them? No one can see us," he said.

They dove in from the edge of the pool. The water caressed their bodies draining their weariness. "This is the life," Maurice said. He dog paddled from one end to the other as Diana floated on her back. He dove and came up under her. They wrestled, then kissed. "Ever make love in a pool?" he whispered.

"Not until now."

When Diana's feet touched the bottom of the pool after Maurice released her, she kissed him.

"I know what was bothering me. I was feeling superfluous."

"*Chérie,* to me you are anything but."

Diana sat at her desk going over the employee survey on their satisfaction with benefits. She had eighty people working for her among all the papers. *Damn,* she thought, *no one seems content.* Pushing the papers aside she picked up the phone and dialed.

"Jane Johnson, how can I help you?"

"I want to order all your books."

"Diana."

"The same. I'm postponing thinking out a problem, how are things going?"

"Kate's great. Andy's adorable. Work sucks."

"I thought it was getting better."

"Martha went to dry out. Now she's back and drinking again. The takeover threat is back."

"Still sending out resumes?" Diana turned her back to her computer screen.

"Still getting rejections. The problem is I'm not sure I know what I want to be when I grow up. I think it comes across. How's it by you?"

"The house is great. Maurice still doesn't have enough to occupy him. We're two chiefs living under one roof, but it's a blip not a problem."

After they hung up, Diana went back to the survey and

made a chart. She plugged in each employee and then marked what they needed, retirement, health insurance, salary continuance, day care, vacation. There had to be a solution, because at the moment the cost was breaking her back and no one was happy.

"Can I come in?" Diana jumped at Bill Reed's voice. He sat down, he looked at his nails, straightened his tie but said nothing.

"Out with it Bill," she said.

"I want to retire."

"But, you're only sixty-two."

"I'm burned out, Diana. Each day I sit at my desk and think I don't want to be here. I don't want to see palm trees, and fight with traffic as soon it gets cold up north. I want to move to where it's cold, Maine. Start a new life. Now, not in three years."

"Maine. Most people from Maine come here."

"I was born there, remember?"

She'd forgotten. "When do you want to go?"

"When you find a new editor. I'd never leave you in the lurch."

Diana got up and went around behind him and put her arms around him. "I hate to lose you. You are this paper, as much as Jim was. But I can't hold you against your own interests."

He patted her arm. "You're a good girl. And you're doing a good job. Jim would have been so proud of you."

Then why am I not having any fun, she wondered? "From you, there is no greater compliment." They discussed who might take over, but no one seemed right. "We'll look outside," she said.

After he left, she called in her personnel manager and told her that they needed to be more creative in benefits.

"Can't be done," the woman said.

"Can't is an unacceptable word. Get our providers in here. And start looking for someone to replace Bill. Use national trade sources, not local ones."

A giant *Garfield* balloon filled the television screen. Maurice sat in front of the television unable to pull away. Smells of roasting turkey filled the house.

Diana stood in the den doorway. She held a wooden spoon in her hand. Her hair was totally frizzed so it looked as if a red halo rested on her head. "When little Maurice is finished watching the parade he can set the table." She pinched his cheeks.

"This is a great parade, Diana. I can hardly wait to see *Père Noël*."

"Santa Claus. I want everything ready by the time Bill gets here."

She went back to the kitchen to recheck everything. This was the first Thanksgiving dinner she'd ever done. Four hours before she'd been staring at the turkey. "It's you or me, bird," she'd said to the pale flesh on the counter. "I mean it. I run five newspapers. You're road kill."

She'd read the directions on the package for the third time. "Wash the turkey." She'd pictured it singing in a bubble bath.

She reached for the phone and called Connecticut. "Hi, Jane. Can I speak to your mother?" Fifteen minutes later she had step-by-step directions.

When the doorbell rang its six notes, do, do, re, re, do, do, she was at step thirty-two: peel six medium-sized potatoes and boil in one quart of salted water with three tablespoons of milk.

Maurice, who had just finished the table, between peeks

at the parade, answered it. Bill entered with a bouquet of yellow roses which he presented with a bow to Diana.

"Oh, Bill. You shouldn't have," she said.

"I can't believe this meal," Bill said. "Don't get mad, Diana, but I didn't think you could do it." He poured himself a second cup of coffee from the Mr. Coffee machine and returned to the table. He couldn't tolerate Maurice's espresso.

Maurice, who considered dishwater a slightly better beverage than American coffee, took a long drag from his cigarette.

"It's a question of national pride," she said. Three perfectly made pies: apple, mincemeat and pumpkin, sat on the table, each with a slice missing. Diana had hidden the boxes that said, "Anne's Bakery—heat 'em up. Your family will never know you didn't bake 'em yourself."

The talk slipped into work subjects. "I'm hearing good things about your benefit plan," Bill said. "I think the unions will buy into it as an addition to their contract."

Diana had coerced the paper's benefits providers into designing a test program where people could pick benefits from a pool based on giving each person points to spend on the things they needed most. "Like walking through a cafeteria line," they'd said.

"It'll save us about fifteen percent as well. But Bill, I'm so tired of doing all this administrative shit. I could manufacture anything with what I do. It's got nothing to do with news." She picked the crust left from her piece of mincemeat pie and nibbled it.

Bill cleared his throat. "Although this isn't the time to talk business, let me throw out an idea." He moved his chair into the table. By the time he finished talking Maurice and Diana were nodding their heads and grinning.

Diana's card to Jane said, "Maurice is the new publisher of the Sarasota Journal Consortium, and I'm the new editor-in-chief of the *Journal*."

1984:
Boston

The clock radio clicked. The WERS disk jockey announced it was 6:00 a.m. As he played a record of Chris Williamson singing about a waterfall, Jane pulled her puff up around her ears.

Main Man put his nose against Jane's. It was cold, but not quite as cold as the room. "Lay down. You just think you have to go out." The dog complied but watched her, his head resting on his front paws.

She half listened to the song and thought, *If I wear my blue suit, my blue blouse is ironed.*

If I don't eat breakfast, that will save some time.

If I put my hair in a braid, I won't have to wash it.

If I buy my lunch, I won't have to make it.

The dog whined.

Three whines and a yip, and I'll believe he means it, she thought, then let her mind drift. Stupid to dread Monday when it was only Thursday.

"Whine."

Monday was the meeting with Martha and Harrison. How much more could she prepare?

The dog moved his mouth next to her ear. "Whine! Yip! Yowl!" She jumped up. Throwing on her robe, she followed the dog as he padded downstairs.

In the kitchen, Kate slathered bread with peanut butter. She added a slice of bologna, wrapped it in Saran Wrap and put it in a Bloomingdale's brown paper bag marked, "Brown Paper Bag."

Jane continued down to the basement where she opened the door to the small fenced-in garden. Main Man took one look at the snow and backed up.

"Oh no. You got me up for this. Suffer." She threw him into a snow drift. He plowed his way to his bush. It had thrived under his daily ministrations. She'd found it in the woods by her parents' house and dug it up and brought it home. Now it was barely visible in the storm. The dog ran back into the house and shook his paws one at a time.

Upstairs the kitchen radio station had been changed to WHDH's no school announcements. "Acton, Bedford, Bolton, Boxboro, Burlington . . ." Kate glared at the radio. "Must be worse west of the city." She poured corn flakes over a banana. Kate, hating soggy cereal, added milk last.

Jane's longing for a snow day was greater than her daughter's. She went upstairs to get dressed. Jeans and a sweater would be OK. Most of the staff lived west of the city and wouldn't make it in.

Back in the kitchen, Jane heard the radio repeat the announcements. "Acton, Amesbury, Ashland, Bedford, Bolton, Boston . . ."

Kate's scream of "Yes!!!!!!" drowned out ". . . Brocton, Burlington, Cambridge . . ."

Jane watched her daughter shove her lunch into the refrigerator and head back to bed. Picking up her briefcase, she left.

Anne made it into the office, one of only five other employees to do so. Living behind Beacon Hill gave her a seven-minute walk. Dressed in jeans, a Harvard sweatshirt and boots, she handed Jane a cup of tea. "You'll need it, Boss. BAP is on the war path." Anne had a series of names for Martha: Chairman Bitch, Yankee Doodle Damnher, Booze Broad. BAP was new. To Jane's raised eyebrow, she said, "Brahmin American Princess."

Jane took the tea into her office. Anne followed, handing her the sales figures from the last campaign. She had the original proposal under them with certain items slashed by a yellow highlighter.

"Is this the reason BA—Martha is on the war path?" Jane asked.

"Yup, now you're armed."

Not entirely, Jane thought, gulping half her tea. Opening her briefcase, she pulled out the miniature tape recorder Andy had given her. "In case you need to prove anything," he'd said.

"But it's illegal," she'd said.

"Still it might be handy in a negotiation," she remembered him saying. Then he'd added, "You still believe the world is a nice place with nice people." This led into their familiar argument which always finished with Andy shaking his head at her innocence, and Jane trying to prove how many nice people she knew, including him.

Well, Martha, isn't a nice person, Jane thought and slipped the miniature recorder into her blouse pocket under her sweater. Hiding the microphone under her large sun pin, bought for the purpose, she gathered her papers and headed for enemy territory.

Pushing the door open, Jane measured how much Martha's hands shook as she lifted the coffee cup to her lips. From the coffee's color, she guessed half was vodka. Mentally chanting her mantra, I won't let her get to me, I won't let her get to me, Jane said, "Good morning, Martha."

"Let me see the sales figures for the Littleton book." The chairman was the only one in the office dressed in a business suit. Her blouse had a small stain.

Jane placed the papers on the desk.

"They're ninety percent under projection," Martha said. Her glasses were perched on her nose. She pushed them back.

"Of course."

"What do you mean, of course?" Martha drained the contents of her cup.

Jane inhaled. "Please remember projections were based on three mailings to in-house list 10A, a law school list, the list Anne recommended, and an ad in *Women's Review of Books.*"

"I wouldn't be caught dead in that feminist rag," Martha said.

Jane gripped the arms of her chair. "You only let me go with part of list 10A. It was a miracle we pulled ten percent." She rolled her eyes at her own stupidity for her phrasing and braced herself for Martha's next attack.

The chairman glared across the desk. She reached for her cup. It was empty. "Jane, I've had it up the ying yang with your insolence. You're fired."

The words stunned Jane into a moment's silence. What to do? Be dignified. She stood. "Thank you, Martha."

The older woman asked, "Don't you have anything else to say?"

"No." Jane returned to what had become her former office. Shutting the door, she sat a few minutes waiting for her hands to stop shaking. As she took her diploma and her New England Direct Marketing Association Award off the wall, Tom, the security guard arrived.

He deposited several cartons on the carpet. His face shone bright red, as it did when anyone made a dirty joke. "I'm here to see you leave quickly and don't take any JRP property." He didn't look her in the eye.

She touched his arm. "Do you really think I'd steal anything?"

He shook his head. "Also, you aren't supposed to talk to anyone."

He helped her carry her boxes past the stares of her former coworkers. One drifted in. The others put their heads down ignoring her. Anne mouthed, "I'll call you later."

Martha stood in the door of her office as they walked past. "Good riddance."

Tom put Jane in a taxi with her boxes. "At least you're out of this hell hole," he whispered.

"I want you back," Harrison said early the next week. "Martha has agreed she was a bit hasty."

Jane leaned against her refrigerator as she talked on the wall phone. Knocking some of the magnets on the floor, she stooped to pick them up.

"She wasn't hasty. She was drunk. I was fired, Harrison, I intend to stay fired. It has to do with quality of life."

He tried dissuading her.

"You'd have to fire the Chairman of the Board for me to come back, and I know you can't do that."

Lucy sat at the counter drinking black coffee and listening. She waved her cigarette around punctuating her words. "I'm going to give him a piece of my mind." She was camping out in Jane's spare room.

"It wasn't his fault. He's caught too."

"But you don't have a job. How will you support Kate?"

"Unemployment and working temp, child support till I find something." *The problem,* Jane thought, *is I don't really know what I want to do, or what I can do.*

That evening, after all the dishes had been washed, Jane stoked the fire in the wood burning stove. She decided not to add another log. They'd be going to bed soon.

Lucy's feet, encased in psychedelic blue socks, rested on the trunk serving as a coffee table. "Now that we're caught up on your news, I can tell you I didn't come just to see old friends. I need to talk to the local Unitarian churches and the Unitarian Universal Association."

"What are you up to now?" Jane had discovered how politically involved Lucy had become when she watched the evening news report an anti–El Salvadorian policy demonstration at the White House. Lucy had filled the screen batting a policeman with a *Jane-Wyman-was-right* sign.

"The sanctuary movement has several Guatemalan refugees who'll cross the border in Texas over the next few months. We need churches between there and Canada to hide them."

"I'll call our minister," Jane said. "Lord, Lucy, you continue with all your politicking, and they'll throw you out of the Helpless Little Old Ladies Club."

Lucy stood up. "They wouldn't dare," she said.

Jane stood in line at the unemployment bureau. She'd filled out enough forms to start a good-sized fire. Then she was shown job postings. She didn't qualify as a truck driver, a computer programmer in either C, C++ or basic or as a legal secretary. There was nothing in publishing and even if there were, she wasn't sure she wanted to do the same thing. She couldn't tell her counselor what she wanted.

270

"It doesn't matter what you want," the counselor said. She was a woman in her mid-forties. "If you want your check you gotta prove you looked." Then she listed what she considered proof.

Discouraged, Jane wandered through Quincy market, thinking that poking into boutiques and to smell coffee, baking cookies, fresh bread, and spices from the food concessions might cheer her up. It had the opposite effect. Now that she didn't dare spend extra money, she wanted to buy everything in sight. *I'm being childish,* she thought.

Outside the main market, in the covered corridors, were the cart merchants. Each had a theme. There was one where everything was purple. Another's merchandise: jewelry, T-shirts, wrapping paper, cards, and miniature paintings, had been decorated with musical instruments.

She stopped at a cart selling gourmet dog biscuits flavored with banana, milk, chocolate, sausage, cheese, onion. Cut into shapes of bones, fire hydrants, cats, and doghouses, they were set out in wooden barrels each lined with red checked gingham.

A woman perched on a stool next to the cart. "Do you have a dog?" She wore a hand knitted sweater with a Saint Bernard covering most of the front. The tail curled around to the back.

"Yes."

"Dogs love these."

Something that had been niggling in Jane's mind for a long time took a giant step forward. "I'll take one banana biscuit. My dog loves bananas." The woman produced a small paper bag decorated with a dog carrying a huge biscuit.

"Is this your business?" Jane asked.

"Sure is."

Another woman came up. She wore a similar sweater, except with a poodle. "Hi, Allison, sorry I'm late. The T is a disaster."

"Don't think I'm pushy, but could I buy you coffee?" Jane asked after Allison finished giving directions to the new arrival.

The dog biscuit lady glanced at her watch. She looked through the glass ceiling at the light snow.

"I need to pick your brain. Ten minutes, I promise," Jane said.

In those ten minutes she learned Allison Barber was divorced, couldn't find a job after being a homemaker for twenty years, created the recipes for the biscuits and was using the cart as a test market along with direct mail.

Jane walked home, a good half-hour hike, her mind occupied. Inside she went straight to her office, switched on her computer and banged away.

Kate brought her Stouffer's Welsh Rarebit on toast at 9:30 p.m. She'd bent to deposit the tray on the floor, noticed the dog's approval of the idea, then put it on the drawing table. She said to her mother, "Whatever you're plotting, good luck."

It was 3:00 a.m. before Jane collapsed into bed. She was up before Kate and back to work.

Andy and Jane entered the Unitarian Church hand-in-hand. It was a typical old New England church with five-foot pews separated by half walls. The founding fathers found that if only their shoulders and heads appeared above the half walls, they could warm their souls during the three-hour sermons while blankets and metal foot warmers full of live coals warmed their bodies. Andy opened the door of one of the boxes.

Jane's tenants, Julie and Barbara, arrived shortly after. Barbara had a bunch of daffodils in her hand and gave Jane one as she joined them in the box.

By 8:00 p.m. the church was filled, something that didn't happen even at Christmas or Easter. Lucy's minister, Alexander, chatted with the president of the Unitarian Universal Association and other church officials. The Roman collars of the several Catholic priests stood out against the sweaters and cords of the Unitarian clergy. Everyone mulled around, then greeted the last arrival, the rabbi who presided at the church's annual seder.

The meeting began with introductions. The youngest Catholic priest stood between the pulpit and a movie screen. He held a pointer in his hand, "Can someone kill the lights, please?" he asked. His dark good looks faded into darkness and were replaced by a slide of a map showing El Salvador, Nicaragua and Guatemala.

"We are starting with the dry stuff. It will get heavy," he said, listing economic statistics for the region. He left the screen blank after the numbers faded before a slide of several hovels flashed up. "Look closely," he said. His shadow loomed on the screen as he crossed to the other side. He used the pointer. "This is an arm. You can see a rotting corpse in that pile of garbage. Sixty people were massacred in this village by the El Salvadorian government."

The next slide was a map with arrows marking refugee routes. "People hitchhike or walk to the Texas border."

"This is the Shah of Iran." The familiar face filled the screen. "He raped his country, ordered thousands killed. Our government welcomed him."

An Indian woman's face filled the screen. The priest cleared his throat. "This is Rosa Maria Gomez. She is thirty-two. She looks sixty. Her annual income was one hundred fifty dollars. She fled after government soldiers stormed her village looking for dissidents. They killed fifty, including Rosa's husband, children, and brother. She is not welcome by our government."

He had nine other faces, each with a story more horrible than the one before. When the lights came on, people blinked but said nothing. They shifted in their seats.

The next speaker was Lucy's minister, who gave the history of the sanctuary movement from the Middle Ages to the present. "Our objective is to bring these people to safety. Our second goal is to get their story to the general public. Missionaries give these victims the names of our contacts in Texas. It is not unlike the slavery underground railroad before the Civil War. This church participated in that movement. We are asking you to do it again, a century later. Injustice is injustice regardless of the time or place."

Chip Baker, Jane's minister, stood up, slowly. If people walked behind him, they might think he was an old man. When he turned around, they could see he was only in his early thirties. He suffered from a bone disease, but since he refused to talk about it, no one knew exactly what it was.

His voice projected into the silent group. "If we agree to use our church to house people, they might stay one night or a year." His hands grasped the sides of the pulpit. "Or anything in between. The Church Council approves, I approve, but because we are breaking the law, we need your approval."

His words launched a heated discussion. Shortly after midnight, a vote was taken. Two hundred ninety-five for, thirty-five against. Andy and Jane voted on different sides. They tried another vote at 1:30 a.m. Ten people had switched from the negative to the positive. Andy wasn't among them.

The twenty-five excused themselves to meet downstairs. A half an hour later they returned.

Dennis Hughes, a lawyer and a member of the church board, spoke, "We have come to an agreement that we will do nothing to undermine your activities, although we still disagree with your actions. Some of us will leave the church. I am one of them. As an officer of the court, I cannot support breaking the law."

Barbara said under her breath, "He's full of shit." Barbara was also a lawyer whose store front practice barely gave her enough to meet her basic expenses. Hughes was a partner in the third largest law firm in the city.

Walking home, because the T had stopped running, Andy said, "I can't believe you would support this insanity."

"I think it is supporting sanity," Jane replied.

Had they not been so exhausted, their discussion would have been more heated than the one in the church.

Main Man tried licking Jane's tears from her face, but she pushed him away. She sat cross-legged on the floor, surrounded by papers. The fan moved the sticky, hot air without offering much relief.

Kate had left at noon with a blanket and her friends to find a good spot on the Esplanade for the Boston Pops Fourth of July celebration. Andy was working, but their affair had been punctuated by fights since the sanctuary meeting.

She wasn't sure if it was her, him or them. He had been wonderful driving her all over New England as she searched for maple syrup, special chocolate, jams, jellies, candied fruit, apple butter, sausages, cheeses, and handicrafts. The last time they had made love was six weeks earlier, after they had met a couple who made goat's cheese outside of Stowe, Vermont. Although it was May, snow had forced them into an inn. After a dinner in front of a fireplace, they'd gone to bed where they'd laughed and tickled, all irritations between them retreating.

Back in the city, when she was once again embroiled in business plans and searching for money, the tension sprang up again along with the spring flowers. She saw less of him. He worked harder than normal, taking as many details as he could for extra money. His kid brother needed help for his Suffolk University tuition payment.

Frustration, not Andy, was the reason for Jane's tears. Despite help from the Small Business Administration, eight banks had turned down her loan application to start her business. She tried reducing her request to a smaller amount, just enough to fund the test, a cart at Quincy Market. The banks said no a second time.

She tried to get an equity loan on the house but was rejected. "Unemployed people are not good credit risks," the banker had said. The banker was a woman with a white blouse, blue suit and prissy little striped bow.

"The house is paid for, you have no risk," Jane told her, resisting the temptation to pull the tie.

"I'm sorry, you don't fit the guidelines," the banker said.

Since banks required application fees for equity loans, most which were half of her weekly unemployment check, she couldn't afford to keep applying.

"Those same banks loan millions to build an office building when there is lots of space unrented as it is, but they can't part with a lousy twenty thousand dollars for Create-a-basket," she had complained to Andy, her parents, Kate, Barbara and Julie.

"You were naive to think they would do anything. I wish

I could help," Andy said. She knew he meant it.

"Maybe you should use the same energy to find a real job with real security," her father said.

"With a good health plan," her mother added.

Jane couldn't think how to say that she'd had a real job and that hadn't offered security. As for the health plan, she wasn't about to tell her parents she used the pray-against-being-sick plan. Paul and Mary Andrews would have panicked.

Barbara and Julie just railed against the white, male establishment. Although Jane gave some credence to testosterone power structures, she knew she couldn't change them fast enough to finance her own business.

She'd thought of asking Diana, but when she called, Diana talked about how she and Maurice had just pulled out of a financial crisis. She had hung up without mentioning the subject.

All this left her on the floor, looking over everything she had done, crying and trying to figure out what next. The dog put his paw on her knee. This time she picked him up to cuddle. He melted against her body.

The smell of grilling chicken drifted into her window. She washed her face and went to the garden where Barbara and Julie were barbecuing. On the way downstairs, she wondered if she were missing something obvious.

"Juan is coming sometime within the next week," Chip Baker said to his congregation on Sunday. Murmurs rustled throughout the group seated in the boxes. People fanned themselves. The sun pouring in the clear windows made the church stifling. "We need around the clock volunteers to stay with him. There is less chance that the government will take him if there is an American with him."

At the coffee hour, Jane stood at the sign-up table. Andy took the pen from her hand, "I really don't want you to do this. I don't believe in it."

"I do, Andy."

"Even if it means the end of us?"

Jane signed her name. "We need to talk."

As they walked into the Public Gardens, a bronze George Washington appeared to look down at them from his metal horse. "Look at him, Andy. He led a revolution for what he believed."

They both kept their hands in their slacks' pockets as they crossed over the suspension bridge. A swan boat drifted underneath. The passengers on it waved. They waved back.

Andy bought two tacos and Cokes from one of the pushcart vendors. They sat on a bench to eat. A squirrel chattered, evaluating his chance of a handout. Jane broke off a small piece and tossed it to him. He ran away.

When she bit into her taco, she had trouble swallowing. She pulled the ring of her Coke can and took a swallow to wash it down.

"I think we should make a major change in our relationship, Andy."

He waited.

"I think we should go back to being just friends," Jane said.

"That's a little extreme, just because we have a political difference."

"It's only the catalyst. I'm ten years older than you. At least once a month you ask me to marry you. I don't want to be married, maybe not ever. You want a family, children. I can't have kids, and don't tell me we can adopt. I don't want to raise another child." She had raised all those issues individually, never as a shopping list.

Andy fiddled with his taco wrapper. "Is there anyone else?"

Pushing a desire to comfort him away, she wondered why he asked that question. "No. I just feel the best thing I can do is to set you free to find someone your own age."

He sat there for a time holding his taco. He threw it in the trash next to the bench, basketball style. Standing he leaned down and kissed her forehead. "I'll call you when I feel better about this. Or when I figure out how to change your mind." He gave that impish smile, which she loved so. "Whichever comes first." As Jane watched him walk away, she cried for the second time in a week.

Going through a drawer, looking for a new ribbon for her printer, Jane found the cassette recordings of her conversations with Martha. She had never needed them. Harrison hadn't disputed her unemployment claim. As she picked them up to throw them out, her hand touched an envelope marked JRP stock. She'd forgotten it. Because Martha had fired the personnel director the same week Jane was let go, no one had asked her to sell them back to the company.

Trying to remember exactly what she had read in the newspaper last week, she went to the pile waiting to go out with the trash. They were gone. "Of all the times for Kate to get so helpful," she mumbled.

She ran to the street. Opening her garbage can, she grabbed *The Boston Globe* as the truck pulled up.

The man holding onto the back dropped off next to her as she shook carrot and potato peels from the paper. He asked, "Are you going to give up your garbage, lady, or do you want to keep it?"

"All but this." She ran into the house.

The business section reported JRP was under another takeover attack from the same company. She called Reiner, Inc. After talking to three secretaries, she still hadn't reached Martin Reiner.

"Andy says I'm naive. He's right," she said to the dog. She made herself a cup of tea and took it to her bedroom where she changed before going to pick up her unemployment check.

The subway lurched and screeched toward Government Center. Leaving the gloom of the entrance, she was almost blinded by the sun. She walked by the flower seller. A few early pumpkins were among the dried wheat.

The unemployment office was crowded. She filled out her card and stood in line. Her counselor asked to see her.

"Did you have three interviews this week?" she asked, tapping her pencil on her desk. Jane thought of Martha, who had the same habit.

"Here's a list of places I sent resumes. Here are the names of people I talked to in follow-up calls." Jane didn't say she annoyed the people she had talked to, nor that she feared if anyone did offer her a job that it would kill her plans. The woman stamped her form and said, "Keep trying."

"Right," Jane said before waiting in another line for her check.

On the way home she passed the Old State House. Across the street a store had a 'for rent' sign.

Jane slammed the phone down. "Damn Andy, he's insufferable about Juan." She had told Andy she couldn't have dinner because she'd signed up to stay with Juan. It had led to a lecture. She'd told him to butt out, further straining their attempts to rebuild a friendship.

Kate came into the room and dropped her books on the counter. She tossed her jacket on the counter stool. "Andy's just trying to make your breakup easier by picking fights."

"What makes you so smart?"

"Diana told me. At the end of one of her visits, I was being really ugly to her. She told me it was OK, I just didn't want her to leave so I was trying to piss her off so we'd fight and then I'd feel better about her going."

"Piss off isn't ladylike," Mary Andrews said through Jane's mouth.

"Being ladylike doesn't get you shit."

Jane thought about correcting her daughter. "Right," she said.

Laying in bed, numbers ran around her head. Her imagination decorated and stocked the empty store she'd found. The wind blew the last of the fall leaves against her window before they fell to the ground. Reiner, Inc. hadn't answered her letter offering to sell her stock. *Probably even megalomaniacs had incompetents working for them,* was her last thought before she fell asleep . . .

Waves of color like scarves trailed by ballet dancers floated then disappeared as Jane walked into a bank. She was dressed in the fashion of the late nineteenth century and carried a parasol matching the scarves. The bank was somewhere in Wyoming.

Harrison Codrington, the teller, sat in a metal cage. He wore a vest, a stand-up collar and a visor.

Andy, in jeans and an Irish knit sweater, came in with two cocked six shooters. "This is a stick up," he said.

Harrison dumped money and tacos into a burlap potato chip

bag that Andy held out. Looking over his shoulder, Andy backed out of the bank.

As he passed Jane, he grabbed her as a hostage. He swept her up on his horse and rode out of town. About a half a mile away, he put her down and threw the taco and some money at her. He disappeared into the scarves.

When she woke, she realized she had found a way to finance her project.

"David," Jane said into the telephone. "One A, five B's and a C is not a bad report card, nor is it a reason to ground Kate." She was tempted to add, "If I ground her she can't babysit for you."

"She's capable of all A's."

"She has one A."

"In art. That doesn't count." His breath came through in puffs over the receiver.

"Kate is also in the orchestra, the band and declaims. She has her friends and her hobbies. She's a well-balanced kid."

"With those grades she'll never get a scholarship. Don't you realize prices go up every year at every university? This isn't ten years ago. With women questioning everything these days, I can't do a few extra hysterectomies to pay for it."

"Right," Jane said.

Harrison agreed to drive in from Concord to meet Jane for coffee on Saturday in the middle of October. They chose *Au Bon Pain* in Harvard Square. Students milled around, drinking coffee, studying, and talking. The chess tables outside were filled, as players took advantage of the Indian summer day.

Harrison scooted between the tables. He carried a red plastic tray with two cappuccinos and two croissants. "It's strange seeing you in jeans and a sweater," she said to him. He had slimmed down considerably since his divorce. With his gray hair and Van Dyke beard, she thought he looked quite handsome.

He sat, making a four with one foot resting on the knee of his other leg. His hand traced the markings of the well-tooled leather of his boot. "I'm becoming the gentleman farmer. There are times I hate to leave the country to come to work."

She bit into her croissant. Crumbs, so many beige snow-flakes, floated onto the marble tabletop.

They watched the chess players at the next table. It was a timed game. Each moved quickly hitting the clock when done. Both the clock and the squares had been built into the table.

"Do you play?" he asked.

"David showed me the moves. I never can think far enough ahead."

"At work, you never had trouble thinking ahead. Anne is good, but not as good as you were. However, she handles Martha better." As he stirred his cup, steam escaped from the Styrofoam. The cream flaked with chocolate disappeared into the liquid. "Why did you want to see me?"

"Reiner offered me ten thousand dollars for my stock."

Harrison started. "I didn't think you had any. We always buy it back."

"Oversight. Comes from random firings. Things slip through the cracks."

The older of the two chess players said, "Check." The younger nodded and protected his king.

"Do you hate me enough to sell it to them?" Harrison asked.

"If I hated you I wouldn't have called you. You were very good to me."

"I tried to be fair."

"Also, I made a lot of money for JRP," Jane said. She glanced at the chessboard. The young player lost a castle. "Do you want the stock?"

Harrison's eyes opened just enough to show he wanted it. The rest of his face remained immobile. He leaned forward.

"I could match their offer."

"Harrison, I'll be honest," she crossed her fingers under the table. "I need fifteen thousand dollars. I want to start a business."

"I'm listening."

"It'll be called Create-a-Basket. People will buy a basket, then fill it with special cheeses, chocolate, jams, coffees, teas, etc. Price will depend on how big a basket and how much is it in. Sort of a *dim sum* of gift giving. I've found the perfect location for a store."

"Lots of stores fail, Jane."

"That's just part of my idea. I want to sell to businesses in place of the usual alcohol or flowers they give at holidays or for Secretary's Day. Someday I'll advance to mail order. I've identified all the products I want. The only thing I don't have is the money." She lifted her cup to her lips. It was hot enough to make her tongue feel fuzzy.

"The bank . . ."

Jane choked on her cappuccino, spewing liquid onto the crumbs. Harrison patted her back. When she regained control she said, "Banks aren't for start up operations." She told him her experiences.

284

Harrison dabbed at the table with his napkin and nodded. "I'll buy your stock at eleven thousand dollars."

"I need fifteen thousand. I don't want it to go to Reiner, because they'll destroy the business. Even if I sold it to Martha, I'm sure she'd turn it over to him. When I left I remember hearing through the grapevine that with just a bit more stock you'd have almost the controlling interest—at least if your older son continues to vote with you."

"Let me buy us lunch," Harrison said. "My treat."

Jane watched the chess players maneuver without either gaining or losing ground. She saw Harrison inside waiting in the line for two hot chicken tarragon sandwiches on baguettes.

He was back quickly. "Have you a business plan?" He saw her look. "Of course you have. May I see it sometime?"

Jane pulled it out of her Kenya bag. "I carry it around in case I run into a funding source."

The two sandwiches grew cold as Harrison flipped through the pages. "I should have known it would be thorough."

Jane said nothing. The older chess player lost his knight but captured the younger one's in the next move.

"I can only go to eleven thousand dollars."

Jane wiped her mouth on the napkin. "Then tell me which is better for you—Reiner or Martha?"

"Bishop to queen," said the younger player.

Harrison said nothing, but flipped through the pages of the business plan again. Jane said nothing. She had no more moves.

"This plan has absolutely no fat in it, no areas for surprise," Harrison said.

"I know that. I didn't dare add anything extra."

He took out a pad of paper and scribbled on it. "I tell

you what, eleven thousand for your stock, and I'll go to my banker for a personal fifteen thousand dollar line of credit for you. They'll do it if I cosign. Fair enough?"

Jane slumped into her chair. Working day and night, she could get the place open before the Christmas rush. As she said, "All right," the younger player echoed the words in her head. "Checkmate."

Jane dragged herself up the stairs and, still fully clothed, fell across her bed. For the past week she had put in eighteen hour days getting the store ready to open.

Everything took longer than she'd expected. Where she calculated an hour to buy the shelving, it had taken her three. When she expected the electricity to be turned on, it wasn't.

Lucy had come down to help, showing up that morning without an invitation. Jane had heard a knock at the door and there was her old boss dressed in work clothes. "What do I do?" Lucy asked brushing past Jane. By dinner time, her sixty-eight years showed.

When Jane noticed her friend paling, she told her to go home. As Lucy put on her down jacket, Jane said, "I wish you'd let me pay you."

Lucy put her hands on her hips. "No way, Jose." Her voice boomed off the empty walls. "You can't do this on your own. So until you can afford to hire people, I'm your helper. Just give me room and board. Oh, I already dropped all my things off at your house. I forgot to tell you."

Jane opened the door to let Lucy out. The new lock was sticky.

Before she could say anything appreciative, Lucy put her dirty hand over Jane's mouth. "I haven't had this much fun since I retired," she said shutting the door firmly behind her.

★ ★ ★ ★ ★

Kate organized her friends into a *let's-help-my-mother-set-up-the-store* party. Three girls and two guys, part of Kate's gang, the same kids who hung out at the house, slept over and confided more secrets than Jane wanted to know, arrived Saturday morning. They found Jane on a ladder preparing the wall for a mural Kate had designed.

"Kate sent us and said not to listen to you when you protested," the tallest girl said as Kate arrived with a bag of Egg McMuffins and a big pot to brew coffee. She directed the team.

By nightfall, everything was painted and the shelving assembled. Freezers that Jane and Lucy had strained to move slid easily across the floor when pushed by teenage hulks.

"I can't believe it," Jane kept saying as she looked around at what she thought was going to take over two weeks. "I can open as soon as my merchandise arrives." With tears running down her face she said, "Kate, kids, Lucy, you're . . . you're . . ."

"Don't get soppy, Mom," Kate said.

"Right," Jane said wiping her eyes with the back of her hand.

A week and a half after opening, Lucy said, "You need to make sales calls if you want to capture the Christmas business. If you can continue to give me a room, I'll mind the shop, even make some phone calls and get you appointments."

The thought of a polite protest almost crossed Jane's lips, when she realized how much she needed Lucy.

"Just continue feeding me," Lucy said.

"It might be cheaper to pay you," Jane said.

Even with Lucy's help, Jane's days began at five in the

morning and seldom ended before ten at night. When things were slow in the shop, she spent the time making the mini-baskets she used in place of business cards when making cold sales calls.

Orders began coming in from old vendors. The printer who had given her Scotch for five straight Christmases placed a five thousand dollar order.

Lucy convinced their old envelope vendor to tie in the size of the basket with the size of the account. "I missed arm twisting when I was sitting around Down East," she cackled.

November 18 had been an OK day for walk-in trade. Jane got in the house a little before ten. The house was dark. A note on the couch said that Lucy had taken the dog out before going to bed. Jane went directly upstairs, dropping her clothes as she went.

No sooner had her head hit the pillow when Kate popped through the door. "Have you got the energy to relate to your daughter?"

"OK." She forced her eyes to stay open as Kate talked about her selection for the next declamation, her Latin homework, the problems she was having with trigonometry, the cute senior who didn't know she existed. Jane made the proper hmms, ohs, and ahs to satisfy her daughter. The phone rang.

"Who'd call this late?" She rolled over and picked up the receiver. It was a *Garfield* phone that Diana had sent her as a good luck gift for the store's opening.

"Sorry Jane, but I'm desperate," Barbara said. "I'm suppose to take Juan to a presentation tomorrow, but I've a client who was just arrested and I need to be in court."

Juan? Juan? . . . Jane thought. Then she remembered. The Guatemalan at the church. Everything but the store had been driven out of her mind. She'd even forgotten to vote for Mondale, although it wouldn't have made any difference. Reagan won every state but Mondale's home state of Minnesota.

"What about Julie?"

"She's in bed with the flu. Honest, I've tried everyone."

"I can cut class," Kate mouthed.

"No you can't," Jane said to her daughter. "What about his translator?"

"Part of the group where he's going. *The Globe* is covering it."

"What time?" Jane said wondering if she'd ever learn to say no. But after Kate left, after her eyes closed, she realized that under any other circumstances she'd have been more active in what she believed was right.

Jane waved at Chip as she passed his office. The minister called to her. When she entered, he gave her a list of instructions. She then headed downstairs where Juan slept in a makeshift area.

To make the Guatemalan more comfortable, the church had added a shower and put in a television. Two members gave him English lessons. He, in turn, did odd jobs around the church. She found Juan dressed in khakis and a sweater. He wore sneakers and carried a coat that they had pulled out of rummage sale donations. He regularly expressed shock at the New England cold.

Jane quickly read over the committee instructions on how to take Juan out for a speaking engagement. She left, not by the front door, but the west side door and glanced around the alley. No one was there. The wall next to the church was solid brick. Reaching the street, she looked around. The only person visible was a Japanese tourist photographing the church.

She'd already bought subway tokens. She and Juan held hands until they reached Boston College, where he was speaking.

Throughout his talk she concentrated not on him, but the things she should be doing. The question and answer period went longer than planned. She found herself growing annoyed when *The Globe* reporter ducked out before the end. *I'm just getting crotchety in my old age,* she thought, glancing yet again at her watch and wondering if it needed a new battery.

It was five thirty. She had lost almost the whole day. On the way back her only thoughts were of getting rid of Juan and heading to the store. She was so engrossed in her plans that she didn't notice the man coming out of the church until it was too late.

"You are under arrest." He slapped handcuffs on her.

"Run, Juan," she screamed. The last thing she saw as the policeman put his hand on her head as he shoved her in the cruiser was Juan being chased.

The holding cell was dingy. A woman, totally wrapped in a blanket, a gray-haired papoose, slept on the bottom bunk. She stank of alcohol and urine.

Jane sat on the one stool, trying to control her terror. All the movies she'd seen of cells didn't compare to the reality. It was too small to pace in. There was a toilet, but anyone walking by could see her peeing.

She wondered how long she would have to spend there. It was better she didn't know, because she could hope that any moment someone would respond to the message she'd left on her answering machine.

The movies didn't lie about allowing one phone call or about a policeman reading her rights. However, no one questioned her. She almost wished they would. Anything would be better than feeling abandoned.

No one came near her. She listened to the noises from other cells she couldn't see. Doors clanked. Footsteps echoed. Jane had never felt so desolate, so alone.

At one point, she wasn't sure of the time, because they'd taken her watch. She climbed into the top bunk. There was no sheet. Her back ached from sitting on the stool.

The one blanket on the bunk didn't take away the cold. As she lay in the gloom she kept trying to tell herself this was better than being an Iranian hostage or a Vietnam POW. It didn't make her any less scared. Maybe she slept, but she couldn't have said for sure.

"You're going to your arraignment, not a fashion show," the matron said when Jane asked for a face cloth and towel the next morning. Unlike the ugly, old matron last night, this one was about Jane's age and a knockout. It made Jane feel even grubbier.

As Jane's escort arrived to drive her to the court house, her cell mate began having convulsions. The matron rushed by, saying, "Shit, shit, shit." The cop escorting her requested help as they passed the entry desk.

In the cruiser, she said, "I don't have a lawyer."

"Don't worry," he said. "The court will appoint one if you can't afford it."

Don't worry, she thought. *That's about as stupid as a dentist or a gyn telling you to relax as they stand with their instruments poised to attack.*

The court room was not that different from the one of Jane's divorce. Since her arraignment was one of many being heard, most of the seats were taken. As she looked through the audience she spotted Andy and Kate. That was the first time in four months she'd seen Andy. He waggled his fingers at her as if he were across the room at a party. Jane's eyes opened wide. He moved his hand up and down several times as if to say, "Keep calm."

Jane concentrated on not throwing up as she listened to the arraignments of two prostitutes, a black for robbery, an Irish kid for vandalism and three drug cases.

As they called her name, she stood up, not knowing what else to do. A man dressed in a suit that was perfectly fitted and pressed, came forth and started speaking—apparently for her—to the judge. She couldn't hear what he was saying.

"Bail at five thousand dollars," the judge said.

The lawyer led her to a conference room. "I'm Douglas Mader, the UUA Attorney. Don't worry."

"Easy for you to say," she said, deciding that when someone said don't worry, that was the time to start. Her hands were hidden under the table so he couldn't see them shaking. She still wanted to throw up, but there was nothing in her stomach.

"This is a church issue," he said, "although they've great photos of you and Juan leaving the alley. Some government group broke into the church and rifled through the records. Juan's folder was left on the table."

"What happens next?" she asked focusing on the hand-kerchief in his breast pocket. It matched his tie.

"The case will probably be continued for years until it's dropped."

"I haven't much money, how can I pay you?"

"The church is taking care of it."

Andy and Kate waited for her outside the conference room. "My mother, the jail bird," Kate said as she kissed her mother.

"Don't say it," Jane said to Andy.

"I wasn't going to say *I told you so*," Andy said. He handed her a copy of *The Boston Globe* which had the story about Juan's talk, her arrest and the raid on the church. "I don't have to. At least I could prove that we're still friends when it counts."

As she walked into the house, Lucy, Barbara, Julie in pajamas, Chip Baker, and several of the church members applauded. "A welcome home party," Lucy said.

Jane cried. Not having eaten for twenty-four hours, she accepted some potato salad and ham. Five minutes later she excused herself to throw up.

David made notices about getting custody of Kate until the girl told him she wanted to stay with her mother. "I'm old enough so the court will listen to what I want."

Harrison called. "What do you need?"

"Nothing, except more time in the day."

Like all news stories, Jane's died when it was replaced by stories of a woman gunned down as she robbed a bank, and a painting vandalized at the Museum of Fine Arts. Juan made it safely to Canada.

As Christmas approached, Jane and Lucy couldn't work fast enough to keep up with the orders. Kate came in after school and Julie and Barbara helped where they could. Even Anne dropped in after work to pack baskets. "If this keeps up, I'll be able to hire someone part time," Jane said.

Christmas Eve, Lucy caught a Greyhound Bus to Maine for a week of rest. Jane's parents arrived carrying all the makings for Christmas dinner.

"Can we at least open the stockings tonight?" Kate asked.

"Excellent idea," Paul said.

Kate had sculpted a small clay statue of Main Man. Jane found it wrapped in bubble paper, then in red wrap, stuck in the toe of her stocking. As Jane put it on the mantle she remembered she'd hadn't sent Diana The Card.

After everyone had gone to bed, she dug it out of her third desk drawer. She chewed on her pen as she thought of all the possibilities. Finally she wrote, "This year was a bitch, but at least I'm out of jail." When she took the dog for a walk the next morning, she dropped it in the mail box.

1985:
Florida

"Are you sure you're OK?" Diana said into the telephone as her dish of Ben & Jerry's Heath Bar ice cream melted next to the phone.

"I'm sure," Jane said.

"Imagine—you in jail. Beats anything I ever did."

"But Diana, I wasn't competing," Jane said. "How are things with you?"

"So perfect it scares me."

They chatted for an hour. By the time Diana hung up, the ice cream was soup. She threw it down the garbage disposal on her way to tell Maurice Jane's news.

Glancing through the kitchen window she saw him asleep on the chaise lounge by the pool with the Sunday paper across his chest and his glasses halfway down his nose. God, I love that man. *He's lost weight,* she thought. *And I've gained what he's lost.* She picked up *Lake Wobegon Days* and went to the bedroom to read until dinner time.

"Maria, Tom, great writing," Diana said. "They'll shit at City Hall when they read it." The two reporters glowed. "Get back to work. You're only as good as your last story."

"Well, that's why we came in. There's a story we wanta

follow," Maria said. She had a heavy Spanish accent, although she wrote English as if it were her mother tongue.

"Lay it on me."

Using his hands to support himself, Tom leaned over Diana's desk. "I just bought a new car."

"That doesn't make a story," she said.

"Let me finish," he said. "I got a really good deal by negotiating the original price down."

Maria put her hand on Tom's. "Wait a minute. Let me get a word in."

Tom's gesture gave her the go ahead.

She nodded her appreciation. "Since I was looking for a new car, I thought I'd go to the same dealer."

"If everyone is buying new cars maybe I'm paying y'all too much," Diana leaned back in her chair to watch her two youngest reporters.

Tom and Maria shook their heads. "Nahhh," they said one after another.

Maria continued. "Anyway the model I wanted cost too much, so I looked at the one Tom got. I knew what he paid. The salesman told me the starting price was $500 higher than Tom said it was." Maria perched on the edge of Diana's desk. "Then the bastard said he couldn't negotiate. I don't know if that was because I'm Cuban or a woman. Or both."

Diana nodded her head. "So present the idea at our Story Conference this afternoon."

Tom ruffled through the last three editions of the paper, folding them to where he wanted and said, "Problem. It was the Grey Agency."

"Holy shit," Diana said. Each edition he had put on her desk carried two full-page ads for Grey.

"I'll talk to Maurice before the SC this afternoon,"

Diana said. She walked across the pressroom but found her husband's office was empty. She dug through his debris to find his agenda. Glancing first at her watch, she checked at the entry for 11:00 a.m. It said, "see P.E.-A" which made no sense to her. She whipped back through the agenda and found that every other Tuesday at 11:00 a.m. he saw P.E.-A.

Had he a mistress—the stereotypical Frenchman sneaking off for regular illicit sex? she wondered. It would explain the extra tenderness combined with their reduced sex life. The preoccupation. No, she decided, there were other explanations—like physical exercises—athletics. He could be going to the gym. That would explain the weight loss.

Thirteen reporters sat around the conference table with notebooks and pens and cups of coffee. Maria doodled with her red and blue felt pens. Maurice arrived as Diana rapped on the table.

"So what's the story?" Diana asked.

"Grey's discrimination," Maria repeated what she'd said that morning.

"But aren't they the paper's biggest advertiser?" Bobby Jo asked.

Maurice said, "Let us find out what we have for news first. Then we will decide what to do about it."

Everyone talked at once.

"Does only Grey do it?"

"Was it only that salesman?"

"Is it just that salesman was a sleaze ball or is it agency policy?"

"One at a time," Diana hollered. She wrote on the flip chart all unanswered questions. Turning towards Maurice she asked, "How much of our income is from Grey's?"

"Twenty-eight percent for this paper." Maurice reached

for his calculator before continuing. "And fifteen percent of the regionals. The question is, if there is a story, can we ethically refuse to do it?"

Diana looked at each reporter. She noticed Maria's eyes were almost closed, the expression that meant she was working out an idea. "Maria?"

"What if we start a consumer investigative feature. We could kick it off by testing all the Sarasota car dealers, go on to funeral parlors or something. Like every Monday, we'll investigate a new industry. Report if we find 'em clean, too. That way we aren't picking on Grey's or car dealerships."

"Brilliant," Maurice said. "Give me the methodology."

"Tom and I go to every car dealer in town, see the same sales person, try and make a deal on the same car at each agency. No trade-in because that would mean using different cars."

"It's race-sex discrimination, not car trade-in value discrimination we're looking for," Diana said. "Good thinking."

Everyone started talking again. Diana raised her hand for silence. Nothing. She pounded on the table. Finally she screamed, "SHUT UP!" They did. "Let's give 'em more of a chance. Four people do it. Damian, you're black, and Leah, you're a WASP woman. And I want all of you dressed in suits when you go in."

Maurice stood up. "I know the meeting isn't over, but I need to call our sales people together to figure out how to replace the lost advertising."

Diana arrived home before Maurice and looked into the refrigerator. Sometimes she wondered how he stood her after Solange's super woman management of career and home. However, if he hadn't made a negative comparison, she wasn't calling attention to it. She dialed the take-out Chinese restaurant.

"Chin's Take Out," the owner answered.

"Hello, I'd like to place an order."

"Good evening, Mrs. DuBois. What do you and your husband want tonight?"

Usually they ate at the kitchen counter. As Diana grabbed two paper plates, she changed her mind. Covering the dining room table with the Catalan tablecloth and napkins which they'd bought in Argelès, she placed chop sticks next to the plates.

After the delivery man left, she emptied the white paper containers into serving dishes for nuking when Maurice came in. As she searched for something to give their dinner more ambience, her eye rested on the candle holder shaped like a ball. It took a four-drawer, two-closet hunt before she found the ten pencil-thin candles to fill it.

When Maurice walked in, she hugged him. As he glanced over Diana's shoulder, he asked, "What is the reason for the fancy table?"

"Because," she said.

"Good enough for me."

As they ate, they discussed the new feature. They had once agreed to separate their working and living worlds. It had led to awkward starts and stops in conversation for the two days the agreement lasted.

"How did the sales meeting go?" she asked as she read her fortune cookie. It said, "Prepare for a change."

Maurice had only picked at his dinner but snapped his cookie in two. "They have some ideas. New special supplements, travel, etc. Toni has been working on getting more nationals. She is putting together a co-op plan."

He looked at his fortune and shoved it in his pocket.

"What does it say?" Going behind him, she put her arms around his neck and kissed his tiny bald spot.

"Don't keep secrets from loved ones."

"We don't have secrets." She picked up the dirty plates and carried them to the kitchen.

He followed with the glasses. "I have a secret. We need to talk."

She wiped her hands on the dish towel. He guided her to the living room couch. Opening and closing his mouth several times, he finally said, "This is so hard."

There is another woman flashed through her mind—someone with elegance and style.

"I have cancer. Of the lungs."

"You can't. I won't allow it," she snapped back.

He caressed her face. "You are a very powerful woman, *Chérie,* however, some things are beyond even your power."

Diana walked to the double glass doors and stared into the night. She could see nothing in the dark, not the canal, not the swamp, not her future. His reflection loomed in the glass. She felt herself being turned. *I should be helping him,* she thought. "We'll fight it. Chemo, transplants, whatever."

"It is too late. It is too far along."

Hundreds of small details that she'd ignored, pushed their way into her consciousness. She saw Maurice coughing and unable to catch his breath, pushing his dinner aside, falling asleep at his desk, his terrible color. "You've known for a while."

He nodded.

"How long?"

"Six months. I wanted—"

"Six months! Bullshit! What fucking right did you have to keep this from me?" She screamed more at fate than at him.

Maurice collapsed on the sofa. "Mostly I wanted to pretend our life was as normal as long as possible. As long as you did not know, I could pretend it was not really true."

"Oh God." She rushed to him. As they held each other, Diana felt as if a chop stick had been shoved down her throat. She knew it would stay there a long time.

"Here are the stats, Boss. I put 'em on the spread sheet." Maria handed Diana a disk. "Look at how consistent they are. The white male makes the best deal, the black male second, then comes the white female, then yours truly."

"Garcia Subaru is the only exception," Diana said scrolling through the figures.

"That salesman asked me out to dinner."

"No way to build that into the stats," Diana said. "Now call each of them and get a statement. Give 'em every chance to defend themselves."

Instead of getting up, Maria asked, "You OK? You seem distracted."

"Sorry. I am. Go to work."

Dr. Philip Eton-Amesbury's waiting room was filled with the walking dead. Although he'd lost another two pounds, Maurice looked robust in comparison to those hunched in their chairs. Maurice patted Diana's fist as the nurse ushered them into the doctor's office.

They sat in the two chairs in front of the largest desk Diana had ever seen. The doctor strode in. He was a head taller than Diana and straw thin. It looked as if his head had grown through his remaining strands of hair. His white coat covered jeans, and he had on a pair of cowboy boots. His Texan style didn't match his English name or accent.

Maurice did the introductions then said, "I will leave

you with my wife. I do not need to hear this story again."

Dr. Eton-Amesbury sat down. He folded his arms on his desk and looked directly into Diana's eyes. "Your husband said you are having trouble accepting this."

A long breath escaped her body. "I'm pissed off. I don't know at what I . . . I . . . I . . . just can't accept it's hope—"

"Hopeless? There are two kinds of hope, Mrs. DuBois. Realistic and unrealistic. There are spontaneous remissions and miracles. Unfortunately, they fall into unrealistic hopes. I never tell someone not to keep a spark of hope alive, but to expect it makes it harder for everyone."

"But chemo, diet . . ."

Dr. Eton-Amesbury slapped up three chest X-rays on the light box behind his desk. "These were taken in August, October and last week." He took his pencil and pointed to dark spots. "Both lungs are involved. If it had been one, we might have had a chance to take it out. Notice the growth."

"Why no chemo?"

"Your husband refused."

She knew why. He'd once said of Solange's last few months, "If I had it to do over again, I would have talked her out of chemo. It is all I regret."

"Your husband has told me you're the kind of woman who needs to do something." He wrote out an address. "This is a support group for people caring for those with terminal illnesses. They have two more places for the one that starts next week. I suggest you call."

Diana shoved the paper in her briefcase. The word "terminal" rolled around in her brain, an out-of-control bowling ball battering everything in sight.

Although the phone rested off the hook on Diana's desk, she heard every word that Phil Grey yelled. Periodically she leaned to the mouthpiece and made proper comments. When he'd finished venting, she picked up the receiver.

"Phil, I know you are upset, but we surveyed all the agencies. We didn't target yours."

"I'm pulling every bit of advertising."

"That's your right. However, even if you don't consider production costs, we're cheaper than either radio or TV."

"You are a bitch."

"Of course I am," she said.

Maria and Tom had come in to listen. Diana rolled her eyes. "Phil, if you want to start a fair sticker price policy, we'll give you coverage. I'm going to make the same offer to all the . . ." She looked at the receiver. "He hung up."

Diana walked into Sarasota Hospital. A candy striper sat behind the reception desk, dredging up unwanted memories of Jim's operation. *I could really learn to hate hospitals,* she thought. Before she asked for the Cancer Support Group, she saw a sign saying the group was meeting in the third floor conference room. When she got there, a small woman drew her in.

"Welcome, I'm Betty, your facilitator. Go help yourself to coffee and a muffin."

Ten people, besides Betty, sat down. "Let's go around the table and say who we are and who we are caring for."

"I'm Bob. My wife has ovarian cancer. She starts chemo next week."

"I'm Melanie. My daughter just lost her second breast. She's gone into a depression."

"I'm Diana. My husband has lung cancer."

The names and stories continued until all six women and four men were identified.

Betty, who had been taking notes, looked up. "We'll

meet twice a week for ten weeks. When I talked to each of you on the phone I asked you to make a commitment to all meetings, the only exception being medical emergencies. We'll get to know each other at a level you can't imagine tonight. There's another commitment I'm asking: be honest about what you're feeling. Do you agree?"

She looked at each person. After they nodded she continued. "We have four ground rules. One, you can say whatever you feel. Two, don't tell others what they feel. Three, don't tell others what they *should* feel. Four, you don't put down anyone else for what they say, do or think."

Bob had a crew cut. Diana bet he was ex-military. "Isn't that contradictory. How can I be honest if I disagree."

Betty said, "It's how you do it. For example, if one says, 'I just want to run away', you can't say, 'Aren't you terrible, you shouldn't feel like that.' What you can say is something like, 'I haven't felt like that, yet.' Get it?"

He nodded.

"Who'll kick off?" Betty asked.

People looked at the ceiling, their hands, out the window. The woman who'd identified herself as Karen stirred her coffee, although she had added no sugar or milk. She said, "I'm scared. When he dies, I don't know how I am going to support our kids."

After Karen spoke, the talk flowed. By the time the evening was over, Diana knew she had once again found what she needed when she needed it.

As Diana lay next to Maurice, she listened to him wheeze. Had he not been ill, she would have found the noise upsetting. Because she didn't know how long he would be there to make the sound, she savored it. He turned over and threw his arm over her. She covered it with hers.

At breakfast the next morning, she twisted oranges, getting the last drop of juice out. When Maurice coughed in the other room, she stopped to listen, the chopstick splintering inside her.

As he walked into the kitchen, he stuffed his handkerchief into his pocket. Both pretended they didn't see the blood on it. She poured his espresso and put the juice on the counter. He picked up of one of the two newspapers. Sitting on the stool, he read the headlines and sipped his coffee.

Diana took her usual notes, although her concentration was scattered. She munched on a piece of toast.

"Do you think we could arrange things for a few days in Argelès?" Maurice asked.

"If you want it, we'll do it."

Diana found a parking place near the entrance of the arrivals area of the airport. She was late. As she rushed in, Bill Reed stood by the carousel his two suitcases by his side. He had lost weight and had the pallor of those cooped up during winter months.

"Diana, I am so sorry," was the first thing he said to her.

She shrugged. "I really appreciate you coming back to help."

"I couldn't do anything but."

Tante Jeanne kissed them on both cheeks. "You've lost weight, Maurice. Probably American food," she said.

The couple unlocked their door. Maurice went straight to bed, exhausted from the flight.

Diana rushed to the shops before they closed, turning up her collar against the *Tramontane* blowing leaves and paper into her face.

Maurice slept through the wind rattling the casement

window and Diana dropping the logs as she tried to start the fire. He woke the next day with an energy that Diana had not seen for over a month.

After he devoured the better part of a baguette, he put on his sweater and pulled the Renault out of the garage. The battery was dead. As Diana puttered in the kitchen she could hear Maurice asking a neighbor to help him jump start it. She heard the engine choke then turn over.

"Beach?" he mouthed the word through the window.

Diana dried her hands and put her coat on. Dusty dishes weren't important. Behind the beach the shops, unlike those in the village, were not open year round. This April day several owners were painting them, preparing for the onslaught of spring and summer tourists.

"Look at the white caps," she said. They sat on the stairs leading to the sand. To their right they could see the mountains and the medieval towers that once protected the region. Diana paid more attention to her husband's color than to the scenery. "Glad you're back?" His smile gave her the answer.

During the first four days, Maurice seemed to gain strength. Diana called Bill to see if he could stay on another week.

"How about if I stay as long as you need me?" he asked.

"Bless you," she said and hung up.

Maurice slept until afternoon on most days. When he woke they took small trips: to Collioure to walk along the sea wall, to the *crêperie* restaurant in the mountains next to a stream, to Banyuls to look at the new aquarium.

"It is time to go home," Maurice said. They had been there two days under two weeks.

"Would you rather stay here?"

"No. There is no time."

★ ★ ★ ★ ★

The return flight left Maurice exhausted. He stopped going to the paper and stayed home to watch television. When Diana came home at night he told her what Phil Donahue had said to the transvestite or how many *Jeopardy* questions he had answered. She told him about the latest advertising campaign.

"There's someone to see you," the receptionist said. Betty appeared at Diana's door two minutes later. The last time Diana had seen the facilitator was at the group's last meeting, the night before she and Maurice had left for Argelès.

The woman refused offers of tea, coffee, Coke. "How are you?"

"Holding together. Barely."

Betty reached out and patted Diana's hand. "Bob's wife is doing OK. So is Melanie's." After Diana acknowledged the remark with a nod, Betty said, "But Karen's husband died, which is why I am here. Could you give her a job?"

"What can she do?"

"Nothing. She never worked. Went from high school to having babies."

"Why not?" Diana called her personnel director in and told him to set up an appointment with Karen. "Find something for her even if we have to send her to some kind of training program."

Maurice's suitcase rested on the hospital bed. A nurse breezed in. "Do we need help getting settled?" she asked. Both he and Diana shook their heads. The nurse pointed to a button. "Call if you need me."

The window looked onto the parking lot. "Nice view," he said. He sat on the bed. Diana unpacked his suitcase for him. She had bought him several new pairs of pajamas after he had told her how much he hated hospital gowns. These had large blue and smaller yellow stripes.

She saw goose bumps on his skin as he changed. Finding the air conditioning dial, she turned it down. Outside it was over a hundred with ninety-eight percent humidity. When she had entered the hospital, the walk from the parking lot to the entrance had caused her to sweat despite the double squirt of antiperspirant.

She had dropped Maurice at the entrance supposedly to start filling out forms. In reality, she knew the walk from the parking lot would have exhausted him.

Holding the sheet up, he climbed into the bed. She fluffed his pillow and resting her hand on his forehead, she said, "You can still come home. We can rent a hospital bed, an oxygen . . ."

He reached for her hand. "We have been over it. When I am gone, I want you to remember our home as where I lived, not died." He closed his eyes. She remembered him telling her how he had walked around Solange's hospital bed in the living room for a month after it had been removed.

The nurse fastened a tube with oxygen into his nose. Her chopstick choked until she wanted to grab some of the oxygen for herself. She sat and watched him sleep.

He woke briefly and whispered, "Go home. Come back tomorrow." He slept again and did not wake when her lips touched his forehead.

The gods chose the moment she left the front doors of the hospital to drop a torrential rainstorm. By the time Diana reached the car, she was drenched to her underwear. Opening her bag, she couldn't find her car keys. The contents of her bag absorbed the water. Diana leaned against the car and cried in rhythm with the rain. "I'm so fucking sick of being strong," she wailed. Her answer was a jagged exclamation of lightning, cutting the sky in two. Diana felt as torn apart.

"Can I help you, Ma'am?" a security guard held a *Sarasota Journal* over his head. Her newspaper was a useless umbrella. He was as wet as she was.

"I lost my key," she said, thinking of serial killers like Ted Bundy who approached victims in parking lots.

"Take your time," the guard said. He held his hand out to hold things as she pulled them out of her bag. Nothing. Then she checked her jeans pocket. It was there.

As she drove home the sun came out, and by the time she turned into their drive all the puddles had been absorbed back into the humidity. She still was drenched, and even though it was only 6:30 p.m. she took a shower and went to bed.

"I don't know how much more I can take, Bill," she said several weeks later. Since visiting hours didn't start until 11:00 a.m., she had gone into the office, where she picked up papers and put them down again without acting on anything.

"You'll take whatever you have to," he said. He patted her hand. "I'm giving you another problem. The personnel director doesn't want to bother you. Karen."

"What about her?"

"She's a disaster. She'd been filing for three months before anyone discovered she's dyslexic. It's going to take months to straighten the morgue out. She can't be on the telephone because she can't get a phone number straight. We all play guess who called."

I don't want to deal with this, was what Diana thought.

What she said was, "Send her in."

Karen came in and sat in front of her. She hid her hands but not before Diana saw the nails bitten as far back as they could go. "You're going to fire me," was the first thing she said.

"I let the personnel director do that, but we have to do something with you. I can't afford keeping nonproductive people or people who create work."

"I understand," the young woman said. "Especially with ads down."

Diana thought of the way Karen had been in the support group—warm. Mostly she always found the right words to say to others, even when she couldn't find them for herself.

"I have a crazy idea. Ever think of selling?"

"I'd be terrified."

"Think about it."

"You hate me," Toni said. She was the ad manager. "You put every obstacle in my way. You piss off our best advertisers, you refuse cigarette ads. Because we have the highest circulation ever, you raise our rates. Now you're giving me Typhoid Karen."

Toni, a former stripper, had been one of the people Jim Bourque saved. She separated advertisers from their money like she once separated herself from her clothes. In both cases she delivered whatever was promised.

"Try it three months, till after Thanksgiving."

"You're Jim's kid, all right." Toni took out a cigarette. As she searched for a match, she saw Diana staring at it. "Sorry." She put it back in the case.

"How much longer can he go on?" Diana asked Dr. Eton-Amesbury. They were seated in a conference room so small, Diana could touch both walls when she stood in the middle.

The doctor folded himself around a chair. He toyed with his stethoscope. He shrugged as he began to talk. "I didn't expect him to survive until Veterans Day. Now Christmas is a week away."

They walked to the hospital bed. Even an old friend wouldn't have recognized Maurice. Tubes put fluids into his body and other tubes let them out again. He hadn't spoken for four days. Diana went up and took his yellowed hand, "Maurice, Love?" Sometimes when she spoke to him, his eyelids flickered, but today she got no response.

"Go home and rest. Go to work. Do something not related to sickness," the doctor said to her.

She still stayed until the nurse arrived and said, "Visiting hours ended an hour ago." They both knew she knew. For the last week they'd stretched the rules as much as they could, feigning surprise when they found her next to his bed.

On the way home Diana passed Marina Jack's. The paper's Christmas party was just beginning inside. She decided to wish her staff a Merry Christmas. They all stopped talking when she walked in.

"You look like hell," Bill said. "But we're glad you're here."

She looked at her staff. Karen was missing. "I don't want to spoil your fun, but I wanted to say thanks for all you've done." The chopstick wouldn't let her say more.

Someone handed her a glass of champagne. Tom proposed a toast, then looked stricken when "Merry Christmas" fell from his lips.

"It's OK." Diana smiled at him. No reason the rest of the world couldn't live normally. "I'm going home," she said to Bill.

"I'll walk you to the car," he said, but Toni interrupted. "I'll do it," she said.

Passing the fish tanks with the live lobsters, Diana said, "You fired Karen?"

"No. She's not here because she couldn't afford a babysitter. Actually, she's working out. Not great, but she's carrying her own weight." In the parking lot, Toni shut the door after Diana got in, "I just wanted to tell you, our sales are up 11 percent this month. With so much on your mind, I want to make sure you know that Bill and I are taking care of . . ."

Diana patted the woman's hand, "Thank you." For the first time in her life she didn't care what happened to the paper.

Diana sat next to Maurice's bed. Tomorrow night was New Year's Eve. Last New Year's Eve they had stayed home and watched the ball descend in Times Square because he loved it. "It is so American, *Chérie*," he'd said. He hadn't been conscious since Christmas Day.

Suddenly his monitor flat lined. Two nurses ran in. She had given the order "Do Not Resuscitate" two weeks ago. Detached, she stood back, her hand across her mouth. Then she picked up her bag and went into the hall.

December 1986: Boston

"This is really something." Paul Andrews wandered around the store. He picked up a chocolate Santa made with various shades of chocolate. "It's like a sculpture."

Jane wrote out the sale price and put it in over the original. "A man in Marblehead makes these. We sold three hundred. I'm glad this is the last one. On second thought, take it home. And not a word about your diet, Mom."

The store was empty, as Jane expected it to be two days after Christmas. Her parents had stopped to say goodbye before they drove home.

Before his wife could say no, he slipped it into her pocketbook. It disappeared into the cavern along with the Band-Aids, scissors, thread, wallet, pencils, paper, aspirin, panty hose—all the things Mary kept "just in case."

After her parents hugged their way out the door, Jane returned to her inventory. She was alone, although she now had a staff of four part-timers plus two retailing interns.

A customer came in. He blew on his red hands. "Hazelnut coffee and a chocolate torte."

"Beans or a cup to go?" she asked.

"Both," he said.

In the back room, continuing with the inventory, her attention kept drifting to Kate's design for the January window. The kid was turning into quite an artist. As she counted cranberry relish jars, the bell tinkled again. "Don't come out, I'll come in," a voice called.

"Harrison." She could smell cold rising off him.

He held up a paper bag. "I came bearing gifts, two lobster subs." He put the bag down and started pulling out the sandwiches, napkins and plastic forks. He poured himself a cup of coffee and selected a mint tea for Jane. "How's the inventory going?"

"Boring. Your interruption is welcome."

"How about dinner New Year's Eve? Or are you booked?"

She'd been planning a hot bath and bed with a good book and Main Man. Kate would be babysitting for Andy and his wife. "Thank you, yes."

By the time she locked the store, snow was falling. The T was almost empty, unlike the days before the holidays when she squeezed herself on board. Sitting across from a tall red headed woman, she decided to phone Diana. She had heard nothing from her since she got The Card.

Although she had tried to be there for Diana after Maurice's death the way Diana had been there for her, Jane had felt shoved away. She'd tried to stay with her friend after the funeral, but Diana had insisted she go back to Boston, even packing for her.

"It's not that I don't want you here, but I know you have to work," her old roommate had said.

"If you need me, call. I'll be on the next plane," Jane had said.

"I know," Diana had said.

★ ★ ★ ★ ★

Diana had called back in May. "I can't face taking Maurice's ashes to Argelès alone. Can you come?"

Jane had thought of the four hundred and fifty orders she had to pack and deliver for Mother's Day and said, "Of course," as she'd mentally juggled who would do what in her absence.

In the week they'd spent in Argelès, Jane had felt another person occupied Diana's body. Gone was the cocky, wisecracking friend. In her place was a quiet person who sat for long periods without talking.

"It's hard being here," was all she would say.

When Jane had said, "You've shut down," Diana had agreed.

As they got on separate planes at Charles de Gaulle, one for Boston, one for Miami, Diana had said to her, "I need to work some stuff out. I will. Don't worry about me."

Of course, Jane did worry. She forced herself to resist going to Florida, she resisted calling Diana daily, she resisted hovering.

A Diana look-alike got off one stop before Jane's. Leaving the station, Jane picked her way carefully over the iced brick sidewalk. At her door she quickly undid the first three locks. The fourth opened easily for the first time in months. It had been a week since she got The Card.

Mail had been shoved through the door slot, but no one had picked it up. She put Julie's and Barbara's bills and their issue of *Mother Jones* in their basket on the table next to their door. Shuffling through her mail, she found nothing of interest. The idea of a hot bath and a nice phone conversation with Diana sent her galloping up the stairs. She shoved the door open.

Kate was playing cards with Diana. Main Man jumped

off Diana's lap and jumped on Jane with his usual ecstasy, but she brushed him aside to hug her friend. "When did you get here?"

"About six hours ago. Surprised?"

After Kate went out with her gang to see *The Name of the Rose*, Diana and Jane made a pot of tea and curled up in their night gowns and robes in front of the wood-burning stove.

"You seem better than in France," Jane said.

Diana hugged a pillow to her chest. "I was destroyed. Losing Maurice was the worst thing I ever faced, much worse than the beating, Jim's death, learning about his, his ah . . ."

"Homosexuality," Jane said.

"So I hate saying he was gay. Shoot me. Did I tell you Bill died of AIDS?" Jane's open mouth told Diana this was news. "That's why he quit early. He wanted to work in a hospice in Maine. It was pretty much under control until September. I only learned about it when a health practitioner at the hospice wrote me that he was gone."

Both women sat quietly drinking their tea. The dog was in his basket near the stove.

"Listen to that wind," Diana said. The windows rattled.

"This will be a real nor'easter," Jane said.

"I hope Kate gets home soon."

"The theater is only a couple of blocks away." Jane reached out and patted Diana. "I wish you'd let me help more."

"I needed to find my own way. For a long time my work was the main thing in my life. Then Maurice. He was really exceptional, you know. Like Jim in many ways. There were

times I wanted to kill them both, but they . . . ." She blew
her nose.

Jane went to the kitchen to heat water. Away from the
fire the air felt cool. She asked as she turned on the faucet,
"How are you now?"

"Fine. I sold the paper, the house and . . . ."

"You what?" Jane walked toward the couch, the teakettle
in her hand, leaving the water running.

"Sold the paper, house, Paris apartment, furniture,
books—the whole kit and caboodle." She paused, "That's
not completely true. I kept Argelès."

Jane set the kettle on the woodburning stove. "But the
paper was your life."

"You're right. It was my life. But it was all tied up with
Jim and Maurice. I hate the business end. The fun part is
reporting."

"So what are you going to do?"

"Look for a regular reporting job. Maybe freelance. I'll
know when the right thing comes along. I'd like to live with
you for a while if you and Kate will have me?"

Before Jane could answer, Kate came in covered with
snow. The dog deserted his basket to greet her. She threw
her coat on a stool and asked, "Why is the water running in
the sink?"

Jane jumped up to shut it off.

"Would you like some tea?" Jane asked.

Kate nodded. She stretched out on the rug in front of
the couch, her feet toward the stove to warm them.

Jane poured the hot water over the tea leaves and stirred
them. "What would you think if Diana lived with us for a
while?"

"Way to go!" Kate said.

The dog jumped back in his basket. He dug at Jane's old

chenille bathrobe, so faded that it was hard to tell it was once pink. He kept trying to arrange it to suit him. When it met with his approval, he turned around several times and lay down. Deciding it wasn't quite comfortable, he repeated the procedure. This time he was content, tucked his nose under his tail, forming a fur ball, and shut his eyes.

Jane and Diana watched, knowing exactly how the animal felt. They too had kept, and would keep rearranging their lives until things felt right.

As the three humans sat drinking their tea, listening to the storm, Kate asked, "If you two are in one house, what happens to The Card?"

"We'll frame it," Diana said.

About the Author

══

D-L Nelson is an American writer who lives in Switzerland and Southern France. She is also the author of the Five Star Publishing novel, *Chickpea Lover: Not A Cookbook*. She is editor and publisher of W3, an almost monthly newsletter that is read by writers around the world. Visit her website at www.wisewordsonwriting.com.